The Perils of Paella

*Also by Nancy Fairbanks
in Large Print:*

Chocolate Quake

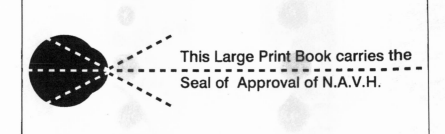

This Large Print Book carries the
Seal of Approval of N.A.V.H.

The Perils
of Paella

Nancy Fairbanks

WHEELER
PUBLISHING

Published in 2004 by arrangement with The Berkley Publishing Group, a member of Penguin Group (USA) Inc.

Wheeler Large Print Cozy Mystery.

The text of this Large Print edition is unabridged.
Other aspects of the book may vary from the original edition.

Set in 16 pt. Plantin by Al Chase.

Printed in the United States on permanent paper.

ISBN 1-58724-652-X (lg. print : sc : alk. paper)

*For my brother and sister-in-law,
Robert and Susan Fairbanks*

As the Founder/CEO of NAVH, the only national health agency solely devoted to those who, although not totally blind, have an eye disease which could lead to serious visual impairment, I am pleased to recognize Thorndike Press★ as one of the leading publishers in the large print field.

Founded in 1954 in San Francisco to prepare large print textbooks for partially seeing children, NAVH became the pioneer and standard setting agency in the preparation of large type.

Today, those publishers who meet our standards carry the prestigious "Seal of Approval" indicating high quality large print. We are delighted that Thorndike Press is one of the publishers whose titles meet these standards. We are also pleased to recognize the significant contribution Thorndike Press is making in this important and growing field.

Lorraine H. Marchi, L.H.D.
Founder/CEO
NAVH

★ Thorndike Press encompasses the following imprints: Thorndike, Wheeler, Walker and Large Print Press.

Author's Note

El Esperit de Gaudí i Miró is a fictitious museum in a fictitious Gaudí building, and the story and characters (excepting several historical and artistic figures mentioned briefly) are products of the imagination. The city of Barcelona, however, with its wonderful buildings, neighborhoods, art, food, and vitality are quite real and a joy to experience.

Books I used for research and authors to whom I owe a debt of gratitude are: *Miró*, Roland Penrose; *Essential Gaudí*, John Gill; *Cultural Atlas of Spain and Portugal*, Mary Vincent and R. A. Stradling; *The Time of the Doves* and *Camellia Street*, Merce Rodoreda; *The Festive Food of Spain*, Nicholas Butcher; *Tapas: The Little Dishes of Spain*, Penelope Casas; *Catalan Cuisine*, Colman Andrews; *Culinaria Spain*, Marian Trutter, et. al.; *Catalan-English/English-Catalan Dictionary*, M. S. Sabater and J. A. Freixinet; *Barcelona*, Robert Hughes; *Art and History of Barcelona*, Bonechi; *Catalonia: A Self-Portrait*, Josep Miquel Sobrer; *Michelin Spain; Spain*, F. Lisa Beebe.

Prologue

From: blue, carolyn
To: hecht, roberta
Sent: Monday, September 1, 2003 9:16 AM
Subject: Barcelona!!!!

Robbie,

Hope you and Hugh are finding marriage wonderful, and what do you mean you didn't appreciate getting a cookbook as a wedding present? What about the crystal goblets? Anyway, WILD WOMEN IN THE KITCHEN is fun to read even if you never approach a stove, which I try to avoid myself. Evidently you are of the same mind. So who does the cooking in your house? Hugh? The stepchildren? And how is that going? Have they fallen in love with you as rapidly as their father did? Or have they decided that you're the Wicked Witch of the West?

So much for chitchat. Jason has a meeting in Barcelona in late September. Naturally I'm going along. Since you're the Miró expert, and Miró's a Catalan native with a big Fundació in his name, you have to write and tell me everything I should do while I'm there — restaurants (of course), museums, wonderful medieval stuff, zany architecture. Did they ever rebuild the opera house?

Jason, Gwen, and Chris send their best. Chris says you're the sexiest lady "of a certain age" he saw during the tour of France. Don't take offense. He isn't even twenty-one yet, and I don't consider either of us "of a certain age."

Send advice.

Love, Carolyn

From: hecht, roberta
To: blue, carolyn
Sent: dijous, 4 setembre, 2003 14:39 PM
Subject: Serendipity

Hi Caro,
I couldn't believe it when Hugh forwarded your e-mail. I'm IN Barcelona. I have a three-month appointment, all expenses paid, to produce a monograph about Catalan and Gaudí influences on Miró's ballet scenery and costumes. The Esperit de Gaudí i Miró, my new sponsor, is doing a show on the ballet stuff next year. Our founder is a gorgeous Catalan industrialist who bought an actual Gaudí building, filled it with his Miró collection, and set up for business, i.e., re-

search, exhibitions, and a tapas café.

Meet me here for lunch at one on Sept. 23, and come early to take in the new performance art exhibit, "Tapas Triage." It's a hoot, and so is the artist.

Love, Robbie

1

El Esperit de Gaudí i Miró

Carolyn

How can one not love an ancient land whose national hero is named Wilfred the Hairy? I thought happily. I had arrived, within the hour, at the Barcelona airport, retrieved my luggage, hailed a cab, and feasted my eyes on Catalonia, a province of Spain that is surpassed only by the Basque region in contrariness and opposition to Madrid. In a state of high anticipation and delight, I climbed out of my cab on Passeig de Gràcia in front of El Esperit de Gaudí i Miró, the newest center for display of and research on Barcelona's most famous modernist architect, Antoni Gaudí, and the city's world-renowned painter, Joan Miró. And what a building it was — a wild, dreamlike construction, all curved lines, fanciful ironwork, and brilliant mosaics.

I paid the driver, took charge of my giant wheeled suitcase, and walked in to meet

Roberta Hecht, old friend, art professor, and Miró scholar. My husband, Jason, was in Salamanca lecturing on something or other to do with toxins and would join me later in the week for a scientific meeting sponsored by the University of Barcelona. In order to spend a few days with Robbie, who had offered me a bed in her apartment, I had flown directly here from El Paso.

Poor Jason — he was going to miss Robbie's personal tour of the permanent collection, the tapas café, and the much-praised performance art exhibit, "Tapas Triage," by the newest darling of the Barcelona art world, Ramon Berenguer, a twenty-three-year-old phenomenon. Could the artist be a descendant of the Berenguer Counts of Barcelona and Kings of Aragon?

The doors of Esperit were a miracle of ironwork leaves and dangerous spears, sharp points upward, thank goodness, backed by stained glass. They did not, however, open automatically, and I had a terrible time getting my suitcase inside. I had to push the left door open, keep it open with my backside, and then try to maneuver my suitcase through. It was wider than the door, and a guard came running over, protesting in his native language. I suppose one isn't supposed to bring a suitcase into the museum, but I couldn't leave it out on the sidewalk. Furthermore, I was feeling, as always, tired,

13

grubby, and short-tempered after the long transatlantic flight, so I protested in return and shed a few ladylike tears, thus cutting off his objections. Clearly disconcerted, he called to the lady at the ticket desk, and she arrived with a box of tissues and the information, once we had established a language in common, namely English, that I had mistakenly entered a museum, not a hotel.

I enjoyed her delightful accent while I took in the curved lobby with colorfully stained, rough stone walls rising to upper balconies. Those floors were accessible by ironwork spiral staircases or one elaborate and fanciful, three-person elevator. Both methods of getting upstairs looked dizzying at best and dangerous at worst. "I am a guest of Professor Roberta Hecht," I explained as slowly as possible, having made use of one of the receptionist's lavender tissues to dab tears from my eyes while she finished speaking. "Perhaps you can store my suitcase behind your desk."

The welcome desk was a flowing, highly polished modernist affair of many woods — very handsome. But she did not want to put my suitcase behind it. "I am to meet Professor Hecht at one," I explained. "She told me to enjoy the exhibit 'Tapas Triage,' if I arrived early enough." I held up my watch. "I have an hour, but surely you do not wish me to take my suitcase through the exhibit."

She looked horrified and informed me that visitors were not allowed to take even handbags into the exhibition sections of Esperit.

"Very wise," I agreed. "The world is full of madmen bent on damaging works of art. There was the slashing of the Rembrandt. And didn't someone take a hammer to the toe of the David? You can't be too careful." Then I smiled at her as winningly as I could and gave her my handbag and the handle of my suitcase.

Disgruntled and evidently at a loss as to how to handle the situation, she told me, I think, that the ticket was twelve euros even if I *was* the guest of a resident researcher — unless, of course, I promised not to look at a single exhibit. I retrieved my handbag and put the twelve euros on my credit card for tax purposes. That way, if someone steals my purse and expense notebook, I have a record. Then, with an hour to wander before my appointment with Robbie, I allowed myself to be directed to "Tapas Triage," which was on the ground floor.

I was actually relieved to be delayed in any journeys upstairs as I paused to watch the mosaic-embellished elevator with eye-shaped windows groaning upward on golden chains in its free-standing, wavy glass shaft. Did Barcelona have an elevator inspection service that checked out that beautiful but unconventional apparatus on a daily basis? Jason

15

would be horrified. He likes his elevators modern, reliable, and constructed according to all the latest principles of physics and engineering. In France he complained about charming French elevators with velvet, mirrored walls, and in San Francisco he grumbled about the effects of earthquakes on glass elevators and the electricity that runs them. Scientific husbands can be nerve-racking companions.

2

"Tapas Triage"

Carolyn

I entered the anteroom of the exhibit through a sort of rounded cave mouth. The temperature dropped ten degrees, and a spotlight hit a picture of the artist, Ramon Berenguer, a dark-haired youth with large eyes and a lean body clothed in black. He was almost uncomfortably handsome and had an amused and wicked smile. I turned quickly to the poster introducing the exhibit. The English version told me that he was a native of Barcelona and an artist of growing reputation for his years, but no real biographical information, not even any art institutes he might have attended. A man of mystery. Either not a descendant of the counts Berenguer or unwilling to claim his heritage. Perhaps a snob in reverse.

"Tapas Triage," according to the explanation, was a performance-art exhibition celebrating the joys of life and the suddenness of

17

death, owing an artistic debt to the spirituality of Gaudí, the art and humor of Miró, and an exhibit at the Fundació Miró called "Goin' Bye-byes," seen by Berenguer when he was a boy. So he was a derivative artist. At his age, that shouldn't be any surprise. The artist personally expressed his thanks to Comte Miquel Xifré i Fontdevila, his patron — also the industrialist who had founded this institute, if I remembered my correspondence with Robbie accurately. I opened another grilled door and stepped into the exhibition.

The long room was divided by a row of elliptical arches — very Gaudian except for the white decor. White tile underfoot, white arches, white walls. Hesitantly, I moved forward and discovered that the arches formed partitions on either side of the aisle. Each partially sectioned space contained a hospital bed with a black iron head and foot, and white bedding. Most of the beds contained a patient, tightly tucked in and sporting a whitened face and sometimes-white bandages, a few with red splotches seeping through the gauze. These patients wore varying degrees of black eye makeup and black lipstick that made the young art students (for that is where the patients came from — art schools) seem to exist anywhere from the verge of good health to the edge of death.

Each bed had a white wooden chair beside it, and on many of the chairs sat visitors to

Esperit. This was performance art that required the participation of the viewers. The visitors chatted with the patients, read to them from art books on Gaudí and Miró, showed them prints, and fed them tapas if the patients seemed inclined to eat. I observed the first patient on the right accepting a wizened black olive from the fingertips of a giggling German teenager, chewing, and then thrusting out his tongue with the olive pit lying on the end. The teenager grimaced and scraped her chair away from the bed. The patient then spat the pit at her.

"Pick it up, pick it up," a six-foot wooden bird squawked in English and several other languages. The bird was painted garishly in the primary colors favored by Miró, both its body and the feathered wings. Its large red beak opened and closed with loud snaps after it rolled out of a cubicle farther down the aisle, bearing a tray of tapas, which it offered to me. Still in shock because, along with the snapping beak, the bird made a noisy clacking sound as it moved and had almost run me down, I hesitated to choose one of the offerings on the tray. The creature then poked me with the tray and flapped one brightly-feathered wing. The German girl, who had been picking up the olive pit, was brushed by the wing and shrieked. The patient began to cry, while I hurriedly chose a potato omelet tapa. When the bird squawked again, I ate my tapa. What a strange and un-settling display!

"That's the Angel of Life and Joy, dear girl," said a passing Englishman, "and the tapas are quite edible."

"Would you please refrain from speaking to strange women," his wife hissed.

The bird folded its extended wing, turned, and clacked away after offering its tray to the English couple. On its hospital rounds it stopped to offer tapas to other visitors, who tempted the appetites of other patients in various stages of health and decay. The scene was surreal but amusing, and I entertained myself by studying symbolism and allusion among the sideshows. One particularly bloody fellow with amazing facial hair might well have represented Wilfred the Hairy. There was a small Catalan flag attached to the foot of his bed. Legend has it that Wilfred carried a plain gold flag or perhaps a shield, into battle with Louis the Pious, who, seeing the Catalan hero badly wounded, dipped his fingers in the warrior's blood and dragged stripes across the banner/shield, thus creating the Catalan flag. Since the two men were not contemporaries, the tale is entirely fictitious but, nonetheless, still popular in Catalan cities and towns.

I was probably right about the identity of the hairy patient. He even had hair on the soles of his feet, which protruded from under the sheets at the bottom of his bed. Robbie later told me that Wilfred, on returning from Flanders, where he had been sent after the death of his father, was identified by his mother because he had hair where none was supposed to grow — on the bottom of his feet, as legend had it. A peculiar sight. Also the hospital chart identified the patient as Guifré el Pelos.

I had just discovered a female patient who might well have been the Aragonese princess Petronella, whose marriage united Aragon and Catalonia, when an ominous rattling commenced. The tapas bird squawked and rolled off to a door on the right of the middle aisle, where it disappeared. The patients set up a wailing that bounced off the white walls and arches, and from a left-hand door appeared a horrible black creature, half bird, half dragon, with long ragged feathers on its back-spread wings, impressive claws on its legs, and vicious teeth in its dragon mouth.

Dragons are much favored in Catalan mythology. Wilfred's father is reputed to have killed one that had been imported from Africa by the Moors to devour Catalan sheep and peasants. St. George, the dragon slayer and patron saint of the province, and Hercules slaying the dragon to get to the golden apples are both tales featured by Gaudí. The Esperit dragon rattled toward me and, forgetting that this was an art exhibit, I scuttled backward beside a bed and fell into the lap of a portly Catalan gentleman of middle years.

The bird-dragon rolled by to the alcove of poor Wilfred and reemerged with the Count of Barcelona flung limply over its shoulder, bushy beard mingling with the tatty black feathers. The two disappeared through the left-hand door. I rose, trembling, from the lap of the Catalan gentleman, who gallantly stood to offer me an embroidered linen handkerchief, evidently under the impression that I was about to burst into tears. I could hear the English couple in the next alcove.

"I believe that was the Angel of Death," said the lady.

"Quite right, my dear," said her husband. "I told you that Wilfred the Hairy would be next. The fellow who gets no tapas has obviously been given up for dead by the Angel of Life and Joy."

"Indeed," said his wife. "Now, can we go to the café? I don't care for this exhibit at all."

"Certainly not. We paid ten euros each for the tickets and would have paid twelve if we weren't over sixty. If you're feeling peckish, you can indulge in the next round of tapas here. In the meantime, I intend to test my hypothesis. If I'm correct, I'll be able to predict the next patient to die. This is most interesting."

Good grief, I thought. *He must be a science professor. That's exactly the kind of approach Jason would take.*

Quince Paste on Manchego Cheese

Tapas are the national snack of Spain and probably originated in Andalusia as "covers" (tapar means "to cover") for sherry, either dry fino *or somewhat dry* amontillado. *These strong aperitifs, which have over 18 percent alcohol, were covered by bar owners with a slice of chorizo sausage or salty cured ham to keep the flies off the drink and/or to induce the patron to drink more because of the thirst induced by the salty tapa. Since Spaniards often eat a hearty lunch at 2:00 or 3:00 in the afternoon and dinner at 10:00, they'd suffer hunger pangs without these tapas and drinks to tide them over and enhance their business and social life.*

On a recent trip to Barcelona I visited a museum exhibition that served tapas to visitors. I was there between 12:00 and 1:00, so got in on the snacks offered by an outrageous bird called the Angel of Life and Joy. Whether tapas were offered to art lovers all day or just during the premeal hours I never thought to ask. Here is an easy recipe for a tapa I tried.

- Cut *1 1/4 lbs. of manchego cheese* into 1/4-in.-thick wedges after discarding rind.

- Cut *quince paste (membrillo)* into 1/8-in.-thick rectangles.
- Place paste squares on cheese wedges and serve with toothpicks.
- If *membrillo* is not available, spread quince jelly on cheese wedges.

Carolyn Blue,
"Have Fork, Will Travel,"
St. Petersburg Sun-Herald

3

In Which Life Imitates Art

Carolyn

I was very relieved that the Angel of Death had disappeared, and hoped that it would not return during my remaining time in the exhibit. Having noticed the hospital charts at the foot of the beds, I went back to check them out. There was a victim of an anti-church riot during Gaudí's time, a retired Roman foot soldier stabbed by his native wife, the mistress of a courtier to King Martí I the Humane, a Jewish scholar from Girona who fell ill during the fifteenth-century Catholic–Jewish debates in Barcelona, an opera singer burned in the fire that destroyed the Liceu, and a Spanish Civil War soldier who had been kicked by a mule. The other patients wouldn't speak to him because he was in Franco's army, not the Republican forces supported in Barcelona.

A late arrival was a female student who had been attacked by an elderly priest when caught passionately embracing her boyfriend in the subway. The priest hit her with a cane because she giggled at his admonitions. A new creature arrived through a door at the end of the aisle and tucked the bruised female student into Wilfred the Hairy's vacated bed.

"That's the Angel of Mercy," said the Englishman.

"Not in my view," said his wife.

I had to agree with her. This figure wore a white habit but had the face of a Miró female monster, a huge black head with splashes of primary colors at the edges and, on top, a bird's beak and eye with several hairs sticking out. A nun's white-winged headdress perched behind the hairs on the lopsided head. Miró's depiction of women is singularly peculiar.

I ducked into the alcove of the burn victim to get away from the Angel of Mercy, and we chatted about opera. The girl, who was supposed to be a Wagnerian soprano, claimed that Wagner was always sung in Italian or Catalan at the Liceu. She spoke English and, in answer to my question, said that the opera house had been rebuilt and reopened after many years of squabbling by various committees. As our conversation trickled into longer pauses, the Angel of Life and Joy came back with more tapas, and my patient urged me to get some. I helped myself to five when the

Miró bird offered them and fed two meatballs and one shrimp to the pseudo-soprano, whose arms and hands were heavily bandaged with stains of yellow salve rising to the surface of the gauze. The other two tapas, one meatball and one marinated shrimp, I ate myself, and very tasty they were.

After glancing at my watch, I excused myself and moved on, planning to glance into the last of the alcoves on the left and then leave for my appointment with Robbie. Since the winged dragon hadn't returned, I was quite enjoying myself and stopped to say hello to two more patients, neither of whom spoke English. The last patient, in the alcove nearest the entrance to the exhibit, was identified as Rosario Segimon Artells. She appeared to be asleep, but more surprising, she appeared to be Robbie. The lush auburn hair, the dark eyebrows, the outline of a voluptuous body.

Standing at the foot of the bed, I stared and blinked and stared again. How like Robbie to play such a trick on me. I said, "All right, Robbie, wake up. Is this what you meant when you said you'd be busy until one?" I plopped myself down on the white chair. The patient didn't stir, so I gave her a shake. Her head lolled to the side, revealing a bit of what looked like dried blood on the pillow.

"This is really too much!" I muttered,

feeling unsettled and, consequently, irritated. Planning to shout in her ear, I leaned forward. Robbie's face was now in profile and — that wasn't Robbie's nose. In fact, the skin, although it had a strange, pallid cast, was not Robbie's skin. It was younger and darker than hers. "Hello — ah — *buenos días.*" The not-Robbie figure didn't stir. In fact — I shivered — the chest didn't appear to be rising and falling. Gathering my courage, I touched an exposed arm. It was cold. Not that mine wasn't too. The room was cold! *All right, Carolyn, I told myself, you're being silly. Just see if there's a pulse.*

But I didn't really want to do that. This was too macabre. They wouldn't have an actual dead body in an art exhibit, would they? Although Wilfred the Hairy may have looked limp when the Angel of Death hauled him away, he was certainly alive — probably on his way to class even as I sat here entertaining lunatic fancies. I grabbed the patient's wrist and felt for a pulse. Then I tried the neck. Then I screamed.

The Angel of Life and Joy clacked in my direction. When that large red beak poked around the arch, I said, "Th-this woman is — is *dead.*"

The English couple entered right behind the bird, which snapped its beak and flapped its many-colored wings. "*Silenci,*" it croaked.

"I guessed right!" exclaimed the Englishman. "This one hasn't had any tapas. Of course, the *franquista* hasn't either."

"You don't understand," I cried. "This person is *dead!* Not acting dead. Dead dead."

"No es morta," croaked the Miró bird, sounding angry.

Other art lovers were crowding around. Then I heard the rattling that had announced the previous appearance of the Angel of Death. Was that supposed to be a death rattle? I shuddered as the visitors made way for the awful winged dragon. Surely it wouldn't just carry off a real corpse without — without — what? Maybe someone died every day here in some — some dreadful artistic ritual. I peeked fearfully at the dead woman and noticed for the first time that she wasn't wearing the usual white makeup or the black lipstick common to the rest of the patients. She just looked horrible in a sort of — more natural way.

"I peeck the dead ones, *idiota,*" shrieked the Angel of Death, who hadn't spoken on its last visit. "Make theese stupeed Amereecan woman leave the exhibeetion!" The order was issued to the Angel of Joy, who wheeled around and shouted, presumably in Catalan, at the black bird-dragon.

A patient joined the argument, evidently a fellow American, saying, "What the hell's going on? I'm supposed to die next. I've got a sculpture class at two."

"Thees ees Catalan art. Speak Catalan," the Angel of Death said to the Civil War patient.

"I say, this is very peculiar indeed," the Englishman chimed in. "Not at all like the previous two cycles."

"Screw you, Josep," the next-to-die patient snapped at the Angel of Death.

"I want to leave, Cecil," said the Englishman's wife. "And if you won't, I'm going myself."

"Please," I said to the American patient, "please tell these people that this woman is really dead. She's not breathing. She has no pulse. And no patient makeup," I added falteringly because everyone, tourists and actors alike, was staring at me with expressions ranging from disbelief to amusement at the silly American woman who couldn't tell art from reality. "That's real blood on her pillow. Can't you see that it's turned brown? Fake blood wouldn't do that."

"That's not Leila," the American patient agreed, staring at the corpse. "Isn't Leila supposed to be in this bed?" he asked the Angel of Death combatively.

The Angel lifted his dragon head off and peered at the corpse impersonating Rosario Segimon Artells, who, now that I thought about it, was the wife of the man who commissioned Gaudí to renovate a plain apartment building on Passeig de Gràcia into La

Pedrera. The woman had changed a lot of Gaudí's innovations and decorations in later years. So people here at Esperit might have reason to wish her ill, but this woman wasn't the real Rosario. Or evidently the real Leila. And I was sure that she wasn't the real Robbie, as I had thought originally, although in many ways she looked a lot like her. So who was this woman?

"What's going on here?"

I whirled and saw, to my relief, my friend.

"You were supposed to meet me at the café fifteen minutes ago, Caro."

Robbie strode through the tourists and patients, most of whom were shorter than she was. That was another thing about the corpse. She wasn't as tall as Robbie, now that I noticed, not that height is easy to estimate in a reclining figure. I collapsed with relief against my friend when she hugged me, and I sniffled about the corpse I'd discovered. Robbie looked over my shoulder and laughed boisterously.

"Isabel, get out of that bed! What's the idea of scaring my friend half to death?"

Of course, Isabel didn't respond. She really was dead. She was also, according to Robbie, a fellow Miró researcher who hadn't shown up for the monthly conference with the patron that morning.

Meatballs in Tomato-Garlic Sauce

- In a 9-in. cast-iron skillet, cook, stirring occasionally, *1 large, finely chopped onion* and *1 finely chopped large green bell pepper* over moderate to low heat in *2 tbs. olive oil* until vegetables are softened. Cool mixture.
- In a large bowl combine the onion mixture with *2 lbs. fatty ground beef, 1/2 lb. fatty ground pork, 2/3 cup fine dry bread crumbs, 2 1/2 tsp. salt, 1/4 tsp. freshly grated nutmeg,* and *1/3 cup minced fresh parsley leaves.*
- Form level tbs. of mixture into balls (about 90). In skillet heat *1 tbs. olive oil* over moderate to high heat until hot (not smoking) and brown meatballs in batches (16 to 20 at a time), shaking skillet frequently so they keep their shape, and adding *3 tbs. more oil* as necessary.
- Transfer browned meatballs with slotted spoon to a bowl.
- In a 6-quart kettle cook *6 large, minced garlic cloves* in *1 tbs. olive oil* over moderate to low heat, stirring about 15 seconds. Add one *33 1/2-oz. can whole tomatoes with juice* and *1 tsp. crumbled, dried oregano* and simmer, breaking up tomatoes.
- Add meatballs and simmer, covered,

occasionally stirring gently, 25 minutes or until meatballs are tender and sauce is slightly thickened.

- Serve meatballs with toothpicks, or use slotted spoon to move meatballs to heated serving dish.
- Boil sauce gently, stirring until thickened.
- Season sauce with *salt and pepper* and spoon over meatballs.
- Serves 8 or 10 at a tapas buffet.

Caper Vinaigrette Marinated Shrimp

- Whisk *1/2 cup olive oil* and *1/4 cup red wine vinegar* together in a bowl.
- Stir in *1 small minced onion, 4 tbs. minced dill pickle, 5 teaspoons tiny whole capers or chopped larger capers, 1 finely chopped hard-boiled egg,* and *1 tbs. minced parsley.* Season with *salt and freshly ground pepper.*
- Add *1 lb. large, cooked, unshelled shrimp* and marinate at room temperature for 2 hours before serving with toothpicks.
- If you have to refrigerate the shrimp, return them to room temperature before serving.

4

The Trials of a
Catalan Homicide Inspector

Inspector Ildefons Pujol i Serra

Murder is never a pleasant business, which is not to say that many of the victims are among society's most admired citizens. However, this victim, a woman, worked in a museum, which seems an innocuous enough pastime. Her death meant that I would have to question not only tourists, whom no sane man cares to meet, but eccentric artistic types. The case promised to be a source of great irritation to me. It had already kept me from my midday meal, which irritated my wife. No doubt in days to come she would complain of having a grumpy husband at her table, when I was lucky enough to get home to eat. My daughter, a university student, would giggle and tell her mother that if I could skip family meals, she should be able to do so as well when her studies demanded it.

Worst of all, the investigating judge on this case was Enric Goytisolo i Llull, a man whose eyes sparkle and whose mustache twitches with delight if he can be of service to a person of noble lineage. And the founder of the museum was Comte Miquel Xifré i Fontdevila, a count, yes, but not all that noble to my mind. The family had been the impoverished owners of small holdings in the country before they sent their younger sons to the New World. One returned a rich *indiano,* set up textile factories in the nineteenth century, and was given a title by the government in Madrid. A traitorous fascist lot, the Xifrés, who drove their workers to exhaustion for slave wages, who sat out the terrible years of the Civil War, and then presented themselves as supporters of the winner, Franco, may he rot in hell for the indignities he visited on Catalonia.

All this caused me great unease as my driver whisked me through the streets of Barcelona to El Esperit de Gaudí i Miró. Goytisolo's admonitions still rang in my ears. The *comte,* a man of great wealth and power, not to mention impeccable ancestry, was to be treated with the utmost delicacy and discretion. The case was to be closed with dispatch and no embarrassment to anyone. Didn't the judge know that, at the least, the murderer would be embarrassed when caught? Maybe it was the comte himself.

Goytisolo would have a heart attack.

We had arrived. Another peculiar Gaudí building. His hand was unmistakable. *How could the son of a cauldron maker, a man of the people, have produced such grotesque buildings?* I wondered gloomily as I studied the museum. Only an unfortunate religious mania could explain such a bizarre design, that and the fact that, although we Catalans are a race of hearty trenchermen, Gaudí was a vegetarian and advocated eating only lettuce with a bit of olive oil and a crust of bread. Perhaps he had hunger- or drug-induced dreams. Although I had never heard that Antoni Gaudí was an addict, just eccentric and priest-ridden.

Police cars and motorcycles already crowded the street in front of the museum, impeding traffic on Passeig de Gràcia, their occupants no doubt inside contaminating the crime scene, which, as I understood it, had been full of tourists when the corpse was discovered.

"One of the wealthiest and most respected men in Barcelona," according to Goytisolo. Respected? Why should an honorable man like myself, whose grandfather had fought for the Republic, respect the son of fascists, who destroyed our liberties and assassinated so many good men who had defended the Republic?

My appearance inside attracted the immediate attention of the uniformed officers who had reached the scene first. They had been lounging about gossiping, ogling a young woman who wept at a large, nonsensically ornate reception desk, and generally acting in an unprofessional manner. Now they descended upon me in a babble of information and had to be silenced and persuaded to speak one by one so that my aide could take notes on the facts of the case. Most were matters of which I had already been apprised — except for one thing. The person who discovered the body was an American female.

No respectable man should be expected to deal with American females — creatures who spend too much money, wear too few clothes, and lack any sense of propriety. The prospect was enough to make a man grouchy, even before the fact. My only consolation was that the victim, at least, was Catalan and had no doubt been murdered for some sensible reason. I sent the officers off to make lists of all the people who had been in the building at the time of the discovery. Then my aide and I went to view the body, trailed by officers who had managed to delegate list-taking duties to those below them in the chain of command. I estimated that there might now be more policemen in the museum than employees and visitors. I could only hope that the police were not attempting to pick the pockets and steal the watches of the visitors.

Such incidents are not unknown and make a bad impression.

The deceased was lying in a hospital bed, covered with a sheet and blanket. Unbelievable! "You moved her?" I roared at the senior officer.

"No, no, Inspector. She was found in the bed," he replied, face paling beneath skin as patchy as that of a shedding snake. In fact, the man had the triangular face of certain poisonous reptiles pictured in a book much cherished by my daughter in her childhood. Happily, she has outgrown that obsession.

"Why would there be . . ." I looked around. "A hospital ward in a museum?"

"It's an-an art exhi-hi-bition, Inspector," stuttered the reptile-faced officer. Evidently he could see my disbelief. "I don't know why — why it's called an art exhibition. Looks like a hospital ward to me too. Except for the rolling wooden angels. They don't look like angels either, but the head guy said they were — angels of mercy, death, and something else. Forget what. I've never been in a museum myself, except for once an alarm went off at the Picasso one night. Me and my partner responded to that. At least they had regular pictures there — well, the ones he did when he was a kid. The later ones are pretty weird. I'm not much into art myself."

"I am here. Is that the victim?" Adolfo Urpia i Garriga, court pathologist and cousin to the judge, had arrived. He looked, as always, like a man in the process of melting into a blob of orange-tinged clay — eyes drooping, nose, cheeks, and chin drooping, stomach drooping. "Good-looking woman that!" he exclaimed on closer inspection of the corpse.

I have always disliked Adolfo's comments on comely corpses. There's an aura of perversion to his enthusiasm. Unfortunately, I can hardly complain to the judge. "You'll want to get on with your examination, Urpia. Let me know your conclusions as soon as possible."

"Well, I can tell you right off, that's a young woman with a fine bosom. Very shapely. And look at those hips. Even under a sheet, I can tell she had a slim waist and a womanly figure."

I ignored Urpia, not to mention the snickers of the men around us. To the snake-headed officer, I said, "I'll need a room in which to interview all the people who were in the building." Sighing to myself, I added, "Naturally I'll want to talk to Comte Miquel Xifré i Fontdevila first. Providing he's available."

"You want to talk to the angels too, Inspector?" asked the reptilian officer.

"Yes, although not necessarily in costume," I replied.

5

Comments on the Late Isabel Almirall i Corberó

Carolyn

Robbie and I were sitting in a lecture hall on folding chairs because the police had shepherded everyone in there after the inspector arrived. Evidently we were stuck until we'd been interviewed. Having come straight from the airport and all those hours on planes, I was beginning to wilt. I needed a nap. No, I needed to sleep for about twenty-four hours. The adrenaline jolt that results from discovering a corpse in an art exhibit had drained away as soon as I sat down. "It's eerie. How much she looked like you," I said to Robbie. "Could she be a relative?"

"Heavens, no," said Robbie. "The woman's a Miró groupie. Or maybe I should say a Miquel Xifré groupie. I doubt she ever met Miró. He died in '83. Even if she was thirty, which I doubt, she was just a kid when he died. Now Miquel — she had a real thing for him, which evidently brought on this little quirk of hers. Looking like women he took an interest in."

"He took an interest in you?" I asked.

Robbie shrugged. "He hired me. He flirted a little. Nothing out of the ordinary, but all of a sudden, Isabel dyed her hair the same shade as mine. She used makeup so she'd look like me. At first I thought it was my imagination. That was before she showed up for work in a dress like mine. And boots. You remember those great boots I bought in Honfleur. She got some just like them after I wore them to a reception. Since she's short, hers came over her knees. Really creepy."

"Yes," I had to agree.

"I asked Narcis about it, and he said she'd done it before. Evidently when she first came to work here, she put a gray streak in her hair because Madrona Brusi had one and people were saying Madrona and Miquel had a thing going. Like I believe that. Madrona's got the hots for Narcis. But she's probably old enough to be his mother."

"Who's Narcis?" I asked, confused.

"The guy whose exhibition Isabel showed up in dead."

"This seems to be a very strange institution," I murmured through a yawn.

"You need some coffee, girlfriend," said Robbie, and she rose to exert her considerable charms on the policeman guarding the door to the auditorium.

Inspector Pujol

As soon as he had entered, I steeled myself to be courteous. "Comte, my sympathies on this unfortunate incident in your museum." Sitting across from me adjusting the razor creases in the pants of his silk suit, the man nodded in that condescendingly gracious way the rich have if they think that you're being sufficiently obsequious. "I realize that Senyoreta Almirall i Corberó was simply a member of your staff, but if you can shed any light on her murder, someone who might have —"

"Good Lord, Inspector, Isabel was more than just a staff member!" exclaimed the comte, who proved his concern by extracting an ebony cigarette holder from his waistcoat and inserting a cigarette into the holder. The man actually wore a waistcoat, some embroidered or brocaded thing; who knows? "We were all exceedingly fond of her."

"She had no enemies that you know of?"

"Of course not. Nor will we ever be able to replace her." He looked pained. "Her explications of Miró's symbolism, especially the birds and ladders, were superb."

42

"I see." The comte's cigarette smelled disgusting. I had to suppress the urge to cough. You'd think a man of his means could find a less offensive tobacco. Although I am only a simple public servant, albeit a homicide inspector of some reputation, my wife assures me that my pipe tobacco burns with a pleasant fragrance. Ah, to be at home with my family, having eaten a fine meal, followed by a pleasant interlude smoking my pipe in our small garden. Well, to the case. The comte's remarks were hardly helpful. The chance that the victim had been murdered over birds and ladders was very small. "You never heard her exchange angry words with anyone?" I asked. "Never heard anyone express resentment against her?"

"Never," said the comte.

The man had thick, wavy hair, threaded rather too stylishly with silver. He probably patronized an expensive hair salon. "She never expressed fear or foreboding to you or to someone who mentioned it to you?" I asked.

"Not at all. Isabel was a very happy girl. Everyone loved her. And she made wonderful paella. Superb paella." The count smiled reminiscently and flicked his cigarette into a strange-looking ceramic blob, evidently an ashtray of the Miró variety, which rested on the desk behind which I was sitting. I pushed the object farther forward, not caring to be showered with ash. "No bones. No shells," the count continued. "She removed them herself so that her guests would not be inconvenienced."

I nodded. "Rich man's paella, I believe it's called."

"Perhaps," said the comte. "Have you ever had it, Inspector? Isabel always included lobster in hers."

"I have to admit that, being a man of simple tastes, I prefer the original Valencian recipe."

The comte nodded. "Chicken and sausage. Very good, I agree, but this is Barcelona. As true Catalans, we must support our fisheries."

True Catalans? No true Catalan would have supported Franco. The comte probably owned a fishing fleet and thought true Catalans should support *his* fleet, buy *his* textiles, and visit *his* museum, which, I couldn't help noting, charged an exorbitant twelve-euro fee. "So you can think of nothing that might assist our investigation?" I added politely.

"No," said the comte, "and I am already late for an engagement to dine with friends. So if you'll excuse me . . ."

"Of course." The comte would dine, no doubt sumptuously, and I would miss my midday meal entirely because someone had killed his employee, the expert on birds and ladders. I signaled my aide to bring in the next interviewee, the museum's director, Professor Jordi Toda i Aguillo, who, according to a newspaper article I had read several years ago, had sold himself for the count's gold. Toda had been a distinguished professor at the university my daughter attends, but had been coaxed into leaving academia for a high-paying job at Esperit.

Carolyn

One moment I was watching Robbie charming that young officer into a state of enchanted bemusement; the next I was fast asleep in that miserably uncomfortable folding chair.

"Wake up, Sleeping Beauty." Robbie gave me a shake and plunked herself down beside me. "Baby Cop over there says he'll check where we are on the list, and if it's far enough along, he'll let us go for lunch to the tapas café. I'll tell you, after all this excitement, I could eat a horse, and for all I know, it may be on the menu. Olives stuffed with horsemeat or some damned thing."

I massaged my neck, which ached after my unplanned nap sitting up with my head fallen over at some uncomfortable and embarrassing angle. "Lunch would be nice," I mumbled.

"Then let's hope that's what he said. I read Catalan better than I speak it, and that kid speaks it better than Spanish, which I'm not too great at either. Did you get a look at that inspector? If he weren't so short —"

"He's not that short. The man's my height at least," I protested.

"Oh, right," said my friend cheerfully. "You and Jason and the inspector are normal, and I'm the jolly, redheaded giant. So anyway, I was saying, before you interrupted me, that he's kind of cute."

"The inspector? Robbie, the man's built like a plow horse."

"Well, he's not a *fat* plow horse; he's a muscular plow horse, and he has that stern, manly expression. Gives you a little tingle, doesn't it?"

"No," I replied. "We're married women, and we're not supposed to —"

"Poof!" said Robbie. "When a woman stops looking, she's dead."

"You, for goodness' sake, are a woman who's practically a bride."

"Yeah, well, five times lucky. That's what I'm hoping for. And the inspector isn't nearly as cute as Hugh." She paused and frowned. "Poor Hugh. Did I tell you the latest on Sammie?"

"Which latest?" Robbie had told me so many things.

"The worst news yet."

6

The Tears of Professor
Jordi Toda i Aguillo

Inspector Pujol

"Isabel was a dear friend," said the director of Esperit. "A dear, dear friend." He wiped tears from his cheeks with a pale green silk handkerchief. It matched the silk scarf he wore in the throat of his cream silk shirt, which went well with his beige suit, a slightly darker shade than the shirt.

"Wait till you see what this cream puff is wearing," my aide had murmured just before the professor entered. My daughter would probably have liked his outfit. In fact, it would have looked more suitable on her. For myself, I found the professor embarrassing. It's disconcerting to question a man whose eyes match his scarf, and his silky goatee and mustache, his shirt. The fellow did not look Catalan to me, although he had a Catalan name, but then most of my fellow Catalans don't look as if a gentle sea breeze would waft them away.

"My condolences, Professor," I replied, pretending his tears weren't still falling. "However, since it seems to be murder —"

"Oh, no," cried the director. "You must be wrong. No one would —"

"Perhaps not," I agreed. We didn't *know* she'd been murdered. Adolfo Urpia might have more to say on that score if he could drag himself away from the admiration of her figure and address the cause of her death. "But we do know, sir, that she is dead and that she sustained a blow to the head, not to mention the unusual fact that Senyoreta Isabel was found in an art exhibit."

"I heard. It's so . . . macabre. So . . . utterly . . . terrifying. Such things do not happen in museums. Who would visit the exhibitions if anticipating corpses on display? This is not only a terrible blow to me personally and to me as the director of El Esperit de Gaudí i Miró, but also to the art world in general."

"Since you and the late Senyoreta Almirall were close friends —"

"We were! We cooked together. My Isabel was a master of paella."

My Isabel? Now that was interesting. "I do not wish to offend you, Professor Toda, especially during this time of . . . great sorrow, but if I may ask, were you and Senyoreta

48

Almirall on . . . ah . . . intimate terms?"

"Of course. We are . . . were devotees and scholars of Joan Miró, the brightest star in the Catalan firmament. Miró, as you must realize, was brilliant. And Isabel . . . Isabel was brilliant. That you will not have known. You should read her article on Miró's birds. Brilliant. Just the other day, she told me of an idea she'd had: that Miró had been interested in parasites and painted them into his canvases as part of the marvelous variety of life forms in our world. Parasites? Our young people know about the most amazing things! And who's to say that Joan Miró did not have an interest in parasites? Isabel knows . . . knew the artist's heart." His tears began to drip once more. "Both as a sculptor and a painter." Out came the green silk handkerchief.

"She was herself a sculptor and painter?"

"No," said Toda sharply. "Miró is the sculptor and painter. Isabel was his emissary to the world, his muse."

"I thought he was dead." Talking to artistic types was not an easy task for a policeman like myself, accustomed to dealing with murder, not art. "How could she be his muse? Doesn't a muse inspire —"

"Stop!" Toda held up a hand with fingernails rather too long and, possibly, painted with clear polish. They looked suspiciously shiny. "Inspector, this is too, too painful a conversation for me to bear. I am sure you are a good man. An admirable man. You have a difficult job to do, but we — you and I — do not speak the same language. We are of different worlds, and the death of dear Isabel has broken my heart. I cannot bridge this chasm between us when I am in such pain and sorrow."

Did my daughter have professors who talked like this? Did she understand anything they had to say? "Then let me ask a simple question, sir. You say you and the deceased were intimate friends. Can I take that to mean that you were lovers?"

The professor stopped crying and, from swimming green eyes, looked at me aghast. "Lovers? Are you asking me, Inspector, if Isabel and I were . . ."

"Yes. Sexually intimate," I replied bluntly.

The professor began to laugh hysterically, a reaction I considered extremely odd, so I stared at him until he got control of himself. "Isabel and I were kindred souls," he said solemnly. "That may not be a concept with which you are familiar, Inspector."

Another condescending witness, I thought irritably.

"Isabel and I were *not* sexually intimate." He looked quite offended. "Even had I been so inclined, that would not have been possible."

Was the man saying he was impotent?

Now, if he had been so inclined, as he put it, and couldn't perform — well, murders have been committed for such reasons. I'd had a case in Barri Xino with just such a motive. An unemployed carpenter, upon finding himself unable to perform his marital obligations, conceived the idea that his wife was unfaithful and beat her to death with a hammer. That was some years ago, but —

"I was her superior and her mentor, sir. No gentleman and scholar would use his position to seduce a younger colleague. Even if he were so inclined."

The professor was wrong about that. I'd had a case when a father, upon finding that his daughter had become intimate with her geography teacher, had cornered the teacher, a middle-aged father of four, and castrated him. The teacher bled to death, and the father was caught, by me, and convicted.

"My apologies for mistaking the nature of your relationship with the deceased," I replied. "Still, if you were intimate friends, you may know of someone who had reason to kill Senyoreta Almirall. Someone who disliked or resented her. Someone she disliked. A lover. An enemy." Good God, would the man never stop dabbing his nose with his handkerchief and answer, or at least say he couldn't provide any names?

"Well . . . Isabel and our new American scholar did not seem on the best of terms.

51

I'm not sure what the problem was."

"The name of the American?" I asked quickly. He provided it. A woman. My spirits fell. I now had two American women to interview. How bad could a man's luck be?

"As for lovers, I do think she had a bit of a crush on Narcis. I saw them on several occasions in intense conversation. But lovers? I think not. No, Narcis was not interested in Isabel." The professor smiled. "Perhaps his affections lie in another direction."

"And Narcis is?"

"Ah! You have not seen our new exhibit? 'Tapas Triage'? It's caused quite a stir. Heretofore, I cannot say that I've had much interest in postmodern art."

"Which is?" I asked wearily.

"Participatory art. Performance art. However, Narcis is very clever, very talented. I *am* impressed. But he is not an artist whose muse has been honed by study, not a scholar by any means. More a natural talent. No, I don't think that Narcis even noticed Isabel's little crush on him, if, in fact, she had developed such an infatuation. Narcis is old for his years. An old soul in the beautiful body of youth. And Isabel was young for her years. Sweet, a wonderful mind, but a girl at heart, if you know what I mean."

I didn't, but I was tired of talking to Jordi Toda i Aguillo. I excused him with thanks and motioned to my aide for the next interview subject, a senior researcher named — I glanced at my list — Senyora Madrona Brusi i Farriols.

Could this Narcis be the creator of the hospital ward in which the victim had been found? Well, it would all come out in the interviews, although I couldn't imagine why the director of the institute would find the artist clever and talented because he set up a replica of a hospital ward in a museum. For that matter, why would art lovers want to visit it? Or critics find it worth their consideration? A long-held opinion of mine had been reinforced — that modern art is a scam, comparable to, say, someone selling a piece of wasteland to a fool who actually believed it when told that the land would be worth a fortune in the near future.

7

The Corpse Was Moved

Inspector Pujol

Before Senyora Brusi could be called in, the court pathologist arrived. As always, Adolfo was sweating, and his odor pervaded the room. This is perhaps an advantage to a man who deals with corpses, some in a state of advanced decay, but right then I'd have preferred the cologne of Professor Toda. Still, information is the meat of a homicide investigation, so I invited the court pathologist to be seated. Adolfo, perched on a narrow-seated, tall-backed modernist chair, was a sight. He overlapped the seat, his buttocks hanging down on either side under his mustard-colored jacket, and the curved back slats of the chair thrust up above his round, bald head.

"I have distressing news, dear friend," he announced, breathless, although he could only have walked across the reception hall from the crime scene to this office. And I was not his dear friend. I tolerated him because his cousin was the investigating judge.

"Have you discovered another body?" I asked.

"What? No! Is there another body?" He mopped his face with a large, soggy handkerchief and shifted on the chair, causing a greater amount of fat to lap over on the left. "The other bodies in those beds were live people. At least I think so. Actually, I didn't go around checking for pulses. Should I have? The ones sitting up were obviously alive, as well as those standing. The rest had left to sit in the auditorium. Not cheerfully, I have to tell you. They are a very aggressive group. Take my word, Ildefons, one of those students killed the woman."

"Is that your distressing news?" If Adolfo Urpia thought the murderer was a student-patient, I could be quite sure that no participant in the exhibit was guilty. Adolfo is an idiot.

"No. No. Not that. I give you that insight out of the kindness of my heart. What I have discovered is even more distressing. Someone," he announced portentously, "has moved the body. Mark my words. The corpse was moved!"

"And why do you think that, Urpia?" I asked patiently.

"The blood on the pillow. It is too little to have killed her. A spot or two only. A woman does not die after bleeding only a few drops of blood."

"Perhaps the blow caused an internal hemorrhage," I suggested.

"An internal hemorrhage?" Urpia shifted and massaged the buttock that was being cut by the chair's edge. "I hadn't thought of that." He rose, continuing to seek relief, this time by slapping himself sharply several times. "I shall investigate. More later, my friend."

He departed. Madrona Brusi entered, a fine-looking woman of middle years with handsome silver-streaked hair, admirably conservative clothes, and good skin. No low-necked blouses or naked arms and shoulders for the senyora, and she had excellent ankles, something I noticed as I rose to usher her to a chair.

Carolyn

Robbie and I had made our escape to the tapas café with the help of Baby Cop. We ordered wine, olives, and little puff pastries stuffed with a potato, tuna, and vegetable salad. Then we snacked while Robbie told me about her stepson, Sam.

"I'll start from the beginning," she said after removing an olive pit from her mouth.

56

They were excellent olives. "Kimmie and I get along beautifully. What a darling she is. We shop together. We giggle together. I couldn't be happier with Kimmie. The poor child was just dying to be mothered, and I — if you can imagine it — seemed to fit the bill. Sam, on the other hand, can't stand me, and he's not even polite about it." Robbie sighed and reached for her wineglass. "This is cava. The local champagne. You'll want to make a note of that."

"I've had cava before," I replied. "You were telling me about Sam."

"Well, I've done everything I could think of to make friends with him. Really, I have. You know that I usually get along wonderfully with the male of the species. Even really young ones. Like Baby Cop. He couldn't wait to help us out. But Sam is determined to hate me."

I thought about the problem. "Sam's a teenager. That's a difficult time under the best of circumstances. And he's what? Thirteen? Fourteen? The worst years of all with boys. Even Chris was hard to love when he was that age. And Sam's lost his mother. He probably feels that if he accepted you without protest, he'd be letting his mother down."

"She's dead, Caro," Robbie protested. "You can't hurt the feelings of a dead person. It doesn't make sense."

"But it's not surprising. You have to give

57

him time, Robbie."

"I have. And I've been nice to him. I've tolerated all his crap with the patience of a saint. I even cooked him things Hugh said he liked, and you know I'm not in love with cooking. Sam wouldn't eat them. I invited him to go kayaking with us. He refused. I bought him a truly dreadful T-shirt memorializing some rock concert. He threw it away. It was Kimmie who rescued it from the trash and started wearing it, and then he yelled at her.

"I'll tell you, Caro, it was kind of a relief when I got this offer, although Sam was at camp part of my time here. You'd think Hugh could have sent the kid away earlier so I'd get a real time-out. But no, I had to go on a parents' visit. What a disaster that was!" She sniffled, although tears are not like Robbie. "Maybe Hugh wanted to get rid of both of us," she said woefully.

"Has Hugh spoken to Sam about the way he's been treating you?" I asked.

"He evidently did after I gave up and stalked off to the car. He admitted when he called last night that he'd told Sam he had a good mind to send him away to military school."

I drew in a surprised breath, thinking that military school would only make things worse. Sam would blame Robbie. He'd feel deserted — by his mother for dying, by his father for sending him away, even by his little sister for taking to the new wife.

"But that's not the worst of it," Robbie continued. "Sam ran away from the camp, and Hugh doesn't know where he is. He's been gone for a whole week, and the police can't find him, and Hugh's beside himself, and I — I don't know what to do. I feel guilty, but I don't know what I could have done to prevent this, and I'm afraid it will ruin our marriage, and Sam will never be found, and —"

I handed Robbie a travel pack of tissues and signaled the waitress for more wine and tapas.

Inspector Pujol

After seating Senyora Brusi, I excused myself and stepped outside. The entrance hall was still full of lounging policemen, so I put them to work — on the off chance that Urpia was right and the body had been moved.

"I want this building searched from top to bottom for evidence that the victim may have been killed somewhere other than in that exhibition. But do not — I emphasize, do not — disturb evidence. Look, but don't touch. Wear gloves to open doors. If you find anything, come to me." I chose those officers who were to lead the search parties on various floors of the museum. I repeated my instructions. Then I returned to Senyora Brusi, who was admiring her chignon in a folding mirror. I couldn't blame her for that. She had a fine head of hair, properly styled.

8

Who Could Have Killed Her?

Inspector Pujol

"You ask who could have killed her?" Senyora Madrona Brusi i Farriols mused. "It was, I assure you, Inspector, not I."

"Senyora, believe me, I had no such thought."

"You may call me Doctor if you wish. I have a doctorate in art history and am an acknowledged expert on the lithographs of Joan Miró."

"Of course, *Doctor* Brusi. My apologies for misspeaking." What an accomplished lady. An air of feminine serenity surrounded her and shone from her dark eyes. She made one want to know more about the squiggles of Joan Miró.

"Isabel was my dear friend, and I, her mentor. One does not kill a dear friend and student," said Senyora — no, Dr. Brusi.

"Of course not." I had a disturbing thought, which, in my position as an investigating authority, I had to voice. "I do not mean to cause offense, but the director, Professor Toda, mentioned that *he* was Senyoreta Isabel's mentor."

Her laugh was low and musical, very pleasant, even to a simple, happily married man like myself. "No, no, Inspector, Jordi may have thought of himself as her mentor, but he was not. A talented young woman such as Isabel Almirall does not take as her mentor a man of Jordi's . . . unfortunate . . . umm . . . proclivities. You understand what I mean?"

"No," I replied, confused yet again by these enigmatic people.

"Jordi, if he were so inclined, would choose a young *man* to mentor."

"Ah. Well, he did say he wasn't inclined to . . . er . . . physical intimacy with —"

"Isabel?" More musical laughter. "I should think not."

"Did the lady have any particular male friends that she mentioned to you, her friend and mentor?" Did the senyora mean that the director was a pervert? "The artist Narcis, for instance?"

"Narcis?" the lady exclaimed with astonishment. "Narcis would not have been interested in one so young and . . . naïve."

"I see. Well, the director would agree with you there."

She squinted at me, almost challengingly.

"And whom does Jordi think Narcis is interested in? Not himself surely?"

I cleared my throat nervously. I'd had no idea what the director thought, or what this lady thought on the matter of Narcis's preferences. Obviously, I'd have to talk to Narcis. "Did Senyoreta Isabel have any enemies that you know of?"

Senyora Brusi considered. "She did not care for the new American woman, Senyora Roberta Hecht."

"Ah." Reconfirmation of bad blood between the victim and the American. "Would you know who has keys to El Esperit?"

"Oh, we all have them," she replied airily.

"And who, if anyone, would be inclined to work here at night? Other than Senyoreta Isabel?"

"I'm surprised to hear that Isabel was here at night. Are you sure of that?"

"It would seem likely since she was found dead in the hospital bed this morning."

"I suppose Senyora Hecht might have worked late. Americans — they are so compulsive about work, so . . . *lower class.*"

"Do you hold workers in low esteem, Doctor?" I asked sharply, for I found her air of disapproval irritating.

"Only pushy American workers," she replied, and gave me a complicit smile, as if we two understood that Americans left much to be desired. I could hardly disagree with that, having heard that Americans willingly worked nights and weekends, never giving appropriate time to their families or their digestions.

Carolyn

"Who could have killed her?" I asked once Robbie and I had received our second round of cava and tapas — mushrooms and shrimp in almond sauce. We had agreed to discontinue our discussion of Sam's disappearance since there was nothing that we, here in Barcelona, could do about the matter.

"The count seemed taken with her, but then, he seems taken with me," Robbie replied, grinning. I frowned at her. "Seriously, I'm quite sure she was his mistress. No one said as much, but then no one says much to me. I don't think they like Americans, except for Miquel. Still, I know the signs. He was boinking her."

"Boinking?" I had to stifle a giggle. "I doubt that he'd appreciate the verb. Do you have any evidence?"

"You'll just have to take my word for it. I've had five husbands and several lovers, and I can tell when people are getting it on. They were."

"And you think he killed her?"

"Oh, probably not. Cheated on her? I'd bet on it. Killed her? Not likely. But his wife does come to mind as a possible suspect."

"He's married?" Rich noblemen with mistresses, wives, and museums of their own. I could hardly take it in.

Inspector Pujol

The confusing Dr. Brusi departed, leaving a light trail of flowery perfume that almost dispersed the lingering odor of Urpia. Before I could call for another interview subject — Narcis Ramon Berenguer had moved up on my list — one of the officers delegated to lead search teams rushed in.

"Inspector Pujol, we have discovered a desk upstairs. Papers have been disturbed. A blue metal statue of a bird has been shoved lopsidedly into its base, and there is dried blood on its beak. Perhaps the victim was struck and killed with the bird."

"Is it the victim's desk?" I asked.

"I don't know," he replied, embarrassed that he had overlooked that information. "But there were papers in disarray, papers typed in a foreign language with notes made in Catalan. The notes I could read, although I did not understand them."

"You touched nothing?"

"Nothing, Inspector." He displayed gloved hands, then stuck them back in his pockets. "I do not take my hands from my pockets. That way I touch nothing."

I sighed. "Good man. Find the director. His name is Professor Jordi Toda i Aguillo."

He nodded. "The pervert."

"Try not to insult him," I advised. "Those who have been insulted are never as cooperative as those who have been treated with respect."

9

Who's Been Sitting at Robbie's Desk?

Inspector Pujol

"Senyor Berenguer?" If he hadn't been well dressed and groomed and presented to me as a promising artist, I'd have taken him for a street punk. He had that predatory look about the eyes, not to mention a certain smell. I am a man sensitive to odor. I can sniff out the criminally inclined, even before they have stepped over the line that separates the good citizen from the bad. Women probably considered Senyor Berenguer handsome. Had the victim? If she was a victim.

"Do you have a key to the museum, Senyor?"

Berenguer relaxed into his chair. He had avoided the tall, narrow model on which Urpia had come to grief and chosen a curved, low-backed chair more accommodating to those who prefer to lounge.

Berenguer sprawled with a covert aura of insolence while replying to my query. "I am not a staff member, Inspector. They may have keys. I don't."

"I understood you to be the protégé of the comte."

"I have that honor, but it does not include keys to the castle." He smiled at his own repartee.

"And the late Senyoreta Almirall? What can you tell me of her death?"

"Why, what more clever and comfortable place could an art historian and critic choose to die than in an exhibit with beds? Isabel seems to have had more imagination than I would have thought."

"You think she killed *herself* in your exhibit, then?"

"How else did she come to be there?" he retorted.

"And how did she manage to hit herself on the back of the head to accomplish that?" I returned.

"She had a head injury?"

"That bled on the pillow."

"Murder, then? Amazing. And in my creation." He relaxed again into the chair. " 'Tapas Triage' should become twice as popular when this story hits the papers. 'Real death in a hospital illusion.' " He spread his hands as if measuring the length of the headline.

A cold fellow, I thought. "You were her lover?"

"Not me," he replied, amused. "There was no personal connection between us. None."

That had the ring of truth. But perhaps this Narcis was an expert liar. "Then what can you tell me that might shed light on my investigation?"

"She was peculiar. Perhaps she had no soul, or at least no vision of herself. She strove to look like others, never like Isabel."

"Why do you think that was?" I asked.

"Whoever caught the comte's eye, Isabel became that person. Robbie, the American scholar, was the last. Look at the two of them, and you will see the resemblance. I heard that Robbie's friend saw Isabel and thought she was Robbie." He chuckled. "I got that straight from the Angel of Life and Joy, a reliable source, wouldn't you agree? Angels have always brought news to us poor humans. And there was another woman before Robbie, and another before that one, although I was not here for all Isabel's reincarnations. She must have spent her entire salary on hair dye and other means of disguise."

"So you think Isabel was in love with the comte? Perhaps intimately involved with him?" I pressed.

"Was he fucking her? Is that what you're asking? I wouldn't think so. The comte is a man of taste. Why would he pay attention to a girl with no identity?"

Carolyn

We had progressed to our third round of tapas, prawns grilled with garlic mayonnaise, and our third flutes of cava. The museum had very nice crystal. I've always been partial to museum food, but I don't remember it being served so royally. Of course, this museum belonged to a nobleman. A rich one. He could afford gold goblets if he wanted them. The combination of wine and exhaustion was buzzing in my head. Goodness knows whether I'd be able to give a coherent account of finding the body when it came my turn to be called into the inspector's presence. He was certainly taking his time. What had Robbie told me? Oh, yes. The count's wife. "You really think she might have killed Isabel?" I asked. "I suppose wives have been known to kill their husbands' mistresses. Is she madly in love with him?"

"Don't ask me."

Robbie was poking through an olive assortment stuffed with various things, but not horsemeat, as she had suggested earlier. At least I didn't think I'd eaten any horsemeat-stuffed olives, although I am aware that Europeans do eat horsemeat. Perhaps it's some historical thing. Their ancestors had been forced to eat the horses during sieges. Or they didn't fall in love with their horses the way cowboys did in westerns. No cowboy would eat his horse. "Then why did you say the countess killed Isabel?"

"I didn't. I don't even know the countess, and I don't know if she is madly in love with Miquel. My guess would be not. They have a peculiar relationship, from what Narcis tells me."

"He's too handsome," I remarked.

"The count?"

"The artist. I saw his picture. That sharp face and shiny black hair. I tend to distrust men who are too handsome."

Robbie grinned. "I tend to take them as they come. Since Narcis does talk to me, he's okay in my book. I wish the others would warm up. It gets lonely working in a place where the women snub you."

"So what's peculiar about their relation-ship? The count and his wife?"

"Well, they live apart, get together a couple of times a month, and fight like cats and dogs. Evidently the big bone of contention is that she still refuses to speak Catalan. She's from Madrid and says Catalan is a bastard language. The count takes offense. Not that he doesn't speak excellent Spanish, but Catalan is his native language, and everyone in Barcelona who isn't a *xarnego,* that's an outsider, thinks their language and culture and — I don't know — productivity are the world's best, highly underrated, foolishly unappreciated by the rest of Spain. They've got some kind of ethnic complex about the whole thing because every time they end up on the wrong side of a war, the winner insists that they stop speaking Catalan."

"That's a strange reason to break up a marriage," I mused.

"They're still married."

"So she could be jealous. She could have killed Isabel."

"From what I've heard about Violante Roca i Navis, she'd hire it out. She's from a nobler family than Miquel. Not as rich, but higher in the Spanish pecking order."

"Maybe he's been spending too much money on his mistress and not keeping his wife in the manner to which she's become accustomed," I suggested.

Robbie giggled. "You're really into this detective thing, aren't you? Oh, goodie. Here comes the sole with raisins and nuts."

Sole with Hazelnuts, Raisins, and Pine Nuts

Noon to 3:00 and 7:00 to 10:00 are tapas hours in Spain, just when we Americans want

---

to eat lunch or dinner, so we, unlike Spaniards, will do just that. I ate at a museum tapas café in Barcelona. It was a cross between a xampanyerie, *which only serves cava and tapas, and a* cervecería, *which serves beer and tapas. The museum café served both beer and cava, but we drank cava and had several rounds of tapas, not all of which could be eaten off a toothpick (elsewhere the customer might be charged by the number of toothpicks he accumulated). We got plates of tapas and forks on one order and received a regular bill. Here is the recipe for a dish we liked:*

- Soak *1/2 cup raisins* for 20 minutes in a cup of warm water. Drain.
- Cut *1 1/2 lbs. sole fillets (around 4)* in half crosswise and dust with *flour.*
- Heat *3 tbs. ea. olive oil and butter* in a large skillet. When butter just turns color, sauté fillets until golden on both sides. You may need to do it in two rounds with more oil and butter, but do not overcook.
- Remove fillets to a warm serving platter, sprinkle with *salt and pepper,* and garnish with *4 slices of lemon* and *2 tbs. chopped parsley*
- Cool skillet a bit; add raisins, *4 tbs. pine nuts,* and *30 split hazelnuts* * (filberts).

- Sauté slowly until pine nuts begin to turn golden. Pour this nut mixture along with any oil and butter remaining in the skillet over the fish and serve immediately.

*The hazelnut bush, having sheltered the Virgin Mary from a storm, not to mention later Christians who believed in its miraculous protection, is sacred in Catholic countries.

Carolyn Blue,
"Have Fork, Will Travel,"
Salt Lake City News

"According to the director, the desk belongs to the American staff member, Hecht," said Porras, leader of an upper-floor search. He was excited by his discovery. "The language of the disturbed papers is English with notations on another piece of paper in the hand of Senyoreta Almirall. The director identified the Catalan handwriting and seemed very upset about the subject of the material, which is . . . paracycles? Is that some sort of bicycle, sir?"

My mind returned to my interrogation of Professor Toda. I asked my aide to read back the last portion of that interview to see if the word was *parasites*.

"Parasites!" exclaimed the police officer. "That's what he said. The paper was about parasites, not bicycles."

"And it was the work of the American woman?"

"Who else? The language was English. Why would anyone who speaks Catalan write in English for a Catalan museum?"

"Why indeed?" So the victim had been at the American woman's desk late at night reading her work and making notes, and she had mentioned the subject as her own idea to the director. And the American woman had come in unexpectedly, discovered the theft of her intellectual property, and —

"The director was furious about the damage to the bird. It's a Miró sculpture, and very valuable, even if it's not a very good likeness of a bird, in my opinion anyway, if you'll excuse me for saying so, Inspector. I mean no disrespect."

"We are policemen, Porras, not art critics. We cannot be expected to admire art that looks strange to us."

"Thank you, sir."

"Get me the American woman."

10

The Unwelcome Insights of a Hungry Englishman

Carolyn

We had eaten and drunk as much as we could in the museum's café, so we returned to the auditorium, not because we wanted to, but because Baby Cop told Robbie she would probably be called next and should be found in the right place. She was talking to the young policeman and I had settled into an uncomfortable doze, when a great hubbub began.

"My watch is gone!" cried the Englishman who had reminded me of Jason. Not that he looked like Jason, who is five seven, in wonderful shape as a result of athletic activities, and has lovely, thick, dark hair with silver touches and a handsome short beard. The Englishman looked like a scarecrow, unstuffed. Painfully tall and thin with a sunken face and colorless, thinning hair.

However, Cecil, as his wife had called him, thought like my husband — logically, no matter what the subject.

"Someone has purloined my grandfather's watch."

"Now, Cecil," murmured his wife soothingly. She was shorter but equally skeletal with limp, gray-blonde hair and lovely skin. "Perhaps it fell off your wrist while you were swanning around that nasty exhibit with the corpse in it," said Mrs. Cecil.

"I do not *swan*," snapped Cecil angrily. "And if my watch had fallen off, I'd have known it."

I believed him. I'd noticed that watch. It looked to weigh about four pounds and would have clanked unless it fell into the exhibition bedclothes. I was just about to suggest that the bedclothes be searched, when Cecil demanded to see the inspector. He was so persistent that Baby Cop went off to tell his superior.

The artist, Narcis, had just returned from his interview and asked what the problem was. Evidently we were all to be kept here until the last of the interrogations had been conducted. And me dropping abruptly into sleep if I so much as lowered my eyelids. To avoid embarrassment I rounded my eyes, no doubt looking like an imbecile in the process, or perhaps someone on amphetamines.

"That young cop who left take your

78

watch," Narcis told the Englishman. "They're all a bunch of thieves, as any native can tell you."

"If you saw it happen, young man, why didn't you tell me at the time?" Cecil demanded. "Maybe you were in league with the thief."

"Cecil," hissed his wife, "that's the artist, the one who thought up that . . . piece of . . . performance art. Didn't you see his picture in the cave?"

"Oh." Cecil looked taken aback, but after he stared hard at Narcis, he said, "Interesting display, lad. I've got it figured out, you know. No tapas, next dead. That's the formula. Am I right? Well, except for the actual dead woman."

"I not plan on her," said Narcis dryly.

"Of course you didn't." Cecil spotted the inspector entering the auditorium in the company of Baby Cop and several other law enforcement persons, actually quite a few. More and more crowded into the room behind the first group. "You!" said Cecil, pointing at Baby Cop. "You stole my watch. You were seen doing it."

"I did not." Baby Cop became red-faced and alarmed. "Inspector," he cried anxiously, "I didn't. On the soul of my mother, I didn't steal —"

"Your mother's still alive," said the inspector's aide.

79

"But she has a soul. An excellent soul. My mother is a saint."

Now Baby Cop, thinking the piety of his mother had been attacked, clenched his fists and took a long stride toward her accuser. "Search him," snapped the inspector.

Interesting. Did the inspector think his officers were the passel of thieves Narcis had labeled them? Baby Cop was grabbed roughly by his fellows and patted down. His pockets were turned inside out. His trouser cuffs, socks, and shoes investigated. His police equipment searched. No watch was found. "Why, sir, did you think this officer stole from you?" the inspector asked the Englishman.

"Because he was seen doing it," snapped an angry Cecil. "The artist said so."

The inspector turned a hard eye on Narcis, who smiled and shrugged. "Maybe other cop. You put uniform on someone, he look like all other uniforms."

"Then you must search all the other officers," said Cecil, "and in the meantime I demand to be interviewed now. I have important information, and I consider it a scandal that I've been kept waiting so long. My wife and I are hungry. We want to go to the museum café and eat."

"The café serves only tapas," said the inspector disdainfully. "We in Catalonia don't consider tapas a meal, just a snack."

"I thought the tapas were lovely," said Robbie. "Didn't you, Carolyn?"

"Quite good," I agreed. "Three lots make a reasonable meal."

"Americans," snorted the inspector. "Which one of you is Senyora . . ." He glanced at a list. "Hecht."

"Dr. Hecht," Robbie corrected.

"You come for the next interview," said the inspector, eyeing Robbie's stylish outfit with disapproval — or was that just interest in her cleavage? Her blouse was unbuttoned one button too many, although she'd tell me I'm a fuddy-duddy if I said so.

"I beg your pardon," snarled the Englishman. "I am Sir Cecil Hawkwood, a former member of the House of Commons of the United Kingdom. Do I have to call the British consul in order to get on with my lunch?"

"Goodness," I said, "are you descended from the famous condottierre whose portrait is painted inside the duomo in Florence?"

"Certainly not," said Sir Cecil. "There are no Italians in my family."

"Sir John Hawkwood was an Englishman."

"Even so, the man, whoever he is, is no ancestor of mine." He turned away from me. "Inspector, I am a person who believes that the police, even foreign police, deserve the cooperation of citizens, even visitors to a foreign country, and I am quite willing to provide that cooperation as long as I can do it right now. Otherwise, I shall call the British consul —"

"And write letters to the *Times* and the *International Herald Tribune*," said his wife. "Cecil is an ardent writer of letters. You'd better take us next. He's also very grumpy when he hasn't had his tea. I do hope they have tea in the café."

"They do," said Robbie, "but it comes in bags. Not, I'll bet, what you're used to."

"Oh, dear," said Lady Hawkwood. "Cecil, perhaps we should go elsewhere for tea."

"There's a discount in the café for ticket holders. I paid for the tickets. I did not finish looking at the exhibition because of the corpse found there. At the least, I intend to get my café discount."

"I didn't know my ticket entitled me to a discount," I exclaimed. The tapas and cava had been rather expensive, and I had insisted on paying the bill since I'd be staying with Robbie for the next few nights, thus saving hotel charges. "Do you think if we go back with the receipt and my ticket, I can get some money back?" I asked Robbie.

"Neither of you can leave this room," said the inspector.

Since Baby Cop sent us a pleading look, we didn't tell on him, and the inspector never realized that we'd been in the café after my discovery of Isabel.

"Where do we go for the interview?" Sir Cecil demanded.

Scowling, the inspector led the English couple away.

Inspector Pujol

No sensible man considers tapas a meal. You might eat a few *before* the meal, but not *as* a meal. I wasn't surprised to hear that the American women thought tapas an adequate midday repast; the Americans are well known to exist on what they call junk food. I suppose I should have expected the same of the English. They do, after all, consider tea a meal, and I've heard that it consists of cakes and tiny sandwiches. Considering the diets of foreigners, it is no wonder that they cannot match us Catalans for hard work and sensible living.

With the English couple seated, I asked just what this insight of his was.

Sir Cecil nodded smartly and replied, "I can solve your case for you, Inspector. By close observation I deduced that the next patient to be carried off by the Angel of Death was the patient who was not served tapas by the Angel of Life and Joy. Which is to say that someone at the museum, perhaps that artist, chooses those who will die. Since the woman in the bed to the left of the entrance was dead, she was obviously chosen. You need only find which one of the museum staff decided. Perhaps it was, in fact, the Angel of Death."

"Cecil, do you mean to say that the other fellow was actually dead — what was his name?"

"Wilfred the Hairy," said Sir Cecil. "Yes, my dear. Although I didn't realize it at the time, he must have been dead too. Inspector, you'll need to send your people to look for his body."

"Wilfred the Hairy?" I echoed.

"Well, his name was written in Catalan, which, of course, I do not speak. I'll wager few people do."

"We Catalans do."

"Ah, well, be that as it may, I did ask for a translation and was told he was Wilfred the Hairy. A rather amusing name, don't you think?"

"I do not," I replied. "He is a national hero."

"Indeed? Well, I did not mean to offend you, Inspector. Many historic figures have strange names. Charles the Simple, for instance. A French king. Or —"

"Thank you for your input, Sir Cecil. We shall certainly keep our eyes open for Wilfred the Hairy."

"And for my watch," Sir Cecil reminded

me. "Just because it wasn't pocketed by that one young fellow, doesn't mean —"

"And your watch," I agreed. "Enjoy your . . . tapas." The eccentric English. I'd read about them, but this encounter certainly supported that reputation. And now I had to interview that American woman with her breasts bulging out of her blouse. My wife would be astounded when I told her about this day.

11

An American Suspect

Inspector Pujol

The officer I sent to the apartment of Senyoreta Isabel Almirall i Corberó called my cell phone to report. There was evidence of a paella dinner for two having been prepared and served. One plate had been eaten and a full bottle of wine drunk, probably by the victim, because only one goblet had been used. The wine was a local Catalan cava, the goblets decorated in blue and violet, and produced in Romania. The officer could make that statement because his wife had bought some herself at a recent special sale at the English department store. The second plate of paella had been thrown against the wall.

He had then taken it upon himself to contact the telephone company because the senyoreta's caller ID indicated a call from Comte Miquel Xifré i Fontdevila. The telephone company also revealed that the late Senyoreta Almirall had then called the home number of Senyora Roberta Hecht (*Ha!* I thought) and another unlisted number that the officer hadn't bothered to follow up on because the first two calls were obviously of the most interest. The concierge at the senyoreta's apartment house reported that she had left the building at eleven in the evening, which was unusual.

Why had the comte called Senyoreta Isabel? I asked myself. Had he revealed that he knew she was stealing ideas about Miró and parasites from the American woman? For whom had the victim been cooking her famous paella? The comte? If she harbored an unrequited love for him, thought him interested in the American woman, and made herself look like the American — pathetic as *that* was — perhaps she had invited him to dinner to try to shift his interest from the American to herself. But having found out about her theft, he had called to cancel dinner.

The angry Isabel had then eaten her paella, thrown his against the wall, and called the American, demanding that she come to the museum. The American, discovering that Isabel was not only stealing her research but attempting to seduce the comte, had killed her at the museum in a fit of rage. A tidy piece of reasoning on my part.

Or perhaps Isabel had been planning to write a paper criticizing the American's parasite work, which she told the American that night. The American woman, fearful for her academic reputation, killed Isabel so that the idiocy of her work would not be exposed. Or perhaps Isabel had invited the American woman to dinner to tell her what she planned to do about the parasite research, then received a call from the comte, accusing her of stealing the American's research. Perhaps he had called the American as well to warn her, and she had failed to show up for dinner. Then Isabel, thwarted, ate her paella, threw the American's against the wall, and called the woman, demanding that she come to the museum immediately, after which one woman killed the other. At that point I had to ask myself whether any of those scenarios made sense.

"The kid who didn't steal the Englishman's watch says you want to see me next."

Senyora Roberta Hecht stood in my door, smiling at me in a lascivious fashion. I wanted to tell her to button up her blouse before she entered the room, but I restrained myself and simply waved her to the narrow, high-backed, modernist chair.

"What a beauty," she said. "Is it a Gaudí design? I've never been in this office." And she sat down. As big as she was, she did not overlap the sides. I did not get up when she entered because I was quite sure that she was taller than I was. Even we simple men have our pride.

"Senyoreta Isabel Almirall i Corberó tele-phoned your apartment last night," I stated, as if I could prove it, which I could, in a manner of speaking.

"No, she didn't."

"Telephone logs show that she did."

"If she did, she didn't get hold of me. Maybe she called while I was talking long distance to my husband." She smiled at me, brazen as a hussy on the waterfront. "Tele-phone logs should show that," she added.

"She asked you to meet her at the museum after eleven."

"I told you. I didn't talk to her. And I certainly wouldn't have come to this museum at night. How creepy would that be?"

"You have a key to the museum."

"No, I don't."

"Dr. Brusi said all staff members have keys."

"I don't. Maybe *she* met Isabel."

"The night guard will know if you came to the museum."

"He can't know something that didn't happen. Good heavens, Inspector, you can't actually think I killed Isabel. Is that where this is going?"

"You were having an affair with the comte."

"I certainly was not."

"And you knew that Isabel was going to write an article making fun of your parasite research." Ah, that had struck home. She was staring at me, astonished. Perhaps she killed Isabel before discovering whatever it was Isabel planned to do about the research.

"Inspector, my *husband* is a parasitologist, not I."

"And you wrote a paper together?"

"Yes, we did." She looked surprised, then giggled. "As a joke. I e-mailed the final draft to him from here in Barcelona. Not too long after we first met, he told me that Miró, as wonderful an artist as he is, knew nothing about parasites. Are you telling me that Isabel read that paper and took it seriously? How did she get hold of it?"

"It was found on your desk today with a page of notes in her hand. And a Miró statue of a bird with blood on it."

"The statue on my desk? Was it damaged? Lord, the comte will have a fit. His father bought it, one of the early Miró acquisitions by the family. Isabel wouldn't have done anything to it. She studied the bird imagery. And the ladders. Symbols of flight."

"Do not think you can confuse me, Senyora Hecht, with these puzzling artistic comments. I consider you a prime suspect in the death of Senyoreta Isabel."

"I've never heard anything so silly in my life," she said.

"You are not to leave Barcelona," I said sternly.

"I don't intend to. My appointment lasts another month and a half."

"Do you have your passport with you? . . . No? Then I shall detail an officer to go to your apartment with you and confiscate it."

12

In a State of Indignation

Carolyn

Because Robbie had gone off to be interviewed by the stern-looking inspector, there was an empty seat beside me. I studied the possibilities for napping on two folding chairs and realized there was no way I could curl up across them. I had to settle for draping my arm over the second chair, turning my body that way, and dropping my head on my arm. As awkward a position as that was, I fell immediately into deep sleep, completely unconscious until Robbie startled me awake by saying my name and giving my hair a mild tug. My head promptly fell off my arm, my body folded onto the adjoining chair, and the top of me pitched into the policeman accompanying Robbie. Startled, he jumped away from me, and I tumbled toward the floor, catching myself with one hand. Robbie's escort grabbed me by the shoulder and arm, and lifted me to my feet.

"Caro, are you all right?" Robbie asked.

"Never startle a jet-lagged woman awake," I mumbled.

The policeman then propped me upright in my own chair, and Robbie sat down beside me. "You must come with me, Senyora," he ordered.

"My turn to be interviewed?" I mumbled.

"You stay," said the policeman, pointing at me.

"They're taking me home so they can confiscate my passport," said Robbie. "You've got the address. Catch a cab after you've been interviewed, that is if you still want to share an apartment with a woman suspected of being a dangerous killer."

"Who?" I really didn't understand the situation, but then I was sleep-dazed and exhausted, nursing the bruised hand that had hit the floor, not to mention suffering from unpleasant pain in my arm and shoulder where the policeman had grabbed me to keep me from rolling ignominiously between the rows of folding chairs.

"Me," said Robbie. "The inspector thinks I killed Isabel last night because we both lusted after the count or because she was trying to steal my research or something. It'll get worked out." She rose and said to the policeman, "Let's go, you cute thing, you." He didn't react. Probably he spoke little English.

"*It'll get worked out!*" I exclaimed. "That's what my mother-in-law said, and it took me a week and an attempt on my life to get it *worked out*."

"Relax, girlfriend," said Robbie.

"Why are you calling me girlfriend? That's black slang. Ebonics, or whatever. Neither one of us is black."

"Go back to sleep, Caro. You're punchy with jet lag."

"We go now," said the policeman, pulling at Robbie's arm. At least he hadn't put hand-cuffs on her.

"If she goes, I go," I said, and took her other arm.

"You stay." He had begun to look worried.

"If I stay, I go to see the inspector." He stared at me anxiously. "Right now."

"Her go, you stay," he insisted.

"Oh, for goodness' sake." I pushed him aside and headed for the auditorium door. "I'll talk to the inspector, Robbie," I called over my shoulder.

"Stay," called her policeman, torn between keeping her in custody and going after me.

Baby Cop tried to stop me at the door, but I held a finger up in front of my lips, shook my head, and murmured "Tapas." Poor Baby Cop stepped aside. He didn't want me telling the inspector that he'd let us wait in the café. Robbie's policeman chased me, calling "Stay," and hauling Robbie along with him,

94

which slowed him up considerably because she wasn't cooperating.

"Go get him!" she called after me, laughing, and I rushed through the inspector's door before anyone could stop me.

Inspector Pujol

The second American woman burst into my interrogation room while I was considering my interview with Senyora Hecht. "Good afternoon, Inspector," she said, offering her hand. I have always thought women who thrust their hands out to be shaken less than ladylike. This one, at least, was wearing decent clothing, although she looked rumpled, and her blond hair was escaping from a scarf that had evidently secured it behind her head.

"I see you don't like to shake hands with strangers," she continued, and sat down without being invited. "Very sensible. I read recently that shaking hands, among other things, such as being coughed on, spreads colds and flu. Happily, I don't have a cough, but I have been traveling for *such* a long time, and I always feel suspicious of the cleanliness of those huge international airplanes. Not to mention the fact that I discovered a dead person today and tried to take

95

her pulse. If she died of a contagious disease, I may have been exposed. And then I fell asleep in the auditorium and fell over. My hand hit the floor, and goodness knows what germs I picked up that way."

"Senyora, I have not called for your presence as yet," I said, afraid she might never stop talking.

"No, but frankly, Inspector, I have two very good reasons for not waiting my turn. One, I am suffering from terrible jet lag and need to get home and sleep for about twenty-four hours. Talking at least keeps me awake. And second, I understand from my old friend Roberta Hecht that you suspect her of killing the woman in the art exhibit, so I felt that I should tell you that is *quite* impossible."

"Perhaps the senyora has never heard of the three branches of a homicide investigation: motive, means, and opportunity. We have motive and means, and she has no alibi except that she claims to have talked to her husband last night on the telephone. That conversation could hardly prove long enough to cover the period of possible death."

"Goodness, you speak excellent English," she said.

"We are not uneducated or provincial here in Catalonia," I replied, feeling additionally irritated.

"I didn't mean that at all, Inspector. I really don't speak any language well enough to converse, except English. I'm always amazed at how well educated Europeans are. Not to mention the fact that Catalans are turning out such fine writers in the language. It must have been dreadful during the Franco regime when you were forbidden to use Catalan."

I was surprised to find that an American knew anything about our linguistic repression during the fascist era. Nor did I believe that this American woman knew anything about Catalan literature. Why would she?

"But I'm digressing," she said before I could take command of the conversation. "You are aware that I'm the person who discovered the body? I thought it was Robbie. Dr. Hecht. That she was playing a joke on me. Then when I tried to wake her up, giving her a little shake, you know, for which I must apologize. I do know that one is not supposed to move a body, but I thought at that time it was a live body. Robbie's body. When she didn't stir, and I found no pulse and noticed blood on the pillow, I panicked and screamed for help. You wouldn't believe how much trouble I had convincing anyone that the person in the bed was not alive. Those strange, birdlike creatures yelled at me and at each other, and then the other patients had their say, and the tourists. It was only when Robbie herself arrived that things began to calm down and the police were called."

I could see that my aide was completely lost in his attempt to take notes, for which I can hardly fault him. The woman was going on and on in American English. I pride myself on my grasp of the language, both spoken and written, but I was becoming lost myself, so I interrupted her, no easy matter, and made her describe slowly and in detail everything that happened from the time she arrived at the exhibit to the time she was sent to wait in the auditorium. I must say, although I had thought her flighty and foolish initially, she did give a clear account of the time involved.

However, the moment she finished complying with my demands, she took back the initiative. "I must tell you, sir, that Professor Roberta Hecht did not kill anyone. She is a world-renowned scholar on the subject of your very own wonderful artist, Joan Miró. You may not realize it, but academics rarely kill one another." Then she hesitated, but added, "Well, hardly ever. And if Robbie says she was in her apartment all evening, that's where she was."

"And the fact that the victim was attacked with the Miró statue on your friend's desk?" I asked.

"Robbie would never use a work of Joan Miró in such a way. She'd consider it blasphemous. What if it were damaged?"

The woman did seem to know her friend's

98

likely reactions. Senyora Hecht had said much the same thing. "Then there is the fact that your friend may have thought Senyoreta Isabel was trying to steal her work on the connection between Miró and parasites."

"Parasites?" The American woman actually giggled. "Robbie used parasites and Miró to catch the attention of her husband, who is a parasitologist. She even showed him Miró prints and pointed out the parasites. This was on a tour of Northern France. Of course, he knew they weren't parasites, but he was head over heels in love by then. Robbie's a very lovable woman."

"So it would seem," I replied as sternly as possible. Again she was saying almost exactly what the Hecht woman had said about parasites. Of course, they could have plotted their responses. Perhaps that was why Senyora — what was her name? I glanced at my list — Blue had insisted on seeing me next. Because she didn't want to forget what she was supposed to say. "It would seem that your friend and the victim were both in love with and competing for the attention of the same man."

"Oh, you mean the count? Robbie's not in love with him. She's a new bride. She's in love with Hugh. Her husband. The parasitologist. Now, Isabel was in love with the count. In fact, she was his mistress. If you're looking for Isabel's murderer, the count would make a good suspect. Perhaps Isabel wanted to marry him, and he didn't want to divorce his wife. Maybe she was even pregnant with his child. So he killed her to get her off his hands. You should have your medical examiner check Isabel for pregnancy."

"Wealthy men rarely kill their mistresses," I replied. What extravagant ideas this woman had! "They simply pay them off if they want to be rid of them."

"Or hire a hit man to kill them," Senyora Blue suggested.

"An American folk tradition, not one of ours."

"Oh, poof," she replied. "European kings, dukes, and noblemen were always hiring people to kill off their rivals. Look at Henry the Second. He said, 'Will no one rid me of this pesky priest?' or something like that, and there was St. Thomas à Becket, stabbed to death in the cathedral. I'll bet we could find examples in a Catalan history book. I have one with me, so I'll look as soon as I return to the apartment and get some sleep."

Of course, she was right, and she had a startling interest in European history. Was she actually carrying a Catalan history in her bags?

"The count's wife is another excellent suspect. She probably found out about the affair and, being a woman of volatile temperament, had Isabel killed."

"How do you know what the temperament

of the comte's wife is?" I asked. "Have you any evidence at all that the wife might have —"

"I have common sense, Inspector. I have always thought common sense a very good guide."

I had to agree with her on that, although I didn't say it. We Catalans pride ourselves on our extraordinary common sense.

"Can I leave now?" she asked, looking exhausted. "I've told you all I know, plus all the suppositions I've made, and I'm so very tired. I came straight here from the plane. I haven't even changed my clothes in over twenty-four hours."

She wouldn't have eaten anything substantial either in some time. Tapas hardly count, no matter what she thought. I could certainly sympathize. My own stomach was complaining of a missed meal.

"I'm staying at Robbie's apartment, Inspector. If you have any other questions for me, you can always call me there, after I've had time for a bath and a good long sleep."

Ha! Staying at Robbie's apartment, was she? That certainly threw in doubt the usefulness of anything she had to say. "Good day, Senyora Blue. We thank you for your information." The woman gave me a sweet smile, rather reminding me of my wife, who wouldn't be happy to be compared with an American, even one respectably dressed.

13

Security Concerns

Inspector Pujol

A Catalan history book? I mused as Senyora Blue departed. If she really had one with her, she'd probably call me to pass on the name and an anecdote about some prominent Catalan who had bought or ordered the killing of a mistress. I shook my head in disbelief and told my aide to bring in the security guard who had been on duty last night, one José Cerdà. The guard had evidently been roused from his bed, because his hair was mussed, more so than that of Senyora Blue, who had been sleeping in chairs from America to Barcelona. Also Cerdà's shirt was buttoned askew. He remembered that Senyoreta Isabel had arrived at about 11:30 the night before and rung the night bell.

"She didn't have a key?"

"Probably," said Cerdà, "but the alarm has to be turned off and on for people coming and going after hours. She wouldn't have wanted to bother. These artistic types don't understand security systems, sir. It's left to my cousin and me to keep the alarms from going off."

"And you didn't notice that she hadn't left?" I asked.

"No sir, I was asleep until my cousin came in the morning to relieve me. He's the day guard. No one set off the alarm, so obviously no one tried to come in or out who shouldn't. Maybe she stayed all night."

I interviewed Guifré Cerdà after that, another slow-witted, sleepy-eyed fellow. He had come on duty at 6:00 when his cousin went home, had checked the alarms, determined that none had been disturbed, made himself some coffee, and read his newspaper undisturbed until the director arrived at 9:00 a.m. If Senyoreta Isabel had been in the building, he hadn't seen her, and obviously no one else was because José hadn't let anyone in but her, which he hadn't mentioned when Guifré arrived.

"I did have a strange American woman arrive at the door late in the morning and insist on bringing in a huge, wheeled suitcase," Guifré Cerdà confided. "When I told her she couldn't, she cried and kept talking, and I didn't know what to do, so the receptionist let her in. Otherwise, it's been an ordinary day, except for finding Senyoreta Isabel in 'Tapas Triage.' The corpses in there have always been alive before. And of course, we never have policemen here, not even to visit the exhibits. Maybe you should talk to the American woman, sir. She might have killed Senyoreta Isabel. She was the one who found her and made such a fuss. What a talker, that one. I'm glad she's not my wife. Would you like me to point her out to you?"

"I know the woman you mean," I replied, then asked, "How long since anyone tested the security system?"

Cerdà looked puzzled. "Test it how, Inspector? When it's armed and someone comes in without turning it off, it makes a big noise. Same if someone goes out while it's armed if they don't put in the code."

I excused him and marveled that all the art hadn't already been stolen from the museum. Someone would have to test the security system. It probably wasn't even working.

Carolyn

I was fast asleep on Robbie's sofa bed when she woke me up after so few hours of rest that I was not yet feeling human again. "Go away," I mumbled, and buried my head under the pillow.

"You've got a phone call, Caro."

"Tell them to call back tomorrow."

"It's Gwen."

"Gwen?" Why was my daughter calling me long distance? It must be some emergency. I grabbed the telephone from Robbie's hand and said, terrified, "Gwen? What's wrong?"

"Nothing, Mom. I just wanted you to know that I got my tickets, and I'll be there on the twenty-seventh."

"Be where?" I asked fuzzily. "Are you sure you're all right?"

"Better than all right!" my daughter exclaimed enthusiastically. "I'm so excited. I still can't believe the university's going to let me go and still get credit for this semester."

"Gwen, what are you talking about?" I demanded anxiously. My daughter tended to get these wild ideas and then insist on carrying them through while I fretted over the consequences.

"My internship with Professor Hecht. Didn't she tell you? Miró did some wonderful set designs. Picasso too. It's a terrific opportunity for me, and my drama professor agrees. I'm already studying Catalan. I put the tapes on every night before I go to bed."

I had been sitting. Now I fell back against the pillow and stared helplessly at the ceiling, which had very nice moldings. I'd have appreciated them much more if jet lag and distress hadn't weighed me down. "Gwen," I began slowly, "you do not have my permission to leave school on some harebrained —"

"I talked to Daddy," she interrupted. "He

thought it would be really neat, especially since I'll get to see you both in Barcelona."

"Jason *agreed?*"

Gwen then asked in a sad voice that I knew was feigned (Gwen is a wonderful actress, which is fine on stage, but not as admirable when practiced in family life), "Don't you *want* to see me, Mom?"

"Yes. I'll come up to visit you at the university as soon as I get home if you're lonely," I replied grimly.

"I'm not lonely. I'm excited."

"Gwen, you know I always do research before we travel, and I can tell you that Barcelona is a dangerous city. I do not want my daughter —"

"Mom, we can't call it all off now. I've got nonrefundable tickets, and I've made all the arrangements with my professors, and I don't see why you'd object. Professor Hecht can keep an eye on me if Barcelona's so dangerous."

Robbie, who is about to be charged with the murder of Isabel? I thought despairingly.

"I'll be fine, Mom. Gosh, if you're that worried, I'll stay with her."

On the sofa bed? I wanted to ask. It wasn't all that comfortable, and Robbie might find she didn't like sharing a small apartment with a teenaged girl. I shot my friend a killing look. She grinned back.

"Whoops. Got to get off, Mom. The lunch

106

bell just rang. See you Saturday."

"Gwen!" She was gone, so I turned to Robbie. "You invited my daughter to drop out of school and come here to intern with you?" I asked accusingly.

"Nope. She called me," said Robbie. "She heard from you what I was doing here and thought it up herself. Of course, I was glad to help out. I got her a stipend from Miquel and permission to live in the university dorms. The money should cover her living expenses. Actually, it's a terrific deal for her."

"Actually, Robbie, this is something you should have talked to me about before you —"

"Hey, I didn't know she hadn't told you. I gather from your conversation that Jason agreed."

"If she'd told her father she wanted to go to the Amazon and join an indigenous tribe to do anthropological research, Jason would have agreed — as long as research was involved. She said maybe she'd live with you."

"Well, I didn't suggest *that*." Robbie looked taken aback.

"And that you'd look out for her."

"Of course I will. I've always loved Gwen."

"How are you going to look out for her if you're in jail for murdering Isabel?"

"Oh, Caro, I'm not going to jail. But if you're really worried about it, you'd better get up and get dressed. Miquel has invited us

107

to join the staff at a dinner to discuss the murder. We can start sleuthing. Wasn't that your idea this afternoon?"

Dinner? When I'd had practically no sleep since goodness knows when? I groaned.

"Up you get, girlfriend. We have to be at the restaurant by nine-thirty. That's just an hour from now."

"Stop calling me girlfriend," I muttered.

14

Paella in Memoriam

Carolyn

I had been introduced to the count, Miquel Xifré i Fontdevila; the count's daughter, Dolors Xifré i Roca; the museum director, Professor Jordi Toda i Aguillo; a museum scholar, Madrona Brusi i Farriols; and the creator of the performance art exhibit "Tapas Triage," Ramon Berenguer, who was called Narcis by all the others. The others no doubt had nicknames too. Being introduced to a group of Catalans was as difficult an exercise in remembering complicated names as reading a nineteenth-century Russian novel. The only reason I still know their names is that Robbie repeated them when we got home, and I wrote them down and still have the list stuck in among my food notes.

We had just been served our soup, gazpacho, when the count raised his glass and suggested that we drink to "our dear friend" Isabel, whom we would all miss. I drank the toast with the others, although I hadn't known her at all, beyond discovering her corpse that morning. With this new infusion of alcohol, I could only hope that I'd be able to avoid dropping unexpectedly into sleep and falling, face first, into my soup. The count expounded on the virtues of Isabel and her wonderful insights on Miró birds and ladders, and I tried the gazpacho. It had cream in it, or so I thought. I was so sleepy that the unusual, to me, ingredient might have been raw egg, and I wouldn't have known the difference. I must say it wasn't as good as the gazpacho I make myself, but I'm probably prejudiced.

Carolyn's Gazpacho

Gazpacho is cold soup that is served all over Spain, not to mention in other countries. The author of Bull Cook and Historical Recipes and Practices, *an eccentric cookbook given to me by my father, claims that gazpacho was born when an Andalusian peasant in the nineteenth century didn't have any firewood so had to eat his vegetable soup cold. He and his guest liked it.*

- Liquefy in a blender or food processor *1/2 peeled cucumber; one green bell pepper, seeds and all; 3 chopped cloves of garlic; 1 small peeled onion; and 42 oz.*

canned tomatoes with liquid. Pour into a large bowl or enameled pan and mix together.

- Mix together in a cup *1 tbs. chili powder, 1 tbs. salt, 2 tbs. olive oil* and *2 tbs. vinegar.* Stir well into the liquefied vegetables.
- Mix in *1/2 cup fine dry breadcrumbs.*
- Mix in *1 qt. cold water.*
- Cover and allow to stand in a cool room five hours or overnight.
- Strain solids from the soup, add extra chili powder and salt to taste, and chill liquid in the refrigerator.
- Stir or shake and serve cold with bowls of garlic croutons.
- **Croutons:** Set oven at 200° F. Remove crusts from *1 lb. sliced, stale white bread* and cut slices into 20 to 25 croutons. Melt half-and-half *butter and Lawry's garlic spread* and dab on croutons spread in baking pan. Bake for 2 hours, allow to cool, and refrigerate until ready to serve. Float on soup.

Carolyn Blue,
"Have Fork, Will Travel,"
Phoenix Sun

While I ate my soup, the others talked about Miró and speculated on who could have killed Isabel. I speculated on which one of *them* could have killed Isabel. Robbie caused a sensation, which seemed feigned to me except on the part of the count, by saying that Inspector Pujol seemed to think *she* had.

"Now, if some of you think I killed her, aren't you afraid of what I'll do when I find out who told the inspector that I was the logical suspect?" She smiled around the table and then scooped up another spoonful of soup. "Carolyn makes better gazpacho than this," she added.

I believe I flushed. I may have thought that very thing, but probably Spaniards would be insulted to hear it. Dolors, the count's daughter, who was sitting beside me, said, "Gazpacho is Andalusian, not Catalan. Do you have Andalusian ancestors, Senyora Blue?"

"No, mostly English," I replied.

"Then it's a wonder you can cook at all," said Madrona. She and Jordi had looked alarmed when Robbie had laughingly threatened those who suggested her as a suspect to the inspector. I assumed they were the culprits.

Narcis was laughing. He said, "Let us feel your muscles, dear Robbie, to see if you are strong enough to have carried Isabel downstairs to the exhibit."

Madrona suggested that Robbie could have used the elevator to transport the body. Narcis said the elevator was so noisy, it would have awakened even the deep-sleeping José Cerdà.

The count said, "Of course Roberta did not kill Isabel. The murder weapon was evidently a Miró bird. None of us would have deliberately damaged the bird."

Now there's a cold-hearted defense, I thought.

"As well as accuse me," said the count reproachfully.

Yes, indeed, I thought.

"But of course I always have the perfect alibi. I have only to put the police in touch with Senyor Bacigalupi, my wife's detective." The count then chortled with delight while his daughter looked miserable. "The man is always with me, poor fellow. But I am sure he is well paid by Violante, who likes to throw my indiscretions in my face when we have family dinners. Isn't that true, my dear?" he asked his daughter.

"Yes, Papa," she mumbled

I felt sorry for the girl and engaged her in conversation when I had the chance, but that was well into the main course because the count had more to say.

"I have taken the liberty of ordering for us all. Seafood paella, the dish that our dear Isabel made so well."

"Ah, she was a maestro with paella," sighed the director.

"Indeed she was. We will always, I am sure, remember dinners at Isabel's apartment." Everyone nodded, including his daughter.

How could a father take his daughter to dinner at his mistress's table? I wondered. The poor girl. No wonder she was thinking of joining a convent, something she confessed to me in a soft voice later in the evening. I patted her hand and let her talk about her religious vocation, which seemed to have more to do with the idea of escape than the idea of becoming a bride of Christ.

"So let us enjoy this fine dinner, although not as fine as Isabel's, in memory of our dear friend. And Madrona, I must tell you that Senyora Blue may, as she claims, be of English descent, but she is a culinary expert. She writes newspaper columns on fine food. For that reason, and because you are a longtime friend of Roberta's, Senyora Blue, I have procured for you Isabel's recipe for paella. I hope that you will put it in your column and mention her name so that she will be remembered even in America." He then passed me a handwritten copy of what I assumed to be the paella recipe. It was in Catalan, and I recognized only the word *paella*.

"She doesn't read Catalan," said Madrona, none too pleasantly.

"I will translate it for you, Senyora," Narcis offered. Madrona looked even more displeased.

The count didn't seem to notice this interplay. He raised his flute, which contained not the native cava but an expensive French champagne, and said, "Let us toast Isabel and commend her soul to God. I am having masses said for her at the cathedral, and I assume you are all praying for her soul."

The last seemed to be in the nature of an order. I thanked him for the recipe and promised to put it in the column with Isabel's name and scholarly credentials. The last pleased him greatly. He ordered Jordi to provide me with a list of her publications. *Surely, he doesn't expect footnotes?* I thought. *"Have Fork, Will Travel," is, after all, a column, not a book.*

The restaurant's paella was wonderful, although without the lobster in Isabel's recipe. It did feature shellfish minus the shells (although some were decorating the edges of the large plates), and perfectly cooked saffron rice. As tired as I was, I had no trouble staying awake for the main course and a motherly conversation with Dolors. I admit to dozing over dessert, a baked apple filled with *crema catalana,* with a burned sugar glaze on top.

Robbie and I were put in a cab by the count himself, who thanked me for being so kind to his daughter. I felt like saying that he might try that himself before she immured herself in a convent, but I held my tongue for Robbie's sake. He shook my hand, kissed

Robbie on both cheeks — but then he kissed Madrona, as well — and took his daughter away in a limousine.

In our cab I said to Robbie, "His wife has a full-time detective to follow him? That's bizarre."

"Evidently, she's had him followed ever since they separated, even before, I suppose. Narcis said she's dreadfully jealous even if she won't speak Catalan and live with him. Also very beautiful. I've always wondered whether they go to bed together after squabbling through those bimonthly family dinners. But I don't suppose they do, or there'd be more children."

"No wonder Dolors wants to go into a convent."

"Really? She told you that?"

I nodded.

"Miquel isn't going to like it. Neither is her mother. She's expected to marry well and add the family name to that of her husband. Miquel has no son; they split before he could get Violante pregnant again, and she won't divorce him, so he's stuck. No male heir. Dolors does take his affairs hard, according to Narcis. You don't think she could have killed Isabel and now be planning the convent thing as an act of penance?"

"What a horrible idea," I mumbled. My last thought that night, before dropping like a stone into sleep, was the question of what my civic duty might be in this matter. Should I call Inspector Pujol and add Dolors to my list of suspects? I didn't like to do that, but if Dolors had killed Isabel, perhaps I owed it to Robbie to bring the matter up. The one person I knew hadn't done it was Robbie.

Isabel Almirall's Paella

The following recipe is often called the lazy man's or rich man's paella and was first made for a young Barcelona gentleman who wanted something different early in the twentieth century. It caught on.

- Sauté *1 chicken (cut into pieces, boned, halved, and skinned)* in a wide, flat-bottomed pan in a little *olive oil* until golden brown; then remove pieces to drain and set aside.
- Sauté in same oil until crisp *1/2 lb. boneless pork loin, cut into 8 thin scallops* and *8 small pork sausages*. Take out, drain, and set aside.
- Sauté in same oil, adding more if necessary, *1/2 lb. monkfish*★ *and 1/2 lb. sea bass or halibut, each cut into 8 small pieces, skinned and boned,* and *8 large peeled shrimp* until lightly browned. Remove, drain, and set aside.
- Sauté until onions soften a bit *3 chopped onions,* and *4 medium artichoke hearts halved and sprinkled with lemon*

juice. Then add *2 peeled, seeded, chopped tomatoes,* stir, and add *1 cup chicken stock.* Bring to boil, reduce heat, and simmer 10 minutes.

- Return chicken and pork scallops to pan; add *1 pound short grain rice*** and *4 red or green bell peppers, grilled, peeled, and cut in strips.* Reserve 12 strips to decorate dish before serving.
- Add *4 1/2 cups chicken stock* and increase heat to medium high.
- Make a *picada* by grinding into a paste with a mortar and pestle *4 cloves minced garlic, 2 sprigs minced parsley, and 8 lightly roasted threads of saffron.* Moisten with several drops of stock and make a paste. Then stir into the pan.
- Stir in shrimp, fish, and salt to taste.
- Boil *4 rock lobsters* until pink, cut in half. Loosening flesh but leaving shells, set aside.
- When stock is partially evaporated, arrange sausages, lobster pieces, and reserved red pepper strips on top of rice. Continue cooking until rice is done and liquid evaporates (20–25 minutes total from second addition of chicken stock).
- When finished, let paella stand 5 to 10 minutes; then serve for 6 to 8 people.

* *Monkfish is delicious, firm, and mild, and we never have to see the actual creature in the United States. However, I saw a whole monkfish in La Boquería, Barcelona's ironwork and glass market. It has a large spade-shaped head with vicious-looking teeth and a scorpion tail with the delicious meat on the backbone in between — no dangerous little bones sprouting out from the spine. But imagine seeing that creature on your plate, teeth bared!*

***Rice came to Spain with the Moors in the eighth century but became an important crop when, in the thirteenth century, Jaume I of Aragon attempted to stem malaria epidemics by having rice planted in certain swampy parts of Valencia.*

Carolyn Blue,
"Have Fork, Will Travel,"
Biloxi Bay Times

15

Consular Advice

Carolyn

When I woke up my second day in Barcelona, Robbie was on the phone saying, "Mr. Barkley? You're the consul, right? . . . Did your secretary tell you what I'm calling about? . . . No, I haven't been arrested, but I'm a suspect in the killing of a Miró researcher named Isabel Almirall at the Esperit de Gaudí i Miró. . . . Well, you should get out more. It's a neat place. Anyway, I'm on leave from my university in the States doing Miró research for three months at Esperit, and Isabel was found dead in a performance-art exhibition. Evidently she didn't like me, so I'm getting blamed. Since I'm innocent, what I want to know is: What should I do? Do you people provide lawyers if I need one or character references or sneak fellow citizens out of the country? . . . Just kidding. I couldn't leave if I wanted to. I haven't finished my paper. . . . Right. Okay. I'll call him. . . . Sure, I'll let you know if they arrest me. Do they give you phone calls in the jails? . . . Should I call you or the lawyer first? . . .

"Now there's this other thing. My husband tells me that my stepson has disappeared from his camp in the U.S. Then in the middle of the night he called again and said Sammie's passport is missing, so naturally we're wondering if he came to Barcelona to see me, but he hasn't shown up at my place, so is there any way you can find out if he's here? . . . Uh huh. . . . Uh huh. Okay, I'd appreciate it, Mr. Barkley. His full name is Henri Samuel Fauree. F-A-U-R-E-E. I'll expect your call." She put down the receiver and for the first time noticed that I was awake and staring at her with dismay.

"What?" she exclaimed. "I called my country's representative because I have a problem, and he gave me the name of a lawyer who speaks English."

"And Sammie? Hugh says his passport is missing?"

"Right. So where would he be going? Hugh doesn't have any relatives left in France, and anyway, Sammie's still mad because Hugh named him Henri for Hugh's dad. Henri is Sammie's first name."

I nodded. "Children can be very sensitive about their names. He wouldn't want to be teased. But even if he has his passport, where

121

would he get the money to travel abroad? Maybe he's run away to Canada or someplace closer. I wouldn't think he'd want to follow you. You said he resents you."

"You're right," said Robbie gloomily. "But I had to ask, didn't I? Hugh is beside himself. As for the money, I'll bet the little bugger took some out of his college fund. Hugh makes a big thing about having the kids' names on the accounts. I'll ask him to check that as soon as I hear back from the American consul, not that knowing Sammie took college money will tell us where he went."

"At least you'll know he's not on the streets starving to death," I told her.

Then I went to the bathroom to shower, relieved to note once again that Robbie had washcloths. European hotels don't. Robbie went into her three- by six-foot kitchen to fix breakfast. I don't know how she could stand it, but then she never did much cooking. *She no doubt lunches on tapas at the museum,* I reasoned. *Maybe they even have tapas to go.*

When I finished dressing, I joined my hostess, who was cracking eggs and throwing them into the sink. "Look at these," she complained. "The shells are brown, and they have chicken embryos in them. Isn't that disgusting? If they'd just keep the roosters away from the hens . . ."

I took her place at the sink before she could discard the last of the eggs, cracked some myself, removed the spots with a spoon, and made scrambled eggs while Robbie tried to cut a loaf of bread into slices that would fit in the toaster. She's a woman with a very colorful vocabulary. My guess was that she went out for breakfast and probably yearned for the delights of frozen toaster waffles.

She did have blood orange juice in the refrigerator, something I love. What a lovely rose color! What a sweet taste! Did they grow in Spain? Or were they shipped there from North Africa or Sicily, where Arab conquerors had introduced citrus trees. To have blood oranges, it would almost be worth being conquered for a few hundred years. Well, not if the conquerors were Muslim fanatics, but as I understand it, the old-time Arabs were more tolerant of other religions.

"What are you thinking about, Caro?" Robbie asked.

"I was thinking the blood oranges in Sicily must have come from North Africa and wondering exactly where these came from."

Robbie laughed. "Is that the kind of thing you and Jason talk about? Now, I'm not criticizing. Since I married Hugh, I find myself in some bizarre dinner-table conversations. It's kind of fun."

"Of course it is," I agreed. "It's better than talking about the neighbor's dog barking early in the morning or whether your university is going to have a winning football season. Not that Jason isn't willing to talk about football."

"It's a male thing," said Robbie. "Not a single one of my husbands has hated football. Now, if it were just a matter of looking at some nice, muscular male bodies — like that inspector, for instance — I'd be all for it, but they put the football players out on the field with a lot of grotesque padding, so all you can enjoy is their tight pants. Then they insist on interviewing the guys between halves, and half or more of them can't speak even moderately grammatical English."

"Oh, that's so true. I came through the family room one Monday evening when Jason was watching a game, and some poor fellow was trying to answer a reporter's questions. Three grammar errors in one sentence. I counted them."

"Right. I've never had a football player in one of my art history classes. I've always thought the coaches warned them away, but I could put up with the grammar if they weren't wearing their padded armor. Probably some of them have luscious bodies."

I laughed and said, "Robbie, you're incorrigible. Does Hugh know you're a fan of male bodies?"

"Well, I only mention his male body to him. There's the phone." She snatched it up and identified herself after saying something in Catalan. "You're sure?" she asked, biting her lip. "When? . . . That's two days ago!" She thanked the person at the other end of the line and turned back to me. "The Spanish government checks the passports of people coming in and records them. Sammie got here Monday." We stared at each other in dismay. "We've got to go looking for him."

"Where?" I asked.

Robbie thought a minute. "Hospitals and youth hostels. If he's here, what's he doing? Why hasn't he come to see me? There's no other reason for him to fly to Barcelona. He could have been mugged or killed."

"Calm down, Robbie," I murmured. "We'll find him. We'll start right now. Hostels — that's a good idea. Kids travel that way — with backpacks and bedrolls, staying in hostels and cheap hotels. Chris did that with friends before he went off to college."

"He was eighteen. Sammie's only thirteen. How come they even let him out of the country without an accompanying adult? God, I've got to call Hugh, and he'll freak. He's probably been thinking Sammie's hiding out with some friend. He —"

"Good. Call him right now. It's what? — nine here, five or six in the afternoon there?"

"No, it's the middle of the night there," said Robbie. "Just having the phone ring is going to scare him to death."

The usually unflappable Robbie wrung her

hands, then wiped her palms on her slacks and reached for the telephone. I went back to the bathroom to brush my teeth. I could hear them talking as I scrubbed and flossed. When I returned to the living room, Robbie was throwing things into her purse.

"Hugh's coming. He has to get people to cover his classes, and he'll have to bring Kimmie because the grandparents are in Mexico looking at Aztec stuff and buying tequila. Celestine loves margaritas. Serves them every time we visit. And he's got to get Kimmie excused from school and get tickets."

"So you're not sure what day he'll arrive," I finished for her.

"Right, but if he gets here before Jason, you're going to have to move to the hotel early because Kimmie will have to sleep here." She pointed at the sofa, where I was folding up my sheets. "And of course, Hugh will share my bed, if he's still speaking to me."

"Robbie, it's not your fault Sammie ran away. You were doing your best."

"Oh, right. And what do I know about dealing with a teenaged boy? Nothing, that's what. Hugh is probably wishing he'd never met me. He might be dean now if it weren't for me, and his boy sure wouldn't have run away."

"I think we should start making lists of the

places we need to look."

"I'll do that. You call the hotel and ask if you can move in early, but not before Hugh gets here. Good thing the museum's closed. We'll spend the day out of the apartment looking for Sammie, and if the cops call or come here when we get back, I'll hide in the bathroom and you can tell them I'm out lighting candles for Isabel or something. Tell them I've gone on a pilgrimage to Compostela. I can't afford to go to jail before we find Sammie. Good Lord, I didn't even think to tell Hugh about Isabel."

"Robbie, take a deep breath. We'll find Sammie," I assured her. "And we'll find out who killed Isabel. Goodness, I'm actually getting used to this sort of thing — I mean investigating murders. You're so lucky I'm here to help."

But we didn't go after all. The count called to say staff members were to meet for breakfast to plan Isabel's funeral. Evidently Isabel had no family.

"Why don't you start calling hospitals, Caro?" Robbie suggested as she flew out the door.

"But I don't speak Catalan," I protested, too late.

127

16

The Meddling Judge

Inspector Pujol

I was called to report on the investigation as soon as I got to my office. Judge Goytisolo would have paid little attention to the case had a sailor in a waterfront bar killed another in a knife fight. The Almirall death, unfortunately, was going to engage his full attention.

"Do you have a suspect yet?" he asked before I could sit down.

On that score I could give him news he might like. I took a chair, quite a comfortable chair. His office is much more luxurious than mine. Not to mention three times as large, with bookshelves lined with leather-bound books, whereas I have battered metal filing cabinets stuffed to overflowing. The judge has paneled walls, a large, handsome desk, and a comfortable leather chair. I have plaster walls and a ceiling discolored by water stains, a scuffed desk, one leg of which has to be balanced by forcing a wad of arrest forms under the glass ball, and an unpadded chair that creaks alarmingly if I shift positions. Still, I am a man of simple tastes and am not bothered by my less than opulent surroundings.

"Yes, I have a suspect, Your Honor," I replied. "Several of the staff members agree that an American researcher and the deceased did not like each other. Isabel Almirall was quite possibly killed at the American's desk while making notes on the American's research."

"Excellent. An American suspect will cause less public controversy than a Catalan. And I like professional competition as a motive. Very believable. Americans are not only known for their violent propensities but for their overweening ambition. It sounds as if we can make a good case against this person. Have you any other reasons to justify an arrest?"

"There's some thought that the two might have been competing for the romantic attentions of Comte Miguel Xifré i Fontdevila," I replied.

"Inspector Pujol, that is hardly a motive we can make public. Some people might take it to mean that the count is susceptible to the . . . er . . . charms of men as well as women."

"The American suspect is a woman, Your Honor."

"Oh, I see." The judge's curved mustache

rose in a smile that revealed both his relief and his neat, white teeth, which looked far too perfect to be anything but man-made. "Well, the count is known to be a charmer of women," the judge admitted. "I can well believe the two women might have been squabbling over him. However, if any attentions of his prove to be the motive, we must try to keep his name out of it."

I said nothing since I was unable to express my distaste for such toadying.

"Wait! A woman as murderer?" The judge glowered at me. "You say the victim may have been killed at the murderer's desk. Was that on the ground floor? I distinctly remember that the body was found in an art exhibit on the ground floor."

"The desk is on the third floor," I admitted.

"Not good," said Goytisolo. "Not good at all. Who would believe that a woman could carry a body, even a female body, down several floors to place it in the art exhibit?"

"There is an elevator," I said.

"Well, that's better."

"But it is very noisy. The guard would have had to be not only asleep, but also deaf or drugged, to fail to be awakened by the clanking and catch the perpetrator."

"Bad. Very bad."

"But the woman could have had an accomplice."

"Do you think she did?" Goytisolo asked hopefully.

"We haven't turned one up. However, even without an accomplice, the American is a very tall and sturdy woman, although voluptuous."

"Voluptuous? Are you saying that she is beautiful? I hope not. And do not tell me that she is charming? It's hard convict a woman both beautiful and charming."

"But remember that she is an American," I reminded him. "And she might well be able to carry a small woman — the victim was short — down those stairs."

"Hmmm." His telephone rang. "I told you I was not to be disturbed," he said sharply, presumably to his secretary, another benefit the judge has that I do not. I have whatever officer is available to take notes for me when I am interviewing suspects and witnesses. Some of these officers have illegible handwriting and are hopeless with a typewriter. It can be days before I get transcripts of their notes. Fortunately, I have an excellent memory. If not, I would never solve a case. I would not be an inspector or have a house with a very pleasant garden and money to send my son and daughter to university.

The judge was taking the call, in fact, speaking in English. His is not as good as mine, for all he is a judge, but then he has connections in high places that I, as a man of the people, do not have. "No arrest yet," he said. "Too soon. . . . What information make you think citizen of your country is — ? . . . *She* says it? . . . *Sí, sí, sí.* I call you my personal self. . . . Good-bye."

The judge glared at me. "You might have kept it to yourself that you suspect the American woman. That was the American consul calling to say she is a famous scholar and he will call the American ambassador if she is arrested. We'll have the diplomats on our hands, making protests, talking about trade and cooperation in fighting terrorism. You don't think she could be a terrorist?"

"It seems unlikely, sir," I replied. Obviously I couldn't make a move in any direction without causing the judge to panic.

His telephone rang again. Not doubt Madrid was calling to criticize us bumbling Catalans for endangering diplomatic relations with the United States.

"Comte!" he exclaimed. "How good of you to call. . . . What, Pujol has closed down the museum entirely? . . . I understand. . . . Yes, of course. . . . The minister of tourism? . . . No, he hasn't called me. . . . Please do not worry, dear sir. I'm sure we can reach an accommodation acceptable to all.

"Senyora Hecht? . . . I don't — Ah, the American scholar. . . . Well, you understand that everyone must be considered a suspect until — No, of course not you, my dear

Comte. . . . We'll certainly take into account your good opinion of the lady. . . . It has been my pleasure, sir, I assure you."

Goytisolo returned the receiver gently to its cradle, then clasped his temples between the palms of his hands, as if developing an unbearable headache. "The comte does not think it possible that the American woman killed his researcher."

"Well, of course, he'd say that," I responded, "especially if he is enamoured with her."

"And he is very upset that you've closed the museum."

"It's a crime scene. We can't have tourists and staff members traipsing through, destroying evidence."

"There has to be a compromise," said the judge.

"I don't see what," I replied.

"Well, think, Pujol. Even the minister of tourism is upset. El Esperit is Barcelona's newest attraction. They've advertised it. Now people will come, only to be turned away. They'll complain that our city is not friendly to guests."

"Even so, sir —"

"We'll close the exhibit where the body was found and block the desk you mentioned with crime scene tape. Assign a man to guard each site. Yes. That's the thing. A solution that should bring even more tourists to the museum. Tourists love a scene of violence. My daughter and I visited a torture museum. People were lined up in the streets waiting to get in. The comte will be delighted when he discovers that the murder, the tapes, and the uniformed officers on site double, even triple his attendance figures. I hear they charge a fortune to get in."

"Twelve euros," I said. "But, believe me, sir, opening the museum, even partially, will be a great impediment to our investigation. When the newspapers hear of it, they'll say the comte is getting preferential treatment."

"Well, of course he is," said Goytisolo. "Now see to it, Pujol. Immediately."

"At least give us until tomorrow to go over the place in as much detail as possible."

"Oh, very well, but the comte and the minister of tourism won't like it."

17

The Hostile Hostel

Carolyn

I spent the morning calling hospitals, trying to find people who spoke English so that I could ask if Sammie was one of their patients. I must say that when I did reach an English-speaking person, most were very kind and helpful. Some thought I was the mother of the missing boy and sympathized; they told me stories of their children who had disappeared on beaches, in subways, at toy stores, and assured me that their children had been found, thanks to the intercession of the Holy Virgin or the child's patron saint or the like. They advised prayer, calling a priest, calling the police, and more prayer. They suggested churches at which I could light candles for the return of my son. They promised to say prayers themselves. What they didn't have for me was news that Sammie was in their hospitals. During these calls I was overcome with hunger and searched Robbie's shelves for food. She had peanut butter (American) and jelly (Catalan, but I wasn't sure what flavor), which I smeared on some of the raggedly cut bread. We'd definitely have to eat out tonight. After my sandwich, I went back to calling.

I was worn out and depressed by the time Robbie arrived, full of breakfast, lunch, and news of Isabel's funeral plans, not to mention the count's anger that the police had closed the museum and were trying to finger Robbie for the murder. I said I didn't know what else they could do about the museum; after all, it was a crime scene.

"What have you found out about Sammie?" she asked, once she had narrated her morning.

"He's not in a hospital," I said.

"Thank God for that." Then her relief gave way to anguish. "But what if he's in a morgue?"

"Well, I don't think he's in the morgue, but I couldn't get a real English speaker there." Then I handed her a list of youth hostels and cheap hotels, which I had picked out of my Barcelona guide. "Anything marked cheap, I listed."

Robbie threw her arms around me and said I was the best friend a woman could have. Then we decided to adopt hope as our motto and visit youth hostels. What a dreadful experience that was! They smelled bad and needed a good scrubbing, and the bathrooms, which I couldn't resist viewing — some had mold growing in between the tiles. Some didn't even have tiles, just grimy, sodden, wooden floors. The thought that my son might have walked barefoot on such a floor made me physically ill. And I was so glad that I had diverted Gwen from going to Europe with friends by talking an acquaintance into hiring her to run a summer children's theater. My mother-in-law was furious; she said I was encouraging her granddaughter to remain interested in a frivolous career option.

Many of the hostels we visited were devoid of youths. They had evidently gone sight-seeing, or whatever youths do while touring Europe. I hoped that it was sight-seeing. None of the adults in these places had seen Sammie. The last place — and the neighborhoods had deteriorated as we searched out addresses on our list — had young people in it. Very grungy-looking young people. Robbie was initially delighted when some of them could answer her in English, but we soon found ourselves in trouble.

A redheaded fellow with a three-day beard — he looked like a homeless person — shouted to the rest, "Hey, mates, look what we got here. *Older women.* You lookin' for some young studs, ladies?"

Robbie laughed and said, "If we were, it

wouldn't be you, sonny. I like my men past the acne phase."

I could see that he took her reply amiss, but she didn't seem to notice. "I'm looking for a young teen named Sammie. Five six, skinny, dark floppy hair, knows a lot about parasites."

"How much is it worth to you, bay-bee?" sneered a friend of the redhead, a boy who obviously hadn't brushed his teeth, much less flossed, in weeks. I could smell his breath from where I stood. He sidled toward Robbie, who gave him a good shove. "Knock it off," she snapped. "This is my stepson we're talking about. If you've seen him, just say so. There might be something in it for you if you can find him for me."

"O-o-oh," cried the grimy redhead. "It's the wicked stepmother. What's in it for *me*, stepmother? You wanna get wicked with me?"

While he moved in on Robbie, the one with bad teeth and a friend whose jeans were falling apart edged toward me. I was so frightened, it was hard to keep my teeth from chattering, and I could think of nothing in my purse that I could use as a weapon to fend them off. You can't carry that sort of thing onto a plane anymore. Oh, for a can of hair spray or perfume. I knew from experience that you could disable an attacker at least briefly by spraying things into his eyes.

Ragged Jeans said, "Fuckin' A. The wicked

stepmother and her blondie sidekick." Then he danced around me and pinched my bottom. I can't think of when I've been so angry, both at his language and his action.

"Your mother would be ashamed of you, young man," I snapped, and I whirled, swung hard, and hit him with my purse. By chance the corner of the bag caught him in the eye, and he staggered back, howling obscenities.

Robbie's cell phone rang. She flipped it open and said, "Of course I'll hold for Police Inspector Pujol. In fact, tell him to send a squad car down here. We're being harassed by unwashed juvenile delinquents." The juvenile delinquents quieted down. A man entered the hall and said something in Catalan. Robbie said into her phone, "Hi, Inspector Pujol. Here's the address. We'll wait out front for the officers." The adult drove the young men away, shouting about the *policia*. That much Catalan I understood. Robbie and I ran out the front door and sprinted two blocks to a safer location, where we hailed a cab.

Gasping for breath, I turned to her. "What about the police car the inspector is sending? I can't believe how lucky we were. What was Inspector Pujol calling about?"

"There's no police car," she said calmly, not even breathing hard. Evidently kayaking, a sport she and Hugh have in common, strengthens the lungs. "And that wasn't Inspector Pujol, thank God. Why would he call me if he didn't want to question me again, or arrest me?"

She was more worried about arrest than she'd let on. "Who did call?" I asked.

"Miquel. He was pretty surprised that I kept calling him Inspector Pujol. He just wanted to tell me that he'd called the police to tell them to get off my back. Pretty nice, don't you think?"

"Very thoughtful," I agreed, alighting from the cab and looking cautiously up and down the street. The young ruffians had not followed us. I wasn't the only one to be fooled by Robbie's pretense on her cell phone. I had to give her points for quick thinking. All I'd been able to do was hit someone with my purse. Goodness, what if I'd put his eye out? We might be sued, if they could find us.

Of course I was acting in self-defense, but would a Catalan court view it that way? I climbed the stairs with Robbie, but I didn't mention to her the decision I'd made. I was going to call Inspector Pujol the first chance I got. He needed my help, even if he didn't think so, and I certainly needed his.

"With the museum closed and the hostels covered, we can start on the cheap hotels tomorrow," said Robbie.

Of course, *when* I'd be free to call the inspector was another matter.

18

Down on the Waterfront

Carolyn

We did eat out that night. Narcis had offered to escort us to a genuine sailor's café. I was somewhat dubious, both of Narcis and of dining with sailors. However, Robbie thought it was an opportunity I shouldn't miss. What a column it would make! she pointed out. "You're not scared, are you? Narcis will look after us." (I'd rather have had Inspector Pujol.) "We'll dress down. No one will even notice us." Jason would hate this idea, but I let myself be convinced, and when he called from Salamanca, I told him we were going out for fresh seafood. He was envious.

I wore slacks, a plain button-down shirt, a sweater, and comfortable moccasins. Robbie's idea of dressing down was a low-necked peasant blouse and a gypsy skirt. I felt as if I were going out to dinner with Carmen and Don José in mufti. Narcis was decked out in tight pants, a shirt unbuttoned almost to his

141

belt buckle, and a gold cross on a chain. If the sailors didn't notice such a mismatched trio, they'd have to be blind or very drunk. Perhaps the latter was what I should have expected.

Narcis ushered us into a waiting cab, and we drove down the famous Ramblas with their parklike medians, lines of plane trees, and crowds of tourists and Catalans. I relaxed and enjoyed the scene, until we turned off and were soon lost in a maze of narrow streets and alleys, ill-lit and spooky. Through the open windows of the cab, the salt smell of the sea with its less than pleasant undertones of rotting fish and petroleum assailed my nostrils. Swaggering, staggering, raucous men became more frequent on the streets. In an alley I saw one urinating against a wall and closed my eyes.

Then we arrived, our destination a place with light and noise pouring out a door and narrow windows onto a dirty street. "Bacallà," said Narcis, and helped us out. "Mean salt cod, but we don't eat cod. I choose." The room was full of rough-looking men, rougher tables with benches, and fish. The smells, the sights — there were even fish scales on the floor — were worrisome. After urging Robbie to slide along a bench until she was beside a huge man in a stained red jersey, Narcis then slid in beside her and pointed me to the last seat on the other side of the table. The man beside me was dozing with his nose in a heavy glass of clouded liquid. During the evening he woke up from time to time, looked at me with complete astonishment, as if I were a mermaid who had inexplicably appeared at his side, then went back to sleep. I never saw him eat anything.

"First, *calamarcets*," said Narcis, and waved a slovenly waitress over to take our order. Almost immediately she returned with a pottery pitcher of harsh white wine. I only hoped there was no lead in the clay of the pitcher. This wine would certainly leach it out. The wine was followed by a large frying pan sizzling with olive oil and the tiniest squid imaginable. They were not more than an inch in diameter, including the tentacles. The woman tossed in minced garlic and parsley, stirred the mixture, and left. We scooped them out immediately at Narcis's insistence.

I hated the café, but the squid were wonderful: tender, crispy, salty, and garlicky. And alas, they are not to be had in the United States. Later research told me that larger squid, cut up in small ringlets would do as well and that kosher salt should be sprinkled on the pan after heating the oil just to the point of smoking. For fear of being disappointed, I haven't tried it.

"Good, eh?" said Narcis. He was popping hot squid into his mouth with his fingers.

"*Anglèsa?*" asked the man in the red jersey,

143

looking from Robbie to me.

"*Anglèsa,*" Robbie agreed, eating squid as if someone might take them away if she didn't finish them fast. Which was the case.

"I spik anglès," said the man, and reached a long arm across the table toward my squid, I suppose because I had more left than the other two. Narcis calmly smacked his wrist with the spoon that had been resting in the hot oil.

"Watch out, pretty boy," snarled the sailor.

Robbie smiled at him and fed him a baby squid. He immediately forgot about Narcis and turned his attention back to her. Narcis shrugged and grabbed the waitress's skirt as she passed. "*Civet de llagosta?*" She shook her head.

"*Rica,*" muttered a bearded man down the table, whose facial hair was dripping fish broth while he dunked bread chunks and stuffed them in his mouth. I believe he was saying we were rich. And why not? *Llagosta* is lobster, and Narcis had just asked for it.

"*Orada al forn a la pescador?*" The waitress nodded to Narcis. "Fisherman's baked sea bream," he translated for me. Then he turned to the bearded fellow. "*Ric,* no rica." The sailor said something in Catalan, something I took to be demeaning, because Narcis's eyes narrowed and he said something back, which I took to be threatening. The sailor shrugged and said, "*Aviat.*"

"Come on, guys," Robbie protested.

"No make unhap pretty lady," agreed her red-shirted admirer.

"*Aviat,*" the bearded sailor repeated. I didn't know what it meant, but it sounded threatening to me.

"Narcis, please don't start a fight," I whispered across the table.

The man with the dripping beard wiped up the last of his soup and began the slow process of rising from the bench.

"Oh, boy," muttered Robbie and leaped to her feet. "*Canta,*" she shouted. Runny Beard looked puzzled. Robbie began to sing. She doesn't have a very good voice, but no one seemed to mind because she was evidently singing in Catalan. In seconds, scores of drunken, scroungy men were belting out the song with her while Narcis sat back watching with amusement and I tried to calm down. At the end, Robbie bowed, the patrons clapped, and she made a halting speech in Catalan that brought more applause and laughter.

"What did you say?" I asked.

"I told them that was the only Catalan song I knew. Now mind your manners, Narcis. I'd like to get through the next course before the riot starts."

"I do nothing," Narcis murmured. The waitress placed a huge baking dish between us. On the bottom were thinly sliced potatoes, topped by sea-bream steaks. Around the fish were piled small pieces of sausage, black olives, slices of green pepper, roasted garlic cloves, and tomato quarters. Narcis served us, and we feasted.

"Oh, God," said Robbie, her mouth full, "if this is what fishermen eat, I'm going to sea."

"I take pretty lady to sea," Red Shirt offered.

"Aren't you sweet," she replied. "You like Miró?"

He obviously didn't know who Miró was, but he was determined to keep her attention in the face of a table full of men who were trying to catch her eye. I didn't know whether to be relieved that she'd defused a dangerous situation or worried that they'd begin fighting over her. However, if I kept fretting, I'd get indigestion from this wonderful dish. It occurred to me that I could probably make it myself if I could get the sea bream. If not, maybe something else would work. The spicing didn't seem particularly exotic.

Since Narcis was sitting across the table from me, I decided to see what I could find out about Isabel and her death. There was still the danger of Robbie being arrested. "So, Narcis, who do you think killed Isabel?" I asked.

"Who say Isabel killed? Maybe died. Maybe suicide."

"She had a head wound."

"Maybe fall down, hit head, stagger in my exhibit, die."

I didn't believe that for a minute. "How did you get along with Isabel? Did you know her well?"

He shrugged indifferently.

"Someone said you were seen in intense conversation with her."

"What is intinz?"

"Heated?" He didn't look enlightened. "Hot? *Caliente?*"

He nodded. "*Calent.* Isabel is jealous."

"Of whom?"

"Me." He grinned. "Think comte pay me too much . . . like. Next month maybe Isabel have black hair like me, *roba* like me."

"Roba?" Was he saying the count was in love with him, not Isabel? Or that she had thought so?

"Roba. *Pantalons.*" He pointed to his trousers. "*Camisa.*" He ran a finger along the silk of his shirt. "*Creu.*" He flipped the gold cross dangling on his chest.

The bearded man had been watching him and shouted something that made Narcis's eyes turn cold. Before he could speak, the fellow knocked aside the snorer next to me and wrapped a hairy arm around my waist. "I take her," he said to Narcis. "What you do, pretty boy?" For a second I froze. Then I stamped my heel down on his instep. It

147

would have been more effective had I been wearing high heels, but I never do. Why deform my feet only to make myself taller than my husband, in whose arms I wished I were that very minute. While I was putting a dent in my attacker's foot, Narcis snapped at Robbie, "Run," and he dove across the table with a feral gleam in his eyes. The bearded man grunted, and his arm dropped from my waist. "Go," said Narcis. I squirmed away and went, but I swear that there was a knife handle in his hand, the blade partially buried in the bearded man's arm.

As I caught up with Robbie outside the door, the café erupted into warfare. Male roars of anger and pain followed us to the corner.

"We should call the police," I said, looking over my shoulder.

Robbie extracted her cell phone from her purse, punched in numbers, and put the phone to her ear. "Dead," she muttered. "I forgot to recharge it."

"They'll kill Narcis," I said.

"No, they won't." She pointed down the street, where Narcis emerged from the café, hair mussed, shirt torn, but sauntering toward us smiling.

"Creep," Robbie snarled at him once he reached us. "You had that all planned out, didn't you? Give the American tourists a little thrill."

Narcis laughed. "What means *creep?*"

"It's a comment on your bravery under dangerous circumstances," I improvised hastily. Robbie hadn't seen the knife. Maybe it was a palette knife, I tried to tell myself. But I didn't believe it.

Fisherman's Delight:
Baked Gilthead Sea Bream

Catalan sailors evidently fix this dish at sea and eat it from a communal dish, each with his own spoon. My first exposure to this recipe was followed by a violent fight among sailors in Barcelona. I recommend the dish but not the fight.

- Preheat oven to 400° F.
- Roast *1 peeled head of garlic separated into cloves* on a lightly oiled baking sheet for 10 to 15 minutes, remove from oven, and set aside.
- Peel *1/2 lb. potatoes* and slice very thinly, blanch for 3 to 4 minutes in boiling water, drain, and pat dry. Brush bottom of baking dish with olive oil and layer slices, overlapping to cover.
- Cut *1 1/2 to 2 lbs. gilthead sea bream* into 4 steaks about 2-in. thick. *If sea bream is unavailable, use red snapper or sea bass.* Arrange steaks on top of potatoes.

- Bake fish for about 10 minutes; then arrange evenly around the edges (not on top) *2 peeled, seeded, and quartered tomatoes; 1 roasted, peeled green pepper* cut into strips, *20 small pitted black olives such as Nicoise,* the baked garlic cloves, *a bay leaf,* and *1 botifarra sausage cut into 3/4-in. lengths.*
- *S*prinkle on top of fish *1 minced sprig of fresh thyme or 1/4 tsp. dried,* plus *salt and pepper.*
- Bake for 15 to 20 minutes more or until fish and sausage are done.
- Serves 4 as a main course.

Carolyn Blue,
"Have Fork, Will Travel,"
Boise Miner Herald

19

Isabel's Enigmatic Autopsy

Inspector Pujol

Attending autopsies has never been a favorite pastime, but since Goytisolo insisted that Dr. Arcadi Zapatero i Sunyer move the autopsy of Isabel Almirall to the top of his list, the doctor insisted that I attend. Zapatero does not like to have his schedule changed, so he was in a bad mood when I joined him at the table.

What a smell! He hadn't even started the procedure, and my nose was already protesting. I was in a bad mood myself because I had awakened with a toothache. I tried to tell my wife that it was the result of having missed my midday meal the first day of the investigation, but she thought differently. She told me in no uncertain terms that hunger does not bring on toothaches; decay does, and I had to see a dentist. I hate dentists. With such a delicate case to solve, I had no time for dentists. My wife and I parted on bad terms, so there I was with my aching tooth and my offended nose, standing across from Arcadi, who was taking a bone saw to Senyora Isabel, for whom I had to feel sorry, even if her dyed hair did not go well with her skin tone.

She looked ghastly and might, in fact, have looked ghastly before she was dead. Those heavily penciled eyebrows were still there. No one had washed them off. Why would she want to look like that giant American woman? Senyoreta Almirall must have been pretty before she changed her appearance and died. And had she actually been the comte's mistress, as the second American woman had said?

If the comte or his wife had killed Isabel Almirall, the judge would be furious. He does not like to arrest prominent people, especially titled people. If I even suggested such an investigative path, he'd act as if I were a traitor to Barcelona and my position as a homicide investigator. Not that his protests would keep me from my duty. Whoever killed the young woman, I would search them out and arrest them. I just hoped that it would turn out to be Dr. Hecht, as she preferred to be called. My sympathies went out to her husband, newly married to a large, flirtatious, suspected murderess.

"I'll tell you one thing, Ildefons," said Arcadi, peering from the corpse to me through his thick goggles. After cutting open the chest and pulling out some organs, he had lifted the victim's head by the hair and peered at the damage to the back of her skull. "This unimportant blow to the head could not have killed her. Her skull isn't even dented."

"Don't you have to look at the brain?" I retorted. "She may have internal bleeding that killed her, caused a stroke or something." If she had died of natural causes, I'd look like a fool, after having all but accused the American woman. She'd go to the newspapers, complain to her ambassador. Goodness knows what trouble such a woman would cause.

But no, I assured myself, Isabel Almirall couldn't have died a natural death. Under such circumstances, she wouldn't have been lying in that hospital bed in the exhibit, tucked neatly under a sheet and blanket. Had she felt ill, she would have dropped dead at the desk or called for help. And there was the head wound.

"Well, of course I'll examine the brain," Arcadi was muttering with irritation. "All in good time. You know I hate to have orderly procedure interrupted."

"You're the one who skipped from her internal organs to her head. Aren't you supposed to be slicing up bits of heart and liver? Weighing and bottling things?"

"Don't tell me how to do an autopsy, Ildefons. Perhaps you'd care to say just why you think she was murdered. Maybe she just died. Maybe she killed herself."

"What? After she hit herself on the head? Can't you just get on with it, Arcadi? I have a miserable toothache, and the smell in here is disgusting."

"You're awfully finicky for a policeman. How many autopsies have you attended? Tens? Hundreds?"

"As few as possible."

"I'll give you the name of a dentist."

"Please don't. Any dentist you recommend would probably pull out all my teeth, save them for analysis, and then embalm my gums."

Arcadi chortled. "All right, my friend, suffer. I'd never have thought you were a man to be afraid of dentists. Ah, what have we here?" Peering at her face, he laid aside the bone saw and stuck a gloved finger into her mouth.

"What?" I asked.

"It's possible — of course, only blood and tissue analysis will tell."

"Tell what? Lab work takes forever."

"True, but this woman may have had some sort of seizure. There are signs."

"Are you trying to irritate me, Arcadi? If so, I'm not amused."

"Have it your way. I'll say no more. You

154

can wait for my written report."

Now I'd offended him. As a result, I might never find out what killed this troublesome woman.

20

Passport Control

Carolyn

I had horrible dreams about that bearded sailor who'd grabbed me around the waist and was, I think, stabbed by Narcis. Both of them chased me through dark, smelly streets so roughly cobbled that running was a suicidal exercise. Although I could not see them, I heard their footsteps and smelled the fish soup in the beard of the one and the copper odor of blood on the knife of the other, and I was terrified. It seemed to me that if I could only run faster, I could reach Jason and be safe, but the slippery cobblestones made me stumble, catch myself, slip, catch myself, and each misstep brought my pursuers closer. Robbie woke me up before they caught me.

"He wants me to come in to work," she complained. "He's got the police to let us use everything but 'Tapas Triage' and my desk. I get to work at Isabel's desk. How creepy is that?"

If Robbie has to go to work, I can call the inspector for an appointment while she's gone, I thought.

"Well, I told him I was sorry, but I'd be late." She chuckled. "I mentioned female troubles. That always shuts a man up, even one as sophisticated as the count. They're terrified you'll go into detail." She then grabbed my hand and pulled me out from under my cover. "So hurry and get up. We can grab hot chocolate and a roll on the corner and head for that cheap hotel. The address looks like it's up by the funicular to Montjuic."

"We could go to the Fundació Miró afterward," I suggested. "I do love that museum."

"We're looking for Sammie. Remember? If we hop to it, we might be able to fit in another cheap hotel before I have to go fill Isabel's chair."

Of course we did as Robbie wanted, had hot chocolate (not my favorite) and rolls, then hopped on a bus she thought would take us close to the hotel. It didn't, or if it did, we got lost, wandering uphill but finding no signs that pointed to the hotel or even the funicular. We did spot a policeman in uniform and asked for directions. He didn't speak English and didn't understand Robbie's Catalan, so Robbie pulled out a map and studied it. "Okay, this way," she decided. We started off again with no better results.

We were stalled hopelessly on a corner in what seemed to be a residential neighborhood devoid of residents, when two men, both wearing ugly sports jackets and wrinkled trousers, accosted us.

"Passport control," said the one in the yellow-and-brown tweed jacket.

We stared at him dumbly.

"*Anglès?* No? We must see your passports."

"I d-don't have mine with me," I stammered. *Could I be arrested for being a foreigner on the streets of Barcelona without my passport?*

"What do you mean, passport control?" Robbie demanded. "I don't carry my passport around. I'll bet you guys don't either."

"Is our work," said the other one, who wore a salmon-colored jacket smudged with dirt at the pocket edges and sleeve ends. "Our duty to check passports. No passport, we look at purses."

"What for?" Robbie wanted to know.

"Drugs. Barcelona is harbor. Many drugs come in. Also drug money. We look at your money."

I was about to hand my purse over, but Robbie grabbed it and said, "In your dreams, buddy."

"There's a policeman right down the street," I suggested brightly, because Plaid Jacket was starting to look mean. "Why don't we walk down there?"

"This our job. We look at purses and do

our duty. Your wallets have identification, no?"

"Fine," said Robbie. "We'll hand over our purses if the policeman down the street supervises."

Salmon Jacket stopped a man walking past and demanded to see his wallet. The man looked scared and produced it. They pawed through it and handed it back. "Okay, you go," said Plaid Jacket. The man scuttled away, leaving us behind. "Now you," one of them said to Robbie while the other one reached for my purse.

I, however, had slipped my camera out. "Isn't this exciting?" I said to Robbie, who looked at me as if I had lost my mind. "We've got to have a picture to take home." I turned to the two men. "Could you stand closer together? Robbie, you can be in the next one with them, and then you can take one of me with the officers." I'd already snapped two pictures of the surprised passport control men.

"This is so amazing — that you'd think we look like drug dealers. I can hardly wait to tell my friends at home. And it would be really terrific if we could get a picture of you officers with the policeman down the street. He has such an adorable uniform."

The "passport control" officers were backing up. Before I could get a third picture, they had crossed the street and were heading away from us.

Robbie started to laugh.

"Sh-sh-sh," I said.

"You're a hoot, Caro."

Grinning, I suggested that we call them back to ask for directions to the hotel we couldn't find.

"Oh, right." She looked at her watch and sighed. "Well, we just wasted an hour and a half. Now I've got to get to the museum."

We headed downhill and actually saw the same policeman again. When he saw us and scurried away, she muttered, "Too bad. I'd like to have sent him after those two grifters."

"Maybe they really were passport control officers."

"Sure, and maybe they were muggers or rapists." Then she whistled through her teeth because she'd spotted a cab. The driver paid no attention. Perhaps that wasn't an accepted way to flag one down. Robbie stepped out in front of him, and he stopped, hanging his head out the window and shouting at her in Catalan. She hopped in, scooted over for me, and gave him the address of her apartment, as if he weren't still berating her. He had wound down to a resentful mutter when I got out and she went on to the museum.

Of course, I didn't mention that I intended to call Inspector Pujol as soon as she was out of sight, which I did, and announced that

I was coming straight over with very important information, not to mention questions I had for him that wouldn't wait. I didn't give him a chance to refuse, which I rather imagine he was planning to do. Before leaving, I attached my camera to the USB port of Robbie's computer and printed out the pictures I'd taken of the passport control agents. The likenesses weren't very good because I had to use regular paper, but still . . .

21

Foreign Exchange

Carolyn

Inspector Pujol looked decidedly grumpy when I arrived for my appointment. *Frankly, if I had an office so dingy and utilitarian, I'd be grumpy, too,* I thought. Then I dropped into an uncomfortable chair in front of his desk, feeling safe for the first time in several days. "I have to ask you, Inspector Pujol, do you consider Barcelona a dangerous city?"

"No more than most, certainly not as dangerous as other Spanish cities. Our people are employed and hardworking." He winced, and his hand went to his jaw. "Elsewhere large percentages of the workers are unemployed and committing crimes."

"Thank goodness I'm here, then. I don't think I could stand any more frights than I've already had." I opened my handbag and extracted the photo printouts. "This morning two men, claiming to be passport control officers, accosted Dr. Hecht and me and demanded to inspect our purses and our money. They said something about drugs. Do I look like someone who would be involved in the drug trade?"

He had begun to frown when I mentioned the agents, but he didn't answer my question because he was busy rubbing his jaw.

"Of course I don't," I said, answering my own question. "Do you have a toothache?"

He grumbled something, which I took to be an affirmative coupled with the opinion that his teeth were none of my business. Men are such babies. They just hate to go to the dentist, even my dear husband, Jason, which was why I happened to have a liquid pain-killer in my purse. After finding it among the many extras a woman traveling abroad needs to have at hand, I told Inspector Pujol to pour some on his finger and rub it on his tooth and gum.

"So you *are* carrying drugs," was his reply.

"This is an over-the-counter painkiller," I snapped. "It's not a prescribed drug. If it were, you couldn't buy it at home without a prescription. Now for heaven's sake, use it so I can get on with telling you about my problems." I handed the bottle across the desk. He stared at it suspiciously. "My husband applies that when he has a toothache. It deadens the pain until I can nag him into visiting a dentist."

My goodness. I think a smile twitched in

the corners of the inspector's wide, grim mouth. He dabbed a bit on his finger, sniffed it, and then gingerly rubbed it onto an upper back tooth. Evidently it helped, because he looked very surprised. "I'd put a bit more on," I advised. "Jason always does two applications." The inspector followed my suggestion and looked much more relaxed.

"Needless to say, these two men made me very nervous. I suspected that they intended to steal our money, and they began to look quite mean when Robbie refused to let them have our purses, so I had a thought. I whipped out my digital camera and took their pictures." The inspector raised his eyebrows questioningly. He had very thick eyebrows. "Well, I didn't say I was doing it so that I could turn them in to you. I said my friends back home would want to see pictures of the passport and drug agents we met. Then I said it would really be wonderful if we could get a picture of them with the policeman in the handsome uniform down the street and one of all of us and so forth. To make a long story short, they left. If they'd been real agents, they wouldn't have left, would they?"

I picked up the pictures I had put down on his desk and handed them over. "I couldn't print these out on photo paper, but I thought if you passed them around, someone in your department might recognize them." The inspector studied the pictures, looking somewhat bemused, nodded, and, folding the sheets of paper, put them in his pocket.

"But that was just this morning," I continued. "Last night Robbie — Dr. Hecht — and I went for dinner to Bacallà."

"Salt cod," he translated. Then he thought a moment. "I hope you don't mean that you and your friend went unescorted to that dive on the waterfront. It's a dangerous place."

"You don't have to tell me, but we didn't know that when Narcis, the artist who set up 'Tapas Triage,' suggested it. You see, I'm a food writer, and he said I should sample true Barcelona seafood. I must say the food was good, although the wine would have taken paint off metal. Given the fact that Catalonia produces many excellent wines, some of them quite reasonable in price, you'd think they could stock something better, but as I said, the food was tasty. We had tiny squid sautéed in olive oil with salt, garlic, and parsley."

Inspector Pujol perked up and told me that I had had a traditional Catalan specialty, one he was very fond of himself, although in better surroundings, such as his own home.

"I'm so envious," I said wistfully. "We can't even buy squid like that in the States. After the squid, we had sea bream baked on top of potatoes with lovely things around it."

"*Gilthead* sea bream?" he asked.

"I think it was."

"One of our great contributions to world cuisine," he said. "My wife makes it superbly."

"You are a lucky man, Inspector. Unfortunately, we'd barely finished the fish when a large, bearded sailor grabbed me around the waist, and Narcis leaped across the table at him and told us to run, which we did. A terrible fight broke out."

The inspector thought about my story, made a phone call, then told me that we were lucky not to be in jail or in the hospital, which was the fate of many customers at Bacallà last night. "You should not have gone there. It is no place for tourists."

"Well, I know that now, but last night and because we were escorted, we thought it would be fine. At least I can tell my readers at home about some wonderful Catalan dishes that they've probably never tasted. Do you think fishermen really make those recipes on their boats?"

"They do. Have you any other tales of danger to relay to me, Senyora Blue?"

"Several," I replied. "I did, after all, find a corpse at the museum, which was not the best introduction to Barcelona. And Robbie's — Dr. Hecht's — stepson has disappeared in the city."

"He ran away from her? She lost him? She does not seem like the maternal type."

"He ran away from his father, got this far, and then, seemingly, disappeared. He's been here several days. That's too long for a thirteen-year-old boy to be on his own in a foreign city. Here's his picture." I had copied a family picture Robbie had in her apartment and circled Sammie's face. "He's about five six, has black, floppy hair, and is thin. As soon as we heard from Hugh that he'd run away and his passport was missing, Robbie called the American consul, who called your government, and we discovered that Sammie's here, so we went looking. Yesterday we had a very frightening run-in with some horrible young men at a youth hostel. They said nasty things to us and threatened us. But Robbie's phone rang, and she pretended it was you and asked you to send a patrol car, so they left us alone when the custodian of the building yelled at them about policía."

"Very clever of her," muttered the inspector, "but then I would expect a murderer to be clever. Perhaps she murdered her stepson and is covering her tracks by enlisting your help in finding him."

"She is *not* a murderer — not of Isabel, not of Sammie," I protested. "But I do have some information for you. You can at least find out if the count killed Isabel. His wife has him followed day and night by a private detective named Bacigalupi, so the detective will know where he was on the night Isabel died. You might also check out his daughter, Dolors." I felt terrible about mentioning her, poor girl, but I had my friend to protect. "She's so upset about her parents' separation and his dallying with other women, like Isabel, that she's thinking of joining a convent. Robbie thought it might be an act of contrition because she'd killed her father's mistress."

Inspector Pujol threw his hands in the air and said, "Senyora, your investigative information only serves to make this case more confusing and peculiar than it was in the beginning, when all I had to deal with was a corpse in an art exhibit."

I couldn't help but smile at him. "I think your tooth is feeling better, Inspector."

"It is, for which I thank you."

"But you will go to a dentist?"

"Why do all women seem to be in league with dentists?" he asked ruefully.

"Because women don't want their husband's teeth to fall out, not that I have matrimonial designs on you, Inspector. I am a happily married woman."

"My wife will be relieved to hear it."

"And that reminds me of my first question about just how dangerous Barcelona really is. To my dismay, I found out that my daughter has gained my husband's permission and the permission of her university to come here for six weeks to serve as an intern with Dr. Hecht."

"In that case, I would say Barcelona is very dangerous for your daughter. I would not want my daughter under the protection of a murderer."

"You are not being helpful, Inspector. You know I don't think Robbie murdered Isabel. In fact, I'm quite sure of that."

"But you think the comte or his daughter might have."

"There's a certain logic to them as suspects. He invited us out to dinner, the whole staff and me and his daughter, and thought it was very amusing that his wife has a detective following him all the time. What kind of marriage is that?"

"An unhappy one, I'd say."

"Exactly. And as I understand it, money and love are the prime motives for murder. Under love one includes, of course, infidelity, jealousy, revenge, and so forth. We did have a lovely dinner — a shellfish paella with all the shells and bones removed."

"Ha! Paella is Valencian, not Catalan. And real paella has chicken and sausage, not shelled shellfish. You were eating some trumped-up rich man's paella. I suppose you think tapas are Catalan too."

"No," I replied. "They originated in the Basque country."

"Andalusia, and no true Catalan would

make a meal of tapas, as the comte seems to expect people to do in his café. We Catalans take our food more seriously than that. If you plan to tell Americans about Catalan food, do not write about paella or tapas."

"What do *you* suggest?"

"I suggest that you take your midday meal at my house. No one cooks better Catalan food than my wife . . . although she is Majorcan."

"That makes her Catalan, doesn't it? Majorca was part of the Catalan Empire in the Middle Ages. Don't they still speak Catalan there — in Majorca?"

"You amaze me, Senyora Blue. For an American, you are a phenomenon."

"And I accept your kind invitation. What a treat to be invited to someone's home. You're very thoughtful, Inspector."

"Or else I've lost my mind," he muttered, rising from his desk.

"What was that?" I asked. Evidently we were going for lunch then and there, although he was already regretting the invitation. Well, I wasn't letting him off the hook.

22

Sea and Mountain

Inspector Pujol

It always amazes me that women seem to feel they have to keep a conversation going while a man is driving. I would have been happier to use the time between my office and my house trying to explain to myself why I had invited this American woman home for a meal. Catalan pride, I suppose. How could a man like myself, who knows the beauty of our national cuisine, let this woman tell a whole nation the wrong things about Catalan food?

But Senyora Blue was one of those talkers. First she told me how she came to be a food writer for newspapers and evidently one book, which she had sent to her publisher before coming here to Barcelona. She said she had a previous visit to Barcelona to thank for her new career because she had eaten, by mistake, a wonderful goat dish at a local restaurant. Goat! Her first publication had been about eating goat in Barcelona. How shameful for us. Surely, they had served her kid, not some old, tough, evil-smelling goat.

Then she went on to comment on a guided tour she had taken during her previous visit. "The guide showed us the bullet holes in walls where battles were fought during the civil war and where those who fought against Franco were killed by firing squads. It must have been a terrible time."

Yes, I thought, *a terrible time.*

"Did your family live in Barcelona then?" she asked.

"No," I replied. "They were from Emporda. It's in the far northeast."

"How lucky," she mused. "Perhaps their isolation protected them from the troubles."

"My grandfather fought with the army that defended the Republic," I replied, feeling again the bitterness of those times, although I had not been born then and my father was just a baby. "I suppose you Americans would say he was a Communist."

She seemed offended. "My reading indicates that the Republicans were working men and women who wanted to be free of kings and dictators. And you might remember that many Americans came here to support the Spanish Republic. Did your grandfather survive the war?" she then asked.

"Oh, yes, he was alive when it ended, but

Franco's soldiers were executing our men and their families. My grandfather and grandmother had to flee to France over the mountains to escape the fascists. As my father was a baby then, not yet a year old, he was left behind with neighbors who had taken no part in the war and agreed to keep him until his parents could safely return."

"That must have been terrible for them," she said with shocked sympathy, "having to leave their child, and I've read how hard that trip into the mountains between Spain and France was. Jews who fled to France ahead of the Nazis came the other way and survived in Spain. Now there's an irony. How long before they came back? Your grandparents?"

"Never," I replied. "My grandfather was caught and died in a Nazi concentration camp. My grandmother joined the French resistance and was executed in a French square. Word of their fate filtered back years later to Emporda, and my father, who had spent his childhood hoping for their return, ran away from the family who had sheltered him and came to Barcelona. Since the Franquistas didn't know that he was the son of a Republican soldier, he got work, spoke only Spanish, as we were forced to do in those days, and kept his own counsel until Franco died and we Catalans could once again claim our language and heritage."

"How did you learn Catalan, then?"

"My parents taught me and my brothers and sisters Catalan at home. I grew up thinking it was a language that could only be whispered behind closed doors."

Senyora Blue stopped talking after that and took several paper handkerchiefs from her purse to pat her eyes and blow her nose. By then we had arrived, and I found myself trying to explain to my wife why I had brought an American woman home for a meal. Sebastiana tends somewhat toward jealousy and viewed Senyora Blue with suspicion when I made the introductions. Why, however, my wife would think me stupid enough to bring home a woman in whom I had an adulterous interest is beyond my imagination. And I have never been unfaithful to Sebastiana, who is a fine figure of a woman and a cook without equal.

Once I had explained that Senyora Blue was an American visiting Barcelona in order to write newspaper articles about our native cuisine, my wife became interested and curious. Then I mentioned that the poor woman had been fed, of all things, goat, paella made of shelled seafood, and tapas. Sebastiana was as distressed to hear this as I had been. I finished my explanation by saying, "I thought she could do no better by her American readers than to eat and write about your own wonderful *mar i muntanya*."

By then Senyora Blue and my wife were smiling at each other like old friends. They left immediately for the kitchen so that Senyora Blue could witness the all-important addition of the picada that makes mar i muntanya the wonderful dish that it is. While the women chattered over the stove, I washed my hands and retired to the patio for a pipe. My daughter, Magdalena, home from the university for the midday meal, joined me to ask questions about the guest inside, then rushed off to practice her English on the subject of food.

It was, of course, a superb meal, as is everything my wife cooks, but mar i muntanya is a particular favorite of mine, a specialty of Emporda that my mother used to fix my father when we had enough money for a chicken and the prawns. Those were hard times, my father making poor wages in the textile mills and my mother working at home sewing piecework late into the night to keep food in our mouths. Still, we survived the bad years and prospered after the death of Franco.

The women chattered throughout the meal, Senyora Blue exclaiming over the flavors of the main course and making notes as my wife told her how to cook it for herself, Magdalena asking questions about the senyora's daughter, who was coming to Barcelona soon. Evidently I hadn't reassured the woman that her daughter would be safe here in Barcelona, but Magdalena laughed merrily at Senyora Blue's fears and assured her that the university dormitories were quite safe. She insisted that only a policeman like her father, who saw nothing but crime and took a grim view of life, would think otherwise. They agreed that the two girls must meet so that Gwen, the senyora's daughter, would have a friend her own age in the city and the two could practice their languages on each other. Senyora Blue said her daughter was listening to Catalan language tapes while she slept, a peculiar and, no doubt, useless method of learning a language. The senyora seemed to find it an unpromising tactic as well.

Then the women were off on a discussion of Merce Rodoreda, a Catalan author of renown here. I was surprised that Senyora Blue had read and admired several of these novels. I myself think Rodoreda should write about women with better morals. I have read *Camellia Street* and refused to let Magdalena read it until she began her studies at the university, when I no longer had any say in the matter. At the time, my wife laughed at my edict and said that at least Rodoreda wrote of real women, not the rich and titled.

She repeated that opinion to our guest, which got Senyora Blue started on Comte Miquel Xifré i Fontdevila and his jealous wife and priest-or-guilt-ridden daughter. Sebastiana disapproved of the marital separation and his womanizing, Magdalena was delighted with the romantic plight of the poor daughter, and I was horrified to hear my case being discussed at my dining room table over *mel i mató,* an excellent dessert of fresh cheese and honey with roasted walnuts. I do not discuss my cases at home, both as a matter of professional propriety and because I don't consider crime a proper topic for the dinner table, at least when the women of the family are present.

I pled the pressure of work as soon as the last bite was eaten and rushed our guest off to the apartment of her dubious friend. Needless to say, I was worried that the American girl might be a bad influence on my daughter. Still, in most ways, the mother seemed a sensible woman, and she certainly had an interest in our culture, which was in her favor. Nonetheless, I regretted bringing her to my home and anticipated that time would increase my regrets.

Sebastiana's Mar i Muntanya

Mar i muntanya, *which translates as "sea and mountain", is a dish mating meat and fish or shellfish that goes back to Roman times and has been a recipe widely used in Emporda forever. The region is in the northeast corner of*

Spain, where shellfish are easy to net but chickens are hard to raise and must be fed. However, besides chicken and prawns, the dish can also contain any combination of monkfish, cuttlefish, mussels, or sole with rabbit, snails, or pork.

- In a Dutch oven sauté *1 chicken cut into 8 serving pieces* in a little *olive oil* until golden brown. Remove pieces, drain, and set aside.
- Sauté *12 prawns or large shrimp with heads and shells on* in same oil until bright red. Remove, drain, and set aside.
- Pour off excess oil, leaving 1/3 in. in pan, and make a *sofregit* of *2 chopped onions and 4 peeled, seeded, and chopped tomatoes* by cooking and stirring onions over a medium heat until golden brown and beginning to caramelize, then adding tomatoes and mixing well. Continue to cook until all liquid has evaporated and tomatoes melt into onions.
- Return chicken pieces, add *2 cups water*, bring to a boil, reduce heat, and simmer, uncovered, for about 20 minutes.
- Add *1/2 cup dry white wine* and *a dash of Pernod*, reduce heat again, and continue simmering ten minutes.

- Return prawns to mix, and simmer 20 minutes or until chicken is very tender, adding more water if necessary.
- Meanwhile make a picada of *4 cloves minced garlic, 2 sprigs minced parsley, 1 slice fried bread, 1 oz. grated* xocolata a la pedra (in the U.S. use the Spanish Ybarra brand of cooking chocolate), and *8 blanched, roasted almonds* by grinding together with mortar and pestle or food mill and making into thick paste with several drops of liquid from Dutch oven.
- Ten minutes before cooking is finished, add *salt and pepper* to taste, and stir in picada.
- Serves 4.

Carolyn Blue,
"Have Fork, Will Travel,"
Hyannisport Harbor News

23

Barri Gòtic

Carolyn

"Where have you been?" Robbie demanded as I let myself into the apartment. "You were supposed to wait here for me." She ran a frenzied hand through auburn hair that was already mussed. "Here I had this huge fight with Jordi and Madrona, who keep dropping these little hints that I must have hated Isabel for trying to look like me and to keep me from taking Miquel away from her. Jesus, I'm not interested in Miquel, and if she was dumb enough to try to look like me when I'm a foot taller than she is, whose fault is that? Not mine. So anyway I slammed out of there, figuring, *Good, Caro and I need to go looking for Sammie anyway,* and now I've been waiting for you for over an hour and . . ."

I dropped down onto the couch on which I'd slept the night. Goodness, but I was full. What a wonderful meal! And what nice people! Well, the inspector could be a bit disapproving, but on the whole I liked him. And I certainly appreciated his inviting me home for dinner. If Robbie hadn't been going on and on, I'd have hooked up my computer and started a column on the wonders of cuisine from Emporda.

"I'm sorry you had a falling out with your colleagues, but I've been with Inspector Pujol," I interrupted in my most soothing manner when it became obvious that my friend wasn't going to stop her tirade. "He's going to circulate those pictures I took of the passport control men and tell the police to be on the lookout for Sammie and —"

"You told him about Sammie?"

"Of course I did. When a child goes missing, you notify the police. I'm surprised we didn't think of it when we first heard."

"I'm surprised you think they'd do anything when they think I'm a murderer," Robbie retorted.

"Well, that's another reason I went to see the inspector — to assure him that you are not a murderer and to make more suggestions about who might have actually killed Isabel. By the way, we were lucky last night to get out of that café when we did. Most of the customers ended up in jail or the hospital."

Robbie shook her head and laughed. "That Narcis! His mother shouldn't let him out of the house."

"Are you sure he has a mother?" I asked dryly, then turned my mind to more important matters than the impish artist. "Anyway, Narcis isn't the problem today, so if you want to go looking for Sammie, let's get at it." Obviously I wouldn't be writing a column as long as Robbie was in the apartment. "Where shall we look now?"

"Well, we've either called or visited the cheap lodging places for kids, and he's not in a hospital. How about the tourist places? Not likely he'd go anyplace I might be interested in — any museum or —"

"What about the Barri Gòtic?" I suggested. "Does he like history?"

"How would I know? He won't talk to me, so I don't know what he likes. Let's try it." She picked up her purse, slung it over her shoulder, and headed for the door. Obviously, I wasn't going to get even ten minutes' rest, so I followed.

We caught a bus at the end of the block and then walked into the Barri Gòtic. Robbie was concentrating on the faces of teenagers while I gave her a brief history of the city: possible founding by Hercules or Carthaginians, both possible sources for the original name, Barcino; the conquest of tribes already settled around Montjuic by the Romans, who stayed in control for six centuries and built walls and towers that still exist; conquest by Visigoths, Vandals, and Arabs; the —

182

"Look, over there," Robbie interrupted. "Isn't that —"

"Sammie? No, it isn't," I replied. "That boy is at least five ten and doesn't look like either Sammie or Hugh." Robbie mumbled agreement, and I continued by telling her how Louis the Pious took the city from the Arabs and made it part of France, after which my favorite, Wilfred the Hairy —

"Wilfred the Hairy?" Robbie groaned, then started to laugh.

"He's the national hero," I retorted. "His bravery against the Arabs made Charles the Bald grant Barcelona independence. Then a period of great brilliance and prosperity ensued during the Middle Ages."

"Charles the Bald and Wilfred the Hairy. Now there's a perfect pair." She stopped laughing abruptly and cried, "Look across the street, that kid with the backpack."

"They all have backpacks, and Sammie's not with that group. Then James the Conqueror —"

"Come on, Caro. Less history and more detecting. I've got to find Sammie, preferably before Hugh gets here. He's really upset."

"Well, here we are at the cathedral!" I exclaimed, as if I hadn't been heading in that direction all the time. "The first church here was fourth-century, followed by an eleventh-century Romanesque church rebuilt by Ramon Berenguer the First."

Robbie stopped and stared at me. "You mean our Narcis is related to some millennium church builder?"

"I wondered that myself." Lord, it was a beautiful sight, Catalan Gothic with a massive four-tiered arch over the doors, topped by a triangle of carved stone and stained glass. I could hardly wait to get inside. "It's dedicated to Saint Eulalia, a young Christian virgin who was tortured in all sorts of horrible ways — hooks, fires, pincers — and then crucified by the Romans in the fourth century."

"Well, that's grisly," Robbie muttered. "I hope they don't have pictures of it inside."

"That's just the sort of thing kids Sammie's age would go looking for — the more grisly and violent the better. Have you ever looked at any of those electronic games they play?"

"You're right." Robbie made no protest at being led into the church so that I could admire the beautiful chapels, the intricate Renaissance wooden choir stalls painted in gold and bright colors. "Not many teenagers in here on their own," said Robbie. "The ones I see are being dragged around by their parents."

"We'll try the crypt of Saint Eulalia," I suggested.

"Good idea," she agreed, but it wasn't what she was hoping for. No gory details, just the stone ceiling and walls with elaborate arches, the long chandeliers and the gorgeous alabaster sarcophagus of the saint with its intricate carving and a female figure on top. Eulalia? The Virgin Mary?

I told Robbie about the miracle when the saint's dried heart was carried from Santa María del Mar to the cathedral. "The heart got so heavy, they had to put it down and pray for strength."

Unimpressed, Robbie dragged me up the stairs, muttering that there wasn't a teen in sight. Accordingly, I never got a closer look at the statue, and I never did see the painting on the keystone of the vault I'd read about.

"Well, that was a total waste of time," said Robbie.

"We could try the cloister," I suggested. I wanted to see it very badly. "I once saw some teens skateboarding in a cloister in Italy." Which was true, but they'd been run off in short order by an indignant nun. I could have spent hours in that Catalan cloister with its long loggia of columns and pointed arches and its pretty washbasin full of mossy green water. However, there were no skateboarders, no teenagers, and no willingness on the part of my friend to loiter there, so we continued through the quarter.

The Renaissance Palau de la Generalitat (or Catalan parliament building; Catalans had had the first bill of rights in Europe) had a pretty loggia on top with an orange garden below, but Robbie saw only two teenagers being lectured by a passing priest for baring their arms in public. Obviously they weren't Sammie. While I looked at Roman walls and octagonal towers and admired the equestrian statue of Ramon Berenguer the Third in front of his royal palace, while I took pictures and tried to cheer her up with delightful historical vignettes, Robbie grumbled and stopped teenagers to stare into their faces, gaining the attention of a policeman who may have thought she was a sexual predator.

"Oh, hell," she snapped when the officer started following us. She whirled and confronted him with a picture of Sammie. "Have you seen him?" she demanded in English and then in broken Catalan.

"Per què?" retorted the suspicious policeman.

"Because he's my son," she snapped. *"Mon fill."*

The policeman mumbled a negative while flushing pink, no doubt because of his unseemly thoughts about a woman who was looking for her son, not an underaged lover. Robbie gave up the hunt and said we might as well go for dinner; then at least she'd get something out of the afternoon. "I know a restaurant that doesn't expect you to wait until the middle of the night to eat." She led me into a maze of alleys that had an unpleasant outhouse sort of smell. When I asked her what it was, she replied, "Broken-up sewers. You said yourself this is the oldest part of town. If they try to dig up the stone streets, they'll find some Greek temple or something that can't be disturbed, and the sewers, which were probably built by the Romans, will keep leaking."

Happily the smell had abated somewhat by the time we arrived at a restaurant with stone walls and wooden rafters that held up a loft. There I was introduced to a rough toasted bread on which we ourselves rubbed ripe cut tomatoes and drizzled olive oil, a sort of do-it-yourself Catalan hors d'oeuvre. While we were thus employed, the cook was roasting hunks of meat — in a giant fireplace, for all I know. The meat was juicy and flavorful, charred outside and rare inside, and it came with a sumptuous bean dish and several kinds of sauces, the best of which was *allioli amb fruita,* a garlic sauce with cooked, mashed apples. Pliny the Elder provided the first written recipe for allioli, and it's not all that hard to make as long as you cheat and use eggs along with the garlic, salt, and olive oil.

"Where can he be?" Robbie moaned as she cleaned her plate. "What if he's hungry? What if he's got no place to stay? Am I so awful he can't come to me for help? I don't see why he'd come here if he didn't want to see me, and now he —"

187

"We'll keep looking," I assured her.

"I have to go to work tomorrow."

"*I'll* keep looking. Inspector Pujol will see that the police —"

"Oh, right. So they find him and throw him in jail. And then they throw me in jail because they think I killed that dumb Isabel. By the time Hugh gets here, both his wife and son will be in some medieval prison, and my poor husband —"

"Let's have a Catalan cocktail," I suggested. "I've read that La Barreja, the Catalans' own cocktail, packs a wallop like a whip." Actually it's a simple mixture of 2 ounces of chilled Spanish Moscato wine and 1 ounce of chilled anisette, but I'd read about it and wanted to try it. A Catalan chef really did say that thing about the whip, but then maybe he'd never tasted a martini. I had a dirty martini in San Francisco, and my head was spinning before I finished it.

"Sounds good to me," said Robbie.

We ordered, and I suggested that tomorrow we find the private detective who kept track of the count. "If the count didn't kill Isabel, maybe the detective will have some idea of who did. I worked with a PI in San Francisco, and he was great."

"Whoa!" said my friend. "Do I detect a little extracurricular romance in your past? Did you fall for a tall, dark, handsome tough guy?"

"Well, he was tall and tough, but he was also gay. Now can we get back to the subject? Do you want to find this Bacigalupi? Or do you have to go back to the museum?"

"Oh, why bother?" she said bitterly. "My colleagues will just snipe at me all day. Hell with it. We'll go after the PI wearing low-cut dresses with lots of cleavage."

"Right," I agreed, already feeling the effects of the Catalan cocktails we were consuming. "We'll charm him into telling us everything he knows."

We clinked glasses, drained the cocktails, and ordered more.

"And we'll take a cab home tonight," I added, "because I don't think I'm going to be in any condition to ride the bus." Maybe that chef had been right about La Barreja.

24

Gentlemen Don't Tell

Inspector Pujol

Having dropped Senyora Blue at the apartment of her friend, I considered the information she had given me. Much as the judge would dislike the idea, I really had to question Comte Miquel Xifré i Fontdevila. If the man had, in fact, been the lover of the victim, he was an obvious suspect. Perhaps even his wife and daughter, as the American woman suggested, had to be considered. Obviously the staff members who had implicated Senyora Hecht were not going to implicate the comte as well. He was their employer. For safety's sake, I pulled my official car, one of the few perks of my position as an inspector, to the side of the street and called the comte on my cellular phone to suggest that he visit my office as soon as possible. Much better to make him come to me than to put myself in a position of subservience by going to him. He agreed with surprising alacrity and presented himself at my door within ten minutes of my arrival.

"How can I help you, Inspector?" he asked, seating himself in one of my creaky chairs.

"By explaining to me a situation that you neglected to mention when we last talked," I replied sternly.

"I believe I answered all your questions as fully as possible," he said mildly.

"But not that you and the victim, Senyoreta Isabel, had an intimate relationship." He showed no dismay at my accusation. "By which I mean a sexual relationship, Comte," I added.

He shrugged. "How would that advance your investigation? Since I did not kill Isabel, it seems to be of no importance."

"Then you admit that the victim was your mistress?"

"I suppose so. You might call her that. I often visited her apartment for dinner and — how shall I say? — dalliance, but it would hardly have been gentlemanly of me to bring that up during our first conversation."

"It was hardly honest of you to omit that important fact, Comte," I retorted. "I believe you called her that evening." She had received a call from his phone, but I did not know for a fact that the call had been from him.

However, the comte did not know of the hole in my knowledge and replied readily,

"Yes, I did call. We were supposed to have dinner together. I called to say that I had other business that evening."

"And you quarreled?"

Again the comte shrugged. "Isabel was not happy, but such changes of plan are often unavoidable. My failure to appear for dinner and her displeasure hardly constitute a reason for me to murder her. I was quite fond of her."

"Perhaps she threatened to tell your wife of the affair."

He laughed ironically. "My wife keeps herself well apprised of my comings and goings. Had Isabel wanted to tattle to Violante, it would have done her no good, but, in fact, she made no threats. She hung up on me, and I went about my business."

"Which was?"

"Well, I see, Inspector, that nothing I tell you will convince you that I am not the suspect you hoped me to be. Therefore, I suggest that you contact a source of information on my activities who may satisfy your curiosity. A Senyor Bacigalupi, who is in the employ of my wife, can tell you what I was doing the night Isabel was killed, not that it's any of your business. He should be listed as a private investigator. No doubt you can obtain his address and telephone number. He may even be parked outside at this minute, waiting for me to reappear."

The comte stood up and gave me a tight smile. "And now, unless you plan to arrest me, Inspector, I think that I shall return to the museum. By the way, it has come to my attention that several of my employees have told you that my new American researcher, Dr. Roberta Hecht, might have killed Isabel. I assure you that that is quite unlikely. I am not sexually involved with Dr. Hecht, nor is she romantically interested in me, although you'll agree that she is a delightful and lovely woman." He then buttoned his suit jacket and bade me good day, as if I were some banker with whom he had shared a fancy lunch at an expensive hotel.

I found the man thoroughly detestable with his fine clothes and negligent manner. And since he had taken it upon himself to defend Senyora Hecht, it occurred to me that they had plotted the murder together in order to dispose of the troublesome Isabel so they could pursue an affair without hindrance. I found this Bacigalupi in the official register of private detectives and called to demand his appearance in my office. The comte may have been right about the detective's whereabouts, for Orfeó Bacigalupi appeared at my door rapidly enough to have been parked in front of the building.

The man was sweating profusely as he took a seat where the object of his investigations had just sat. "My papers are in order, I assure you, sir," he said apprehensively.

"This is not about your papers, Senyor Bacigalupi." He was not a man one could look in the eye, because his left eye tended to wander away. Nor was the rest of him particularly attractive: the bushy mustache, which had wet, straggling hairs in the middle where he had licked them nervously; the pot belly protruding from a loudly checked sports jacket, a pink flower of some sort stuck into his buttonhole. It looked as if it had been plucked surreptitiously from someone's garden.

"What, then?" he asked.

"It has come to my attention that you are employed to follow Comte Miquel Xifré i Fontdevila."

"There's no law against that. I'm a private investigator. That's what I do. Follow people. I don't bother them. I do my job. That's all. I haven't caused him any trouble. Just because he's a big shot, doesn't mean I don't have a right to make an honest living."

"Unpleasant, but true," I agreed. "As long as you don't break the law —"

"Which I haven't."

"Good. And now you are being asked to assist in an official investigation."

"You mean you want to hire me?" Bacigalupi beamed. "I've never heard of such a thing. However, if you can meet my hourly rate —"

"I do not wish to hire you, Senyor. I want you to tell me what the comte was doing from, say, seven in the evening on twenty-two September until you gave up surveillance for the night, if you did. I want a complete report from you on his activities."

Senyor Bacigalupi looked appalled. He tugged at the wilted collar of his yellow shirt. He took out a grimy handkerchief and wiped sweat from his face, but missed a drop that fell off the end of his bulbous nose. "I cannot do that," he said. "Much as I would like to cooperate with the authorities, that information belongs to my client."

"And who is your client?"

"I can't tell you that either. Confidentiality is the gold standard of a private detective. I am an honorable man, Inspector. My client would have every reason to fire me if it became known that I had given out confidential information. My best client, I might add. A client whose business I cannot afford to lose. You understand, Inspector. I am a poor man, but an honorable one. The information I gather for a client is like — like confession is to a priest. It cannot be told. It is sacrosanct." He looked as virtuous as he could, which was not particularly impressive because his eye kept wandering away as if in search of a hiding place.

"You realize that I can go to the investigating judge and obtain permission to search your records?" I said threateningly.

The sly look that came into his one focused eye made me believe that he planned to rush back to his office and burn any material he had that related to the comte. Or perhaps he planned to pass it on to the comtessa, thinking that I didn't know who his client was. Not that getting anything from the comtessa would be an easy matter. The judge might grant me permission to search the private detective's office, especially if I failed to mention that I was in search of information about the comte, but Goytisolo would never let me pursue the comte's wife.

"You may go, Senyor, but keep in mind that refusal to cooperate with the police has its consequences. See to it that you do not destroy any material that might be relevant to my investigation."

Bacigalupi shuddered and scurried away.

I then tried to get in touch with Senyora Roberta Hecht, but she was not to be found — not at the museum, not at her apartment. *Very suspicious*, I thought. *Has the comte advised her to avoid the police? Perhaps he arranged for her to leave the country, even though her passport has been confiscated.* These speculations caused me great unease. If she proved to be the murderer, it would be the very devil extraditing her from the United States.

What have I learned that is new and helpful? I asked myself. That the comte admitted to an affair with the victim. That his had, in fact, been the phone call Isabel received the night of her death, canceling their dinner, at least according to him. That story did explain the paella she had made, the bottle of wine and dish of paella consumed by one person, Senyoreta Isabel, and the second plate of paella thrown against the wall. Then she had called two numbers: the comtessa's and the American's.

Senyora Hecht insisted that she had not taken the call and that she had been in her apartment during the whole evening, at one time talking to her husband in America, which was true, although it did not clear her of the murder. Isabel Almirall might have insisted that Roberta Hecht meet her at the museum to have it out over the man they both coveted, the result being that Isabel was killed — either for reasons of jealousy or because she was caught stealing Hecht's research. Two motives for the American.

Isabel could have insisted that the comte meet her at the museum later in the evening after he refused to come to dinner. When she told him that she had called his wife, he might well have given in to rage, no matter how indifferent to that prospect he seemed to be, and killed his mistress, or killed her because she was a hindrance to his desire for the American woman.

Last, having been called and told of her

husband's affair, the comtessa might have agreed to meet Isabel at the museum and killed her rival there. Or the comtessa might have paid Bacigalupi to commit the murder, which was why the detective refused to cooperate by telling me the comte's whereabouts that night. He didn't know. He had been killing the comte's mistress instead of following the comte.

Obviously I needed to question the comtessa. Not a happy prospect. And I needed to ascertain that Senyora Hecht had not left, and would not leave, the country.

25

Drinking Lunch

Carolyn

Robbie and I woke up with headaches as a result of the experiment with Catalan cocktails, but she mixed up some foul-tasting concoction that did make me feel better. After that, we talked it over and decided that we would present ourselves to the countess's private detective as prospective customers. "In fact, I'll hire him to look for Sammie. Then we won't be telling a lie," Robbie suggested. "I don't have any more ideas about finding him anyway, and Hugh will be arriving in a day or two. I'd like to meet him at the airport with good news."

"That's an excellent idea," I agreed. "Once the detective is comfortable with us, maybe we can worm some information out of him."

"We'll tell him we need references, get him to tell us about his work so I'll know if he's the person to hire."

"Very good," I agreed. Whatever Robbie

decided, Bacigalupi didn't have a prayer of keeping anything from her. I truly thought there wasn't a man alive who could resist Robbie, unless it was Inspector Pujol or Jason, of course.

Robbie got the number from the telephone book after I found the Catalan word for detective in my paperback dictionary: *detectiu*. He couldn't give her an appointment, but he did agree to meet us for lunch. He even chose the restaurant. I looked that up too. Three stars. Evidently we were expected to pay. Robbie went off to the museum, bad-tempered from the lingering pangs of her headache and ready to take the offensive against her snide colleagues. I almost felt sorry for them.

I decided to treat the last of my headache with fresh air and spent the morning at the Parc Güell, Gaudí's fantasy park. It was to have been a garden city financed by his patron, Eusebi Güell i Bacigalupi. How odd. Gaudí's patron's mother had the same name as the countess's detective. Eusebi Güell had been a count, too. I'd have to tell Robbie.

At any rate, no garden city evolved. Only two houses were built: Gaudí's and that of a friend, but the entrance, the porter's house, and the double staircase to the room of a hundred columns are there to see. Those columns, of which there are really only eighty-six, bend like tree trunks to hold up the wave-form vault, and everywhere are colorful mosaics and dragons, not to mention the wonderful, curving mosaic bench that edges the upper terrace and overlooks the city. I took pictures; I sat on the bench, thinking of the worker who had been asked to sit naked in wet plaster so that the bench would have human form. When I was a child, I took an ashtray home to my mother that had my hand imprinted in plaster, then was garishly painted by me. It wasn't as pretty as Gaudí's mosaic reptile bench, and my mother didn't smoke, but she kept it by her bedside until she died when I was twelve. I wonder if my father has it stuffed into a box in the attic of his house.

Last I went to Gaudí's house, which still holds his belongings, although he ended his life sleeping on a cot in the unfinished Sagrada Familia, his wonderful church, until he was run down by a streetcar. They didn't know who he was and took him to a hospital to die as an indigent. What a sad end to such an amazing talent. The first thing I asked the detective was if he was related to Eusebi Güell's mother. He looked confused at my question, and he certainly didn't look as if he came of noble stock. He smoked a disgusting cigar until the food was served and wore a wilted red rose in his buttonhole. It looked terrible with his brown-and-yellow checked jacket.

Robbie ordered a good bottle of wine first off, and the detective cheered up immediately. I whispered that I didn't think I was up to drinking anything so soon after last night. She whispered back that "a hair of the dog" was supposed to help what ailed us. However, we were still sipping our first glasses when Bacigalupi finished his third and Robbie ordered a second bottle. In the meantime, she had been flirting shamelessly, while I asked admiring questions about his "fascinating" profession. Fortunately, he spoke English, although rather peculiarly. Not that I could fault him for that. I didn't speak Catalan at all, and Robbie spoke it badly. How would Gwen ever get along here with only her sleeping lessons in the language?

We ate sardines crisscrossed on a plate, and Robbie told Senyor Bacigalupi that I was a connoisseur of private detectives, having worked with a famous San Francisco PI on a murder case. Consequently, I was part of this negotiation to assist her in evaluating his skills and experience. Over the second bottle of wine, our detective told us stories about his expertise in finding missing persons. This paean of self-congratulation took us into the entrées. I had lamb, which Orfeó, as he insisted we call him, advised against because it wasn't the right season.

"If you find Sammie," Robbie asked, "will

you be able to follow him and find out what he's been doing?"

Orfeó assured us that he was a master of tailing subjects and ferreting out all their secrets.

"Well, you say that," I demurred, "but I'm sure it's not that easy in a city this size. Have you any cases that would recommend you for this task?"

Indeed he had. He was ascertaining every movement of a very important person for a client, a delicate matter, we were to understand, and the subject was none the wiser after having been followed closely for months, for years. Even the police wanted information from him on this person, but being a man who understood the meaning of confidentiality, he could not help them.

We, of course, were overcome with admiration and curiosity. Bit by bit, we weaseled more information about the count from Senyor Bacigalupi, who, much the worse for wine and desirous of gaining a rich American client, could not resist providing details to two such charming ladies, as he called us.

By the time we had consumed dessert and brandy, the very *indiscreet* Senyor Bacigalupi had told us that Comte Miquel Xifré, who was supposed to be eating paella at the apartment of his mistress on a certain night, had actually been playing baccarat at a private club, had lost 150,000 euros over a period of five hours, and had then made a gift of a solid gold cigar case to a fado singer who had taken his fancy. The two then went to his mansion in his limousine and spent the night together.

"Surely you do not mean to say that a man of such importance let a *singer* share his bed for a whole night," said Robbie, acting both titillated and dubious.

"A fado artist, Senyora," said Bacigalupi. "She is beautiful woman and very admired for singing, a greatest popular form of entertainment at this club, where many Portuguese millionaires gamble when in Barcelona."

We both nodded, wide-eyed. "And you saw her leave in the morning?" asked Robbie.

"Sí. A limousine, not the comte's, is called for her."

"And the count, did he leave with her?" Robbie asked breathlessly.

"But no. He leave in his own limousine in a half of hour. But both looking very pleased." He smirked. "Very . . . satisfied."

"And did his mistress find out about his indiscretion?" I asked.

"That is best of story," he replied, squirming with pleasure. "She kill herself in his *museu* while he sport with fado singer. Very tragic. No? Very dramatic."

"And what did your client think of all this?" asked Robbie.

"Ah, that would be not for me to tell. My

client, she is secret. No?"

"Of course," Robbie agreed. "I shouldn't have asked." She gave him a picture of Sammie and wrote him a check on the spot. "I do hope you can find my stepson in the next few days."

"Of course, dear lady. I find and bring him to you."

"Excellent." She waved imperiously for the bill, and we departed while Senyor Bacigalupi finished his second cognac and admired the check that paid him to search for Sammie.

"What a dreadful man," I said.

"A real creep," Robbie agreed. "But maybe he can find Hugh's boy. People like that have connections. Still, he's not getting any more money out of me, so we'll see how far that much gets me. Hugh should be here by the time Bacigalupi —" She started to laugh. "Can you believe it? He actually thinks he's discreet." At that moment her cell phone rang. I could tell from the conversation that it was Hugh.

When she'd clicked off and returned the phone to her purse, Robbie looked full of dread. "He'll be in tomorrow morning, he and Kimmie."

"So soon?" I was surprised.

"And I haven't found Sammie."

"Maybe Bacigalupi will be able to —"

"He's following Miquel. He'll put some underling on Sammie, and anyway — oh, this is so awful!"

We climbed into a cab, and I told her that having Hugh here would make her feel better. "At least you'll be together, and maybe Hugh will have ideas about finding Sammie, who's his son, after all. Goodness, Robbie, I need to move out. You'll need the sofa bed tomorrow."

"You can stay until they get here," she protested.

"Believe me, after that trip, they'll want to go straight to bed, and they won't need me packing up and moving while they're trying to recover from jet lag. I'll call the hotel as soon as I get back to the apartment. Unless you don't want to be by yourself tonight."

"It's not that," said Robbie gloomily. "In fact, maybe it would be better if you moved today. I'll have to change the sheets and wash the dishes. Hugh's kind of picky about things like that."

"It's easy to be picky when you're not the person doing the work," I said dryly. "I can change the sheets for you."

"No, you can't. I have to take the ones I've got on the beds to the Laundromat tonight, and don't try to tell me you'll be able to master a Catalan Laundromat in one afternoon. It can't be done. They haven't got them changed over to euros, so it's an unbelievable hassle, not to mention the fact that you have to know which machines work and which don't before you use up your money on the duds."

I had to agree. I'd once tried to wash the children's jeans in a foreign Laundromat. I'd been washing my own things in the sink at the hotel but put them in with the rest. The results were disastrous, even after I mastered the machines.

The cab dropped Robbie off at the museum and then me at the apartment. While I packed, I thought over the revelations of Bacigalupi. It would seem that Comte Miquel Xifré i Fontdevila hadn't killed Isabel himself, but that didn't mean he hadn't paid to have it done, or that his wife wasn't responsible, or his daughter.

As a good citizen, and because the private detective evidently hadn't told the police anything, it was probably my duty to call Inspector Pujol about my findings. He had been awfully nice to me. On the other hand, Robbie was my friend long before the inspector took me home for mar i muntanya, so as long as he persisted in suspecting my friend, he'd have to get his own information on who *hadn't* killed Isabel.

26

The Inspector and the Comtessa

Inspector Pujol

The rich are an arrogant lot, I thought as I pondered my next move while driving back to work from an excellent midday meal. Comtessa Violante Roca i Navis would not take my call, would not make an appointment to come to my office, and would not grant me an interview at her home. The replies to my requests had been relayed through a secretary, who at least had the good sense to apologize for his mistress's refusal to cooperate with the authorities.

The woman wasn't even Catalan. She came from some noble family in Madrid, the center of a government I detested, although some autonomy had been granted to us Catalans after the death of Franco. Still, we should have complete independence. As matters stand, we have no recourse when xarnegos flood into our province to take advantage of our prosperity. Our schools still teach Spanish, even if our children now learn Catalan as well.

No doubt, had this comtessa seen fit to grant me an interview, she would have refused to speak in Catalan. Perhaps she hadn't even condescended to learn the language after her marriage, which she no doubt contracted to provide herself with Catalan wealth rather than a husband she loved. Why else had they been separated for so many years?

Well, she had information that I needed. She might even be the murderer. The sensible Senyora Blue, who did not think herself too fine to appreciate the beauties of Catalan civilization, considered the comtessa a good suspect. I knew better than to go through the judge, Enric Goytisolo, who would never command a noblewoman to do anything she did not wish to do, much less consider her a possible suspect in a murder. Therefore, I would visit the comtessa's house, uninvited, and interview every one of her employees at length. Perhaps I could corner the daughter and get a statement from her.

Resolved on my course of action, I called for my aide and two uniformed officers and set out to visit the comtessa's house. The officers took the front seat as driver and passenger while my aide and I rode in splendor in the back. I even let them open the car door for me and knock on the door of the house. And what a house it was, an old stone villa from an earlier age, gloomy and forbidding both outside and inside. It was like an underground crypt in a church or castle, lightless, cold, and heavily draped. A maid informed me that the comtessa was not taking calls that day.

"Very well, senyoreta," I replied. "Round up the household. I will question everyone here since the comtessa is unavailable." The poor girl looked terrified, torn no doubt between fear of bringing down upon her own head the wrath of her mistress and of getting herself into difficulties with the police. Although I could understand her plight, I insisted that she obey my orders, and she did.

I had the uniformed officers keep the whole household in a large salon with stiff, uncomfortable chairs on which they were afraid to sit, while I interviewed them one by one in a room with a fine desk, which would be of little use because the light was so dim. My aide had trouble taking notes in the twilight as I questioned the butler, the secretary, the housekeeper, the cook, the maids, the gardeners, and the comtessa's chauffeur. Evidently the daughter and her driver were out, but I was prepared to take my time in hope not only of information but also of her return. One of the uniformed officers was stationed at the door to the salon so that he could keep an eye on the huge double doors to the entry hall through which the daughter would presumably enter if she returned.

The answers I got from the staff were only marginally helpful. They were sure that the comtessa had been in the house the night Isabel Almirall died, but no one had actually seen the lady after 11:30, when, dinner over, she retired to her rooms. The secretary confirmed that the comtessa had received a telephone call from a woman who would not identify herself earlier that evening, but he insisted that the comtessa had not taken the call. In fact, he claimed to have had an argument with the caller, who became somewhat hysterical when she was not allowed access to the comtessa.

Well, he would say that, I thought. He was an employee and said what he was told to say. I asked each person whether the comtessa could have left the house without being observed, an idea that seemed to astonish the various employees. Her personal maid was sure her lady would not have dressed herself and left; she would have called her maid. The secretary said the comtessa never kept outside appointments that he himself had not made for her. So it went. What a downtrodden lot they were.

I went over with the relevant persons any outings she had taken immediately before and after the death of Isabel Almirall and was told of shopping trips to expensive stores, visits to expensive friends, charity functions, religious missions, and so forth. I asked about people who had come to the house and met with her. Dressmakers, wealthy friends, her lawyer, her banker, her priest, and Senyor Bacigalupi. No one could tell me the purpose of his visits, but the maids did giggle behind their hands. Obviously, they knew that he kept track of the comte for the comtessa, but they would not say it, and of course, none knew what she and the detective said to each other.

I asked if the comtessa had a key to El Esperit de Gaudí i Miró. No one knew, but they also had never heard of her going there. She did not like the buildings of Gaudí or the art of Miró. Evidently the architect and the artist were topics of hard words between the comte and his estranged wife when he came for dinner. The servants were very reticent on this matter, but I could read between the lines.

I got no farther at the end of these interviews than I had been before I came here. The comtessa could have returned Isabel Almirall's call after refusing to take it in front of her secretary. She could easily have slipped out of the house, and no one here would have been the wiser. She could have arranged with her lawyer or her private detective to have Isabel killed, and no one here would have heard the plans. All I had accomplished was to make sure that the comtessa, if she was really upstairs, could not summon her servants because I was holding them hostage in the salon.

Then the daughter came home and was stopped by a uniformed officer in front of a suit of armor that had probably belonged to Ramon Berenguer el Gran or some such person. From the desk behind which I sat, I heard the girlish voice crying, "But who are you? And why are you here?"

"Bring her straight in," I said to my aide.

She was a pale girl with dark hair pulled back in a stark knob at the base of her neck. No curls for this one. Her clothes were as dark and conservative as a nun's, which, if I remembered correctly, Senyora Blue had said Dolors Xifré aspired to be. And her lips trembled. She did not look like a murderer.

Hardening my heart, I asked her all the questions I had asked the household, and she answered timidly and with some confusion. She had dined with her mother on the night in question and received her mother's blessing before the two of them retired to their suites; she was aware of and obviously embarrassed by her mother's employment of Bacigalupi; she knew of her father's relationship with Isabel Almirall but found it too painful to discuss; she had no idea where her father was the night Isabel had died; and she didn't know whether her mother had a key to Esperit.

"But surely you don't think my mother or father killed Isabel," she exclaimed, as if I had driven her to distraction with my questions. "I have a key to Esperit, but I didn't kill Isabel." Then she burst into tears and ran out of the room.

Well, that hadn't been very successful. My three men and I left the house under the reproachful eyes of the household. A simple policeman like myself shouldn't be expected to deal with the arrogant rich or even the pathetic rich. And if I had to, I should have the power of the law behind me, rather than one toadying judge who thought that only the poor should be accused or even suspected of crimes.

I was in a very bad humor by the time I got back to my office and told my aide that Orfeó Bacigalupi was to be in my office at 9:00 the next morning if he expected to keep his license. He was my only conduit to that accursed Xifré family. Perhaps I was a fool for letting Senyora Blue convince me to look elsewhere and not at her friend, the brassy American Miró scholar.

Sebastiana, however, would be interested in hearing about the household of a comtessa. I felt that I could tell my wife that much without compromising my integrity or that of the investigation. No doubt she would scold me for making the daughter cry. Perhaps I'd leave that part out.

27

On the Passeig de Gràcia

Carolyn

The hotel was a comfortable haven for businessmen, a short walk from the fountains that played delightfully with color and music at night. It was also quite reasonable; Jason found it on the Internet. I unpacked, hung my clothes, and placed my toiletries in the very acceptable bathroom. It didn't have washcloths, but it did have an enclosed tub and shower so that I wouldn't be forced to wade through shower water after bathing.

So, what to do with myself for the remainder of the afternoon? I had checked the hotel restaurant and discovered that, as was the custom, it did not open until 9:30. Therefore, I could write some columns before dinner and still have time for sightseeing activities. Obviously, not a visit to the Sagrada Familia; that wonderful structure required much more time than I had. But I could stroll on the Passeig de Gràcia and view the modernist (as the Catalans call Art Nouveau) buildings. I could take pictures. I could sit on fanciful benches. I could admire elaborate street lamps. I rushed right out to do it, camera in hand.

My favorites are Casa Batlló and Casa Milà. The first was a once-boring apartment building restored inside and out by Gaudí. Everything is curved: the walls, the columns on the ground floor, the strange balconies that look like masks or perhaps mouths with teeth, all the way up to the dragon-backed roof with its garlic-bulb tower and four-armed cross. The walls seem to undulate, and they sparkle with the multicolored mosaic that adorns them.

Casa Milà is even more amazing, five stone stories, rolling horizontally, with windows curved into the walls like caves. It's called La Pedrera, the stone quarry. Gaudí decorated window ledges with metal sculptures that resemble twisted plants and topped the building with a waveform roof and bizarre hosts of chimneys like giants and knights wearing carnival masks, some with mosaic armor. You can go in, admire the courtyard with its variously painted walls rising up to sunlight, the lovely columns, and the staircase. You can visit the roof and stare, astonished, at the surrealist armies who stand guard there. I went. Then I visited the gift shop. What woman can resist a gift shop?

There were Gaudí books, Gaudí household ornaments, Gaudí jewelry. Spendthrift that I am, I bought a pair of matte silver earrings and put them on immediately. I was tempted by the matching pendant but restrained the impulse, reminding myself that Jason might ask me what they cost when I showed them off. He can be a bit thrifty.

Of course I had taken dozens of pictures, which I admired after going outside to sit on a bench under leafy trees that had not yet bowed to fall. While I was sitting there, having clicked back through the photos on my little digital screen, I watched the passing crowd, well dressed, bustling. Barcelona is a hive of activity. I have seen students standing in bookstores, reading books in the middle of the night, and wondered if they ever slept. The Rambla certainly doesn't with its hordes of tourists and natives pouring through the flower and bird markets, in and out of the cafés and shops. Here there were fewer young people in casual jeans and T-shirts, and more adults in designer clothing, carrying shopping bags and briefcases.

Well, I had best get back to the hotel, I thought, and stood to make my way to a bus stop. On the corner at which I was to turn, I saw a boy, none too clean, with dark hair falling over his forehead. He was begging and held his hand out to me, hardly looking up from under lowered eyelids. "Sammie?" I said uncertainly. He stiffened and began to move away. "Sammie? Is that you?" I grabbed the boy's arm, excited that I might have found him, worried that I might be mistaken and about to make a terrible fool of myself on this very fashionable street.

A uniformed policeman moved toward us and asked something in Catalan. "No . . . habla . . . er . . . Catalan." I was now nose to nose with the reluctant boy, who looked both terrified and confused.

"Henri Samuel Fauree, look at me," I demanded.

He did, wide-eyed.

"I'm Carolyn Blue." He blinked. "Remember me? Your father and my husband are friends." The policeman spoke to us again, aggressively to poor Sammie. "I knew your mother," I persisted. "Your new stepmother is an old friend of mine." He burst into tears. I sighed and waved the policeman away as if he were a troublesome gnat. For a wonder, he left. Whatever was going on, this was a very unhappy, frightened child in my grasp, so I put my arms around him and patted him consolingly on the shoulder, although he was just my height, and we must have made a peculiar sight there on Passeig de Gràcia — a respectably dressed, almost middle-aged woman (the forties aren't really middle-aged, do you think?) and a weeping youth who looked homeless and disheveled.

"Come along now," I said. "I'll take you back to my hotel." He rubbed his fist against one eye and then the other. "I'll bet you're hungry." He sniffed and allowed himself to be hustled toward the street. "We'll order room service," I promised. My children had always loved room service on the few occasions when their father allowed them to order.

"Are you really Mrs. Blue?" he asked.

"Of course I am. Surely I haven't aged that much in the few years since you last saw me." I hailed a cab. "You've certainly grown a lot." I pushed him into the cab and gave the driver the card I'd picked up from the hotel desk. No sense in trying to communicate in Catalan or Spanish at a time like this. "Here's a tissue," I said to Sammie, who accepted it and blew his nose. Goodness, but the boy needed a bath. He *smelled.*

I chattered all the way to the hotel, giving him news of Chris and Gwen, tactfully not mentioning Robbie again since my first move in that conversational direction had brought on the tears. But why was he in Barcelona, if it wasn't because of Robbie? He'd never been here before. It was unlikely that he had any friends here, for instance someone he'd met at that camp he ran away from. I doubted that Barcelonans sent their children to camp in the Midwest.

I whisked him through the lobby before the

management could see or smell him, into an elevator, which, thankfully, was empty, and into my room, where he stood on the carpet, becalmed. Obviously, he didn't know what to say or do. I took a deep breath. "About Robbie," I ventured. I had to call and tell her I'd found him, but I didn't want him running off at the prospect. "Sammie, are you all right?" He'd turned pale under the dirt. "Sit down," I ordered, pushing him toward a chair. He fell into it and began to shake.

"Are you ill?" I asked.

"I killed her," he mumbled.

"What?"

"I killed my dad's new wife." He looked up at me miserably. "I'm a murderer. And he'll never forgive me."

What in the world? I sat down abruptly myself. I'd just seen Robbie at lunchtime. How could he have killed her? Maybe he was feverish.

"Maybe you'd better tell me all about it," I suggested cautiously.

220

28

The Confession of
H. Samuel Fauree, Minor

Carolyn

He looked so pathetic, trembling on that ornate chair with his hands clasped between his knees, his hair falling over his face, and those thin shoulders that heaved as he gulped in tears of what was evidently remorse, and/or fear. He thought he'd killed someone. Surely not Robbie, unless it happened this afternoon. The only dead person was Isabel, but why would he kill her? All he had to do was take a good look, and he'd have known it wasn't Robbie, if that's the person he meant to kill. The thought gave me pause. Had this boy, the son of longtime friends, come all this way to kill another friend of mine? Should I be worried for my own safety? Was he likely to grab that lamp on the table by his chair and whack me on the head with it?

I considered my options. I could call

Robbie. I could call the police. I could get him to talk to me and find out what had happened. Or I could make him take a bath while I sent for food, which would give me time to think over my other choices. *When in doubt, delay.* It isn't usually the best course, but I acted on it all the same. "Sammie, I want you to go into the bathroom and take a shower. Through that door." I pointed.

He didn't look up. I rose, took his elbow, and tugged. "There are clean towels and shampoo," I said to tempt him. "No washcloths, unfortunately." I wasn't going to offer him mine. "And there's a toweling robe on the hook in the bathroom. You can put that on and throw out your clothes. They're . . . ah . . . in need of washing. While you're having a bath, I'll call for room service. And ask about laundry service."

"But . . ." He looked at me anxiously. "Didn't you hear what I said?"

"Sammie, it seems unlikely, but we can talk about that later."

"You don't *believe* me?" He was obviously dumbfounded. "Why would I —"

"Exactly. Why would you? Now into the bathroom. You'll feel a lot better once you're clean and fed. I'm afraid I don't have an extra toothbrush. Can't believe I neglected to pack one, but you can use my toothpaste. Just rub it over your teeth —"

"But, Mrs. Blue —"

"And swish it around your mouth. Clean teeth are very comforting, don't you think?" I ushered him into the bathroom, handed him the toothpaste, pointed out the amenities, including the robe, and took his dirty clothes when he handed them out. "Use the detachable showerhead to wash down the shower floor when you're through," I called through the door. I hate a dirty bathroom, and teenagers aren't usually very fussy about such things, especially male teenagers.

What would a Midwestern boy who was probably half-starved — he certainly looked half-starved, and shaky to boot — want to eat? Not paella or mar i muntanya or goat, I thought wryly. I ordered a steak dinner for him, a whiskey sour for me, and told them to pick up the laundry bag in the hall. But wait. What if he *had* killed Robbie this afternoon? By having his clothes washed, I'd be destroying evidence, which was against the law. I called housekeeping, canceled the laundry order, and hid the bag of clothes under my bed. He might want to get back into them and escape, which he couldn't do in a bathrobe.

Considering the state of his person, he was out of the bathroom with wet hair and skinny legs extending under the toweling robe in less time than I would have expected. My whiskey sour had come up from the bar, but his steak was still undelivered. "Your food should be here soon, Sammie. Don't you feel better?"

"Yes, ma'am." He sat down gingerly on the chair and then wrapped one long, naked foot around the other, his hands clutching the robe closed.

"While we're waiting, you can tell me all about it," I said. I hadn't even had time to call the museum to see if Robbie was there, alive, or elsewhere, dead. "Why don't you start from the beginning?"

"The beginning?" He looked confused. "Like when my dad brought her home?"

"Fine. Start there."

"I couldn't believe it. He'd only known her a couple of weeks. He and my mom —" He gulped back tears. "They dated a couple of *years* before they got married, and now he's gonna, like, marry this strange woman, and he thinks we're gonna forget all about Mom and give this Robbie a big hug. Jeez, she's taller than me. I bet she weighs more too."

"Well, you'll certainly grow to be taller than Robbie by the time you're eighteen," I assured him.

"You think?"

"No question. Look at your feet. And hands. Outsized feet and hands are an indicator of height to come."

He looked at those long appendages woefully. "I thought I was just going to be geeky-looking all my life."

"But Sammie, your father's tall."

"But Mom —" He choked up again.

"Her father was quite tall. I met him several times."

"Yeah." He looked happier at the thought of the height genes at his disposal. Then his expression tightened. "And Kimmie, like, thinks it's great — Dad's getting married and all. She practically climbed into Robbie's lap at the wedding reception."

I nodded wisely. "You resented Robbie. That's natural."

"I *hated* her! I was — like, really mean to her, and my dad got awesomely mad. He said I had to shape up and start treating her okay, and I said, 'Yeah, sure,' but I didn't, so he sent me off to this lame-o camp, which I hated. And on Parents' Day who does he bring along but Robbie, who's got these brownies she made and gives me a kiss on the cheek, and all the guys make smooching noises. Jeez, Mrs. Blue, Chris wouldn't have liked that, would he? If you died and Professor Blue married some woman with big — ah — bosoms and —"

"I imagine Robbie was trying to be friendly, Sammie. Goodness, I didn't even realize she knew how to make brownies."

"Yeah, she's an awful cook, but I didn't mean to kill her. I don't even know, like, how it happened."

"Not at camp, I assume," I prompted.

Sam hung his head. "No, it was later. After I threw the brownies in the trash can and she looked like she was going to cry, and Dad told her to go back to the car. Then he grabbed my arm and said, like, 'I told you about making an effort, Sam,' and a bunch of stuff like that, and he said I was going off to military school as soon as I got home from camp." A few more tears leaked from Sammie's eyes. "I didn't want to go to military school or leave Dad or even Kimmie. He went home, and I thought and thought about it, and I decided I had to call Robbie and tell her I was sorry, because, man, was I sorry by then, only she wasn't home. She'd gone off to Barcelona. Grandma told me. Dad was out of town at a meeting and Grandma was staying at the house with Kimmie until school started.

"Anyway, there was no way for me to fix it. I was going to get sent off, and Dad probably wouldn't even let me come home for Christmas or anything, so I — I —"

"You came to Barcelona to see Robbie?" I asked when he seemed stuck at that point in the story.

He nodded glumly. "I snuck out of camp and hitched home — got into the house while Grandma and Kimmie were at the mall. I needed my passport and the bankbook for my college account and some clothes and stuff. A suitcase."

"How did you get out of the country? Doesn't a boy your age have to have an adult escort or —"

"I forged a letter from Dad saying I was going to see my stepmother in Spain. Well, I printed the letter on his computer and forged his signature. That wasn't too hard." He looked rather pleased with himself, I suppose because something in his crazy scheme had been successful. "I got the name of the place she was working and figured I'd go straight there as soon as I got off the plane and tell her how sorry I was and . . . like that."

I nodded encouragingly. "So you got to Barcelona. What then?"

"Then it cost a lot more to get from the airport to the city than I figured, and I was really tired, and I had to buy a map too, and still got lost trying to find the museum or whatever it is. Then it took the last of my money to buy a damn — sorry, Mrs. Blue — a ticket to get in, and after all that, the woman at the desk wouldn't let me go upstairs to see Robbie because I didn't have an appointment. So there I was in this weird museum, looking at freaky stuff and wondering how I could get past the receptionist. They had this exhibit that looked like an old-time hospital with big birds serving food — at least I got something to eat — and carrying supposedly dead people off. Way cool. Anyway, I finally decided that I'd hide out in the men's room until the museum closed and then sneak up there and leave her a note about where to find me. I still got the note." He reached for a pocket and realized that he was wearing the bathrobe, not his jeans.

I fished the note out of the laundry bag later while he was asleep. It read:

Dear Robbie,
I'm here in Barcelona, but the lady at the desk wouldn't let me go up to see you, so I'm leaving this note so you'll know to look for me in the first-floor men's room or maybe I can go to sleep in one of the hospital beds for the night. Please come and get me. I'm sorry I was rude to you and promise I'll be nicer.

> *Yours truly,*
> *H. Samuel Fauree*

"So I sat in that bathroom, and whenever anyone came in I, like, pulled up my feet so they wouldn't know I was in the stall. Finally everyone left, and the guard went to sleep in his room, so I ran up the stairs to the offices. Those stairs behind the receptionist's desk, and I found the office with Robbie's name on it. At first, I was pretty nervous and thought maybe I should go back downstairs because there was a light on in there. The offices all have these weird windows looking in, so I took a quick peek, and it was her.

"Man, I thought I was one lucky kid. She was working late. I mean I was scared about talking to her. In fact, I was shaking, but I walked in and said, like, 'Robbie, it's me, Sammie.' She was kind of leaning over her desk, reading something, I guess, and she didn't even answer. So I said it again and walked up behind her, and she made this funny noise, like maybe she was laughing, and her shoulders wiggled. I asked her to please talk to me, because I'd come all this way to tell her I was sorry and would she talk to my dad and tell him not to send me away. And she wouldn't even turn around. It was like I could never put it right. She'd never let me back in the family, and it was *my* family." At that point, his voice broke, and it was all I could do not to hug him.

"And I guess . . . I guess I, like, lost it. There's no excuse. I know that." Tears were leaking out of his eyes again, and his nose was red. "There was this dumb metal bird on her desk, and I grabbed it, and I yelled, 'Talk to me,' and when she wouldn't turn around, I . . . like, poked her with it. Not that hard, I swear. But she went flat on the desk. Maybe she's got one of those really thin skulls. I saw a program on TV about someone who died when they shouldn't have because they had, like, an eggshell skull instead of thick bone. I killed her."

Good Lord, he must have killed Isabel,

thinking she was Robbie. "Why did you take her downstairs to 'Tapas Triage'?" I asked.

"What do you mean?" He looked genuinely puzzled. "I got out of there as fast as I could. I found a window in the basement and shoved it open. I was so scared, I ran until I fell down. I don't even know where I was. All I could think was that I'd killed my stepmother and the police would get me and put me in some moldy prison before they executed me."

"I don't think Spain has capital punishment, Sammie," I said, bemused. "When was this? That you hit the woman with the bird?"

"I don't know. Three or four days ago. I've been sleeping in churches and alleys and begging to get money for food ever since. I can't use my round-trip ticket to go home. They're probably watching the airports for me. And where would I go if I got home? Dad won't ever want to see me again. Anyway, I've never gotten together enough money to get back to the airport."

He looked so bereft, I could have cried with him.

"I guess you've got to call the police now, huh? And my dad. He's probably wondering why she isn't e-mailing him."

"He is," I replied. "You didn't kill Robbie, Sam. You killed Isabel Almirall. She works at the museum."

There was a knock at the door, and

Sammie looked terrified. "It's room service." I tipped the waiter at the door and took the cart without letting him in. "You better have something to eat," I said to Sammie.

He looked longingly at the steak, as if he hadn't eaten in days. Maybe he hadn't. Then he looked up at me. "You're wrong about who I killed. It was Robbie."

"Believe me, Sammie, it wasn't. She and I have been looking for you ever since Hugh said you'd run away from camp and the American consul told us you were in Spain. Robbie's fine. I saw her at lunchtime."

"Today?" he asked. I nodded. "I killed some stranger?"

"Eat your dinner, Sam." *What am I to do next?* I wondered, picking up the fork from the tray and putting it into the boy's hand. I sat there until he'd consumed every bite, which didn't take him long. Teenage boys, even those who are regularly fed, can consume large amounts of food in small amounts of time. Then I told him to get in bed and go to sleep. Goodness knows, he looked like he needed it.

Then I called Robbie.

29

Robbie Takes Over

Carolyn

Robbie couldn't thank me enough when I called to tell her that I'd found Sammie and had him safely at my hotel. "Don't let him get away," she ordered. "Does he know I'm coming straight over? Maybe you shouldn't mention that."

When I tried to tell her that he thought he'd killed her, she laughed heartily. "I hope you assured him that I'm in good health. Well, no matter. I'm on my way. Where did he *get* such a weird idea? Oh God, he's not on drugs, is he? I'll take a cab. Just keep him there. I don't know how to thank you, Caro. You've saved my life. When Hugh gets in to-morrow, I can say, 'Here he is. All safe and sound.' He is, isn't he? Oh, listen to me, will you? Borrowing trouble. If there's something wrong with him, we'll get a doctor. I'm on my way." And she hung up.

I sighed and put the telephone back into

the cradle as soundlessly as possible. The few words I'd managed to say to Robbie had been whispered. Sammie was still asleep, and I planned to let him stay that way until Robbie arrived. Then *he* could explain to his stepmother why he thought he'd killed her. She might not be so happy to see him after that.

I pulled a chair over by the twin bed into which I'd put him. He was having bad dreams, eyes moving behind closed lids, small moans and cries coming from his mouth. Although it was only forty-five minutes until I heard the knock at my door, it seemed like hours. I let my friend in and, always emotional and impulsive, she hurtled straight to the bed and wrapped the sleeping boy in a tight hug. He came awake, terrified. She cried, "Oh, Sammie, you monster, you've scared us all to death. Thank God, Carolyn found you. We even hired this seamy detective to look for you."

Sammie cowered away from her.

She gave him a hearty kiss on the forehead and re-enveloped him. "You poor boy, you've lost weight. I can feel your bones. Where have you been living? Haven't you been eating? And why didn't you come to me? You weren't suffering from amnesia, were you? Good Lord, was someone holding you captive?"

"Robbie," I intervened, "I think Sammie

wants to tell you some things if you'll just let go of him."

"Oh, of course." She dropped him back on the pillow as if burned. "I'm sorry, Sam. I know you don't want me hugging you. What was I thinking? It's just that —"

"Sam, why don't you pull that robe around you and get up," I suggested. He looked as if he'd prefer to disappear under the covers.

"Clothes," said Robbie, snapping her fingers. "Carolyn told me yours were filthy. What happened to your suitcase?"

"Someone stole it at the airport," he mumbled.

"Of course. We had two men trying to steal our money and passports while we were looking for you. Caro, clever woman, took their pictures, and they ran off. Well, I can't seem to stop talking. I bought you some clothes." She held a shopping bag out to him. "I hope they're all right. There's underwear and everything. Well, not shoes. I assumed your shoes were wearable. Was I wrong?"

"Go in the bathroom and change, Sam," I said. He scuttled out from under the covers, hugging the bathrobe around him, and headed for the bathroom.

Robbie and I sat down in the two armchairs to wait. Robbie was actually biting her fingernails. "I'm just no good at this," she moaned. "Here the first thing I do is give him a hug. He doesn't even like me. He probably hated that. In fact, he looked terrified. I suppose he's worried about what Hugh will say. Did you tell him Hugh and Kimmie will be in tomorrow?"

"Actually, he did most of the talking."

"Well, you're obviously way ahead of me. He didn't say word one to me. Of course, I guess I didn't give him a chance."

"Then I fed him a steak dinner and put him to bed. Well, he took a bath before we talked. I'm afraid he really needed it. He's been living on the streets and begging for money to buy food."

"Oh, poor Sam." Tears came to her eyes. "Am I so awful that he couldn't come to me? I can't believe this. I don't even understand it."

"Just let him tell you the story, Robbie."

Sam edged out of the bathroom shortly thereafter wearing a pair of khakis with a snakeskin belt and a T-shirt that said: "Gaudí is Gaudy. Miró is the Most." I wondered if the shirt had come from the museum shop. Maybe she had bought it for herself. No, it would have been too small for her, cup-size-wise. She must have bought it for him. To take home to him as a peacemaking present. I felt so sorry for both of them.

Sam sat down on the end of the bed, his head hanging once again, his hands pressed between his knees. I could see the tremor in his bony shoulders, as if we'd gone straight back to the beginning, except that he was now clean and fed.

After I prompted him, he told his story haltingly, casting glances at his stepmother from time to time. Robbie bit her lip, frowned, even growled at the reception he had been given when he arrived at Esperit. When he tried to explain why he had struck the woman he thought to be her, she froze. Finally he got through it, the scramble downstairs, the window in the basement through which he exited. "I'm sorry," he said at the end of his recital. "I really, really didn't mean to . . . I was just so scared when I thought you wouldn't even speak to me. I don't know what —"

Robbie stood up in the middle of this fumbling apology and said, "Well, I'm fine. See." She spread her arms, flipped her hair. "You didn't kill me. It was Isabel, stupid woman. I'll bet she's sorry now that she got herself up to look like me."

Sammie's mouth dropped open. "But she's dead."

"Did you leave fingerprints on that statue?" Robbie asked. "Or anything to show you'd been there?"

Sam stared at her in helpless astonishment. "I don't know."

"Well, no matter. They don't have your fingerprints. They don't even know you're here.

Your father arrives tomorrow, and he can take you straight home."

"Ah . . . Robbie," I ventured. "I asked Inspector Pujol to look for Sam. Remember? What if he asks me —"

"Lie," said Robbie decidedly. "But I can't keep Sam at my place. What if they come to arrest me? I don't want them finding him."

"Arrest you for what?" asked Sam.

"Oh, they think I killed Isabel."

Sammie looked stricken. "Then you have to turn me in."

"Nonsense. I didn't kill her, so obviously they can't find me guilty. No problem. You'll go straight home. Have you got a ticket?"

"He does," I answered, "but Robbie, they'll be looking for him at the airport. He's a missing foreigner now."

"Damn it, Carolyn. Couldn't you have kept your mouth shut about Sammie? I didn't ask you to go to that straitlaced, tight-assed inspector."

Sam gaped at her language. I glared at her ingratitude. After all, I'd found Sammie for her, and I told her so.

"I know. I know," she muttered. "Sorry. I can't think of what to do."

"Talk to Hugh tomorrow," I suggested, "and of course Sam can sleep here tonight. I've got two beds."

Sam looked rebellious. "I could —"

"Just let us fix this, Sam," Robbie interrupted sharply. "Your solutions so far haven't been very sensible."

He huddled down further on the bed and said nothing.

"Oh, don't look that way," said Robbie. "I'm not mad at you. I'm just scared. Somehow, we've got to get you out of the country tomorrow, and I'm not sure how."

"Dad's not going to leave you here to take the rap for what I did," said Sammie.

"Much you know," she snapped. "He loved you before he ever even saw me."

"But —"

"And he'll do what I tell him to. Only I don't know what to tell him," she finished hopelessly.

"They can take a train," I suggested. "They can go up the coast and over the mountains to France. No one will be looking for him in France. The four of you can leave from Paris or someplace."

"The three of them. I don't have a passport, and I have to stay a suspect until we get Sam safely home to the States. But the train. That's a great idea. We'll do that." Robbie couldn't be budged from her position. She would stay. Hugh, Kimmie, and Sam would go home. Immediately. By way of France. "You're a smart woman, Caro. Thank God, you were here. You found him, and you're going to save him. Sorry I snapped at you. I'm a bit frazzled here."

"Small wonder," I murmured, and gave her a hug before she left. She looked as if she was thinking of hugging Sammie, but she restrained herself. I'd have been worried about how things would turn out for this strange family if I hadn't been preoccupied with how I'd keep Sam's presence in my room from the management. Robbie and I couldn't take him to the airport with us tomorrow to meet the plane. I'd have to hide him in a closet or something, make his bed myself, as if it hadn't been slept in, then stay close while the maid was cleaning the room. Thank goodness, the room service waiter hadn't seen him. The fellow would just think I have a big appetite. But I wouldn't be getting any dinner. Rats.

30

Orfeó Bacigalupi Gives Up His Honor

Inspector Pujol

As I drove to work, resentfully because it was Saturday, it occurred to me that there was a way to convince Judge Enric Goytisolo to help me force information from the reluctant private detective who was to appear at my office that morning. Goytisolo would be filling in for all the investigating judges this weekend, so I went straight to his office, only to receive the information that he had ordered El Esperit de Gaudí i Miró completely reopened and the police presence removed.

"The Office of Tourism insists," he said piously. "And the comte has been most upset that people could not enter to enjoy the full delights of his museu."

I was not pleased to hear this, but at least I had kept the tourists out long enough to give my officers a chance to investigate the crime scene. I must admit to taking pleasure in the information I had to impart that morning: that Comte Miquel Xifré had been the lover of Isabel Almirall. "Furthermore, it is likely that they quarreled the night she died, the comte preferring not to see her, the lady taking offense."

"This is terrible, Ildefons," cried Goytisolo. "We can not bring in a comte for questioning."

"Justice is for rich and poor alike," I murmured.

"Yes, but unless we have proof that he is guilty, there will be repercussions. I assure you, Inspector, that there will be protest and scandal. We will regret that —"

"Perhaps there is another way, Your Honor. A way to clear him. Or, if we are unlucky, to excuse ourselves in the embarrassment of accusing him."

"What is it?" he asked eagerly.

"It seems that the comte's wife is a jealous woman."

"Do not tell me that you wish to shift suspicion from him to her. Comtessa Violante has friends in the highest places in Madrid. We would find ourselves in even greater difficulties if we were to bring her in under suspicion of —"

"Of course, she may be guilty in some way," I interrupted soothingly. "But my information is that she has a private detective following her estranged husband at all times. This man will know if the comte could have killed Isabel Almirall."

"May the saints protect us from such misfortune!" cried the judge. "Have you questioned this fellow?"

"I have tried. He considers any knowledge he has of the comte's movements on the night in question the property of the comtessa and as sacred a trust as the knowledge of a priest in the confessional."

"Balderdash," snapped Goytisolo.

"Now, if you were to tell him that he must cooperate or lose his license —"

"I do not wish to speak to this person."

"But you could issue an order."

The judge bit his lip, sipped his coffee — he had neglected to offer me any, although there was a small china pot steaming on his desk. It would only have been a matter of calling his secretary for an extra cup.

The judge mused and fretted. "I will do it," he announced finally. "Such a person cannot refuse to cooperate with the proper authorities." Goytisolo called for his secretary, who rushed in with sugared rolls and honey. "No, no," he said. "Take this down." She juggled the rolls and managed to slide them onto a console by the door. When her stenographer's pad was on her knee, Goytisolo dictated a stern order to Orfeó Bacigalupi, Private Detective.

Although I had been offered no coffee or sugared rolls, I left quite pleased with my success. In my outer office I found the sweating detective, who had been awaiting my pleasure now for 20 minutes or so. I waved him to a seat in front of my desk. My aide followed with pencil and pad.

"You will now tell me, Senyor Bacigalupi, everything you know of Comte Miquel Xifré i Fontdevila on the night of twenty-second September and the early morning following."

"But, Inspector," squeaked Bacigalupi, "I thought you understood that —"

"Neither I nor the investigating judge, Enric Goytisolo i Llull, understand your reluctance to do your duty as a citizen." At the mention of Goytisolo, Bacigalupi turned pale and drops of perspiration ran down his face into his gnawed mustache and onto the collar of his pink shirt. I could see a growing spot where the sweat was puddling above his belly as I handed him the judge's memorandum.

"My license?" he cried. "Can this be done?"

"Most assuredly," I replied.

"Then I have no choice. The comte could not have killed this Senyoreta Isabel Almirall, although she was his mistress. On the night that the lady died, he was playing baccarat at his club. Then he took the fado singer, María Catalina Ibaris, to his house and spent the whole night with her." The man pulled a soggy notebook from his pocket and wet his finger so that he could flip pages. "The comte was at the club from eleven to three and lost a hundred fifty thousand euros. Then he gave the singer a gold cigar case and took her home with him at three-fifteen. I followed them. She left at eight-thirty, and he left an hour later for the museum, where he held a monthly staff meeting." Bacigalupi slapped the notebook shut, shoved it back into his pocket, and stared at me with reproach. The look reminded me of those I had received from the comtessa's household after I questioned her daughter.

"You have deprived me of my honor, Inspector," said Bacigalupi. "Will you now at least leave me my livelihood? Do not let it be known that I betrayed a client, I beg you."

"And you were outside the club and the comte's house this whole time that you mentioned? Can you prove that?"

"Me? Why should I have to prove anything?"

"Perhaps you are using this information, which is false or not of your own observation, to give yourself an alibi for the night of the murder."

"Why would I need an alibi? I have done nothing. I have given you what you wanted. I am a simple man of the province, earning a meager living at my trade. I —"

"If the comte did not kill Senyoreta Isabel,

244

perhaps the comtessa commissioned you to do it. You are her man. Only the threat of losing your license induced you to give us information."

"I did not say the comtessa was my client," he gasped.

"You did not need to tell me. It is well known. The comte laughs about it."

Bacigalupi groaned, collected himself, and said, "I killed no one. I was at my post that night, following the comte. What else can I say?"

"Or the daughter? Perhaps she paid you to kill her father's mistress."

"The lady Dolors?" He looked quite astounded. "She is a . . . a very pious girl, always in church or doing good works, more even than her mother would wish."

"You have no information that would link either of the women to the death of the Miró scholar?"

"I have given you what I have. I can give no more."

I stood abruptly. "You are excused, Senyor Bacigalupi, but we will have our eye on you. If you have lied to me in any way —"

"I have not." Bacigalupi gave his nose a huge, honking blow into a pink handkerchief that matched his shirt but nothing else he was wearing, including the bedraggled posy in his buttonhole.

I waved him away and he left, as rapidly as

245

his little feet could carry his fat body. So it would seem that the comte was not, as Senyora Blue had thought, the killer. Which left me with three women: the American, the comtessa, and her daughter. Poor choices in my opinion. Women, especially women of good family or education, seldom bash one another's heads in. Well, perhaps American women did. Americans are a violent people; but happily, they are, generally speaking, an ocean away from Barcelona.

31

Sir Cecil's Watch

Carolyn

When I awoke the morning after Sammie turned up, he was still asleep in the next bed, but he had been thrashing all night, and I was very tired. However, even in my exhausted state — I hadn't had an afternoon nap since arriving here — I did find an answer to the problem of keeping the hotel unaware of Sammie's presence. I'd order a big breakfast, enough for both of us; goodness knows, I was hungry. I'd had nothing since lunch yesterday but some peanuts left over from my transatlantic flight.

After I'd intercepted breakfast at the door so the waiter wouldn't see Sammie, I'd tell the waiter that I was so jet-lagged, I planned to eat and go straight back to bed and didn't want to be disturbed all day. In the event, he advised me to hang out the Do Not Disturb sign. Perfect. I wouldn't have to make beds or hide Sammie in a closet when the maid came in. Sammie could stay safely behind the Do Not Disturb sign while I went to the airport, which I had to do because in all the excitement and confusion of the last few days, I'd completely forgotten that my daughter was coming in today.

I got up and called Robbie to tell her that I'd be going to the airport. She thought I should stay in the room to protect Sammie and let her meet Gwen. However, when I explained my plan, Robbie gave in and told me to be at Esperit at 10:00. "I'm back in my own office," she said, "sitting where Isabel presumably died."

I then called room service and said I wanted a big Catalan breakfast, something I could write about for my newspaper column in the United States. A three-way conversation ensued between the chef, a member of his staff who spoke English, and me, as I took advice on and helped to plan the meal. Then I took a shower, dressed for the day, woke Sammie, and sent him into the bathroom, where he was to stay until room service arrived.

Everything went according to plan, and the two of us settled down to a meal that Sammie considered peculiar. He objected to the sardines, not to mention the hot chocolate. He wanted milk. Or even coffee. But he had to take what was there. I told him to listen carefully while I was gone and sprint for the closet if he heard anyone knocking at or trying to enter the room. He became very nervous. I assured him that the sign on the outer doorknob should protect him from discovery.

Then I left surreptitiously, making sure that no maids saw me, took the elevator down to the last floor with rooms, and the stairs to the lobby, from which I managed to escape without being noticed. Esperit was just a cab ride away.

Once there, I was sent straight upstairs in a special staff elevator behind the receptionist's desk. She didn't even try to make me pay for a ticket. I noticed that there were lines waiting outside the newly reopened "Tapas Triage." *Nothing like a murder to draw in the kind of people who stop to ogle car wrecks,* I thought wryly. Robbie was in a conference room with the comte; Jordi, the museum director; Madrona, who was an expert on something Miroesque; and the artist, Narcis.

Narcis invited me to sit in the chair beside him. "Started any riots lately?" I asked under my breath. "Inspector Pujol said I was lucky to get out of Bacallà without ending up in jail or in a hospital."

"Why you discuss our dinner with police?" he asked, also quietly. Around us the others were discussing the best way to capitalize on the publicity the institution had received of late.

"I could change patients in Triage to all murder victims," Narcis offered. "One bed for Isabel. Others for people kill this year and show up in news."

"That would be a bit tasteless, wouldn't it?" asked Robbie.

"But clever," Jordi chimed in, sending an approving smile at Narcis.

"Indeed." Madrona was sitting on his left and stroked his arm. "What talent is here in such a pretty package." Narcis half rose from his chair to bow to her.

"Absolutely not," said the comte. "We would defile Isabel's memory with such a stunt."

Narcis immediately said, "I take back idea. Our patron know what is best taste for Esperit." He shot a meaningful glance at the comte and adjusted his cuffs. That's when I noticed the watch on his wrist and knew that I'd seen it before. While the discussion continued, I watched for glimpses of it and searched my mind.

Then I had it. "Sir Cecil!" I exclaimed. The discussion stopped, and they all stared at me. "The Englishman who claimed his watch was stolen by the police. Narcis is wearing one just like it."

"And you know what is Englishman's watch how?" Narcis asked with indolent amusement.

"Because I kept running into him at 'Tapas Triage,' and he was always pulling back his cuff to look at his watch. It looked just like yours."

"So you say I steal this anglès watch? Mine is gift from admirer." He looked smug. "Is nice. No?" He displayed it for all to see.

"Very nice," said Madrona. "You owe Narcis apology, Senyora Blue, if you suggest he steal watch." She turned to the young artist and stroked his cheek. "Narcis is not bad boy, are you, dear one?"

Narcis gave her a wicked look. "You like I be your bad boy, nice lady?"

Madrona shot him an intimate look from beneath lashes heavy with mascara. She was a handsome woman, but surely she was old enough to be his mother.

"Do stop flirting, Madrona," said Jordi. "Narcis doesn't need you to speak up for him." Now *he* was smiling at the artist in an overly fond way. "Narcis can always count on me to come to his defense if someone is so silly as to attack him." I then got a malicious look from the director.

I distinctly heard Narcis murmur, evidently meaning for me to catch his comment, "As if I need be defend by old queer." Good grief. I had stirred up a hornet's nest.

"Well, we've got to be going." Robbie stood up. "We've got planes to meet. Come along, Carolyn." She hustled me out to the staff elevator, which creaked louder than the public elevator.

"Jesus, Caro, did you have to make it sound like you think Narcis is a thief?"

"He may be," I said defensively. "He's the one who said a policeman stole the watch, and no watch was found on the poor fellow."

"Oh, the police are always stealing things or taking bribes. Everyone knows it. As for Narcis, they all love him here, including the count, so lay off. He's the museum pet. And he is sooo pretty. Tell the truth. Have you ever seen a handsomer boy?"

"He nearly got us killed."

"Oh, poof." Robbie laughed and pushed me out the front door. She had a cab within seconds, and we were on our way to the airport. Since Robbie had little to say, I was left to question my own motives. Had I deliberately tried to embarrass Narcis because I resented the trouble at Bacallà? What, after all, were the chances that the comte's protégé was a thief?

32

A Rude Surprise from
Dr. Arcadi Zapatero i Sunyer

Inspector Pujol

After a successful morning and an excellent afternoon meal at home, I returned to my office to find a message from Arcadi Zapatero, indicating that he had more information for me on the death of Isabel Almirall. Good, I thought. No doubt he'd confirmed that the blow to the head had been fatal. Some skulls are more fragile than others, although it seemed to me that he could have reached that conclusion sooner.

I ordered men out to talk to neighbors of the victim and the three female suspects and to find out more about Orfeó Bacigalupi, particularly his activities the night of the murder — had he really been at the comte's club and his mansion, that sort of thing. Then I paid a call on Arcadi. I could have asked that he send the report up, but I like to treat with courtesy those who extend it to me.

I found him taking organ samples from the corpse of a tram driver who had died on duty, causing an accident with injuries to his passengers and the passengers in the car hit by his tram. "Probably drunk as a sailor," said the medical examiner jovially. "Well, we'll know soon enough, and then the lawyers can start suing. In cases like this when there may be liability on the city's part, I'm often asked to skew my results. When will they learn that I am immune to bribes and threats?"

"You're feeling unusually cheerful today," I remarked, turning my head away from the gaping innards of the corpse.

"Always cheerful when I've been proved right," he replied, flourishing a razor-thin knife. "The blood and tissue results came in on your Senyoreta Almirall. You're going to be surprised, Ildefons. I certainly was. By the look of her, I'd never have taken her for a drug user. A suicide maybe, but —"

"What was she addicted to?" I asked.

"The woman had enough pure heroin in her to kill a horse," said Arcadi. "Now what do you think of that?"

"Heroin?" I didn't know what to think. "But what killed her?"

"Oh, the heroin, undoubtedly."

"And the blow to the head?"

"A minor injury. Nothing more."

"Which occurred before or after the heroin?"

"Well, she was still alive, because she bled, but she was probably dying. I imagine she injected herself, fell over, hit her head, and died."

"The head injury was caused by a blow from a Miró statue."

"Then perhaps she fell onto the statue."

"And then dragged herself downstairs to die in an art exhibit on the first floor?" I asked dryly. "That seems unlikely. How long does that much heroin take to kill someone?"

"Hmmm." Arcadi gave it some thought. "Probably depends on how much tolerance to the drug the person's developed."

"And she showed signs of long usage?" I asked. Arcadi did like to make a production of his findings. I should have sent for the written report.

"Only the one injection site," he admitted, "but she could have been using some other narcotic — cocaine, for instance."

"Her mucous membranes were —"

"No, but she could have been ingesting things. Smoking things. Although her lungs —"

"It sounds to me as if she was murdered upstairs by someone who hit her with the statue, rendering her unconscious —"

"I'm not sure the blow would have caused

unconsciousness," he interrupted.

"— then injected her with enough heroin to kill her, carried or dragged her downstairs to the exhibit, and placed her in the bed, although why the murderer would have done that is hard to imagine."

"Well, you're the detective. If that's what you think happened, you just need to find a murderer with access to pure heroin and a peculiar sense of humor."

"Access to heroin." I thought it over. "Americans are known drug users, but would the American professor have sources in Barcelona? Is she herself a user?"

"You have a female American suspect?" Arcadi looked up from a microscope and eyed me with surprise.

"Yes, but she seems very lively for someone on heroin."

"You'd want someone either jittery or nodding off unless you happened to observe them at just the right time," Arcadi advised.

"I know that." Then I considered the noblewomen. "No doubt Comtessa Violante or her daughter, Dolors, would have enough money to buy the drug, but why would they choose that particular way to kill Almirall?"

"What a case you have!" Arcadi exclaimed. "A noblewoman and her daughter? Well, the answer to your question is that they wanted to make the death look like suicide and might well have gotten away with it if they hadn't moved the body. So the real question is, why move the body?"

"This is not a case that simple men like ourselves can easily understand, my friend," I said. "The nobility, artistic types. Bah. Give me a good working-class case of spousal murder."

"Well, the discovery of the corpse, according to the morning paper, is expected to bring in a flood of customers at the museum. Maybe your comte killed our victim."

"He's alibied," I said with disgust. "Unless Bacigalupi lied about that. And Bacigalupi could have found a source for the heroin and killed her himself."

"Who's Bacigalupi?"

"The comtessa's detective."

Arcadi laughed. "Good luck to you, Ildefons. Even if your find the culprit —"

"Which I will," I said with more certainty than I felt.

"Our esteemed judge, Enric Goytisolo, won't let you make an arrest. Not if it means inconveniencing important people."

33

A Gathering of Families

Carolyn

Gwen's plane got in late. Her first words after we hugged were: "I thought Robbie would be here too."

Robbie and I had discussed in the cab to the airport how much the children were to know about Isabel's murder and the attendant suspects, not to mention the housing situation, which would be a clear sign that something was amiss. Robbie got her way in the end. Nothing about the murder and Sam's confession would be mentioned to Gwen and Kimmie. We'd tell Gwen that Robbie's small apartment would be filled with Hugh and his daughter, and that Sammie was staying with us at the hotel until he, his father, and Robbie had a chance to deal with his running away.

"That's cold," said Gwen as soon as I spun this tale. "Kids run away. Aren't they going to forgive poor Sammie? He'll feel awful about not being able to go home with his family."

"Barcelona's a long way to run," I mumbled. "Hugh and Robbie have been terribly worried about him. In fact, Robbie and I went out hunting for him." Had I said too much?

"Cool," my daughter exclaimed. "Where did you find him?"

"Actually, I ran into him on the Passeig de Gràcia and took him straight back to the hotel."

"I wish I'd been here. And how come he's in Barcelona anyway? Don't tell me he's got a crush on Robbie, and if he does, why didn't he go straight to see her?"

I sighed and had a few hard thoughts about my friend. I did not like lying to Gwen. "Honey, I think the less said about this the better. It's a touchy situation, so don't even mention it to any of them. Please."

Gwen shrugged. "Well, if she's got all these problems, how is she going to break me in at the museum? And what do we do with Sammie when Daddy gets here? That's only a few days, right? I suppose you've got two rooms, but you can't put Sammie and me together." She grinned at me. "I mean, that wouldn't be proper, right?"

"I don't have a second room. Sam will have to sleep on the floor."

"With us?" Now Gwen did look astonished. "Very cozy. How old is he now?"

"And we can only hope that he and his family will be reconciled by the time Jason arrives. I'm sure Hugh has to get both kids back to school as soon as possible, so they'll probably be leaving."

"Well, that's good. If you've only got one room, I suppose I'll have to sleep on the floor after Daddy gets here, unless I can move in with Robbie."

"My understanding is that you're to move into the dormitory at the university."

"Right away?" she asked, again surprised.

By then we met the Faurees — Robbie, Kimmie, and Hugh — coming from their plane, and I didn't have to answer any more questions. Hugh evidently knew that Sam had been found, for he was looking quite cheerful. Of course, he didn't yet know that his son had confessed to trying to kill Robbie and succeeding in killing Isabel. That news would come later. In the meantime, we took a cab back to the city, Robbie insisting that she, Hugh, and Kimmie be let off at her apartment, while Gwen and I went on to the hotel. Which left me to oversee the meeting of Sammie and Gwen. That would be awkward. Gwen would have questions. Sammie would feel orphaned because his father hadn't come to fetch him.

"What about Sam?" Hugh asked before

Robbie could bully all of us into doing what she wanted.

"Sam's at Caro's hotel," she said.

"Why isn't he at your place?" Hugh demanded.

"I bet Robbie's still mad at him," said Kimmie with a hint of little-sister satisfaction.

"I'm not mad at Sam, Kimmie," Robbie protested. "As soon as we drop off our luggage and your father and I have a few words, we'll be heading straight for the hotel to see your brother."

Kimmie giggled. "You mean you're going into the bedroom to kiss?"

Hugh looked embarrassed. Robbie and Gwen laughed, and Robbie said, "How did you get so smart, Kiminski?"

"Kimskaya," the girl corrected.

"Well, let's get to it," said Hugh gruffly. He looked much less cheerful than when I had first seen him. Poor man. Little did he know what was coming.

Reluctantly he allowed himself to be urged out of the cab at Robbie's apartment. Shortly thereafter, I was opening the door to my room at the hotel. The first thing I noticed: Sammie wasn't in the room. My eyes went immediately to the bathroom door, but it was open.

"Looks like he's run off again," said Gwen.

Oh, Lord, I thought, *Hugh is going to be so upset.* Then I remembered that Sam was to

261

hide if someone came in. "Gwen, wouldn't you like to freshen up?" I suggested hastily and pointed toward the bathroom.

"I don't need to pee."

I couldn't very well push her in and close the door, but with my daughter in the room, I couldn't call Sam out of the closet, providing he was in there. Maybe she wouldn't notice that it was a closet.

"I think I'll unpack a few things and hang them up," said Gwen. She hefted her smaller bag to the luggage rack, zipped it open, pulled out two outfits, which she had rolled together in the bag, and headed for the closet door.

"Why don't we go downstairs for lunch," I said desperately.

"They served brunch on the plane," Gwen replied, opening the closet door and sweeping my clothes to the side. There was Sammie. Behind the toweling robe, looking scared to death.

"Well, look who I found," said Gwen and pulled him out. "Hi, Sam. You remember me, don't you? It's Gwen. Mind if I hang up a few things? I think there'll still be enough room left for you in there when I finish."

"I . . . was . . . looking for my shoes," Sam stammered.

"With the door closed?" Gwen gave him a hug. "Obviously, something's going on that no one's telling me." She laughed. "But I can wait." She turned to me. "So what now? We all go down to lunch. Sam looks like he could use some."

"Actually, Sam's fine," I said, although he hadn't had anything to eat since the Catalan breakfast.

"Maybe we could get room service," he said hopefully.

"Your dad and sister should be here any minute, Sammie," I said. "Robbie too."

That evidently killed his appetite.

"So how come you ran away?" Gwen asked him.

"Gwen!" I exclaimed.

"Dad was going to send me off to military school," said Sam morosely. He probably didn't know that Gwen was to be kept in the dark. This whole situation was impossible.

"Military school? Bummer," said Gwen. "I'd have run away too."

Before things could get any stickier, the knock came at my door. Sam turned a ghastly gray, and Gwen, ever a girl with a sympathetic nature, pulled him down on the end of the bed and put her arm around his shoulders. "Don't look like that, Sammie. What are they gonna do to you, after all? Kill you?"

Sam stared at her in horror, then turned to me with reproachful eyes. He thought I'd told Gwen something that Robbie had promised would be a secret.

34

The Conclusions of a
Scientific Mind

Carolyn

Hugh came in with a black cloud hanging over his head. Kimmie was clinging to Robbie's hand and looking from one to the other, still, I assumed, unaware of her brother's problems. As soon as she saw Sammie sitting on the bed beside Gwen, she dropped Robbie's hand, squealed, "Sammie!" and hurled herself across the room. I'm sure he would have been embarrassed by this welcome from his sister had he not been in dire need of an overt display of affection from someone in his family.

Gwen, meanwhile, had risen and, smiling, said, "Come to claim the prodigal son, Dr. Fauree?" She kissed his cheek, then turned to Robbie and hugged her. "I have to thank you again for offering me this opportunity, Dr. Hecht. I guess I'd better get used to calling

264

you that now that I'm working for you. The other majors are so envious. Evidently, Barcelona has an active theater, not to mention the theater program at the university, and researching Miró's sets is so cool. I —"

Hugh interrupted by saying, "Gwen, I wonder if I might prevail upon you to take Kimmie downstairs for lunch?"

"I ate on the plane, Daddy," said Kimmie.

"Then you can have an ice cream sundae." Evidently this was an unusual offer, because she looked tempted. "Are you trying to get rid of me, Daddy?"

"Robbie and I need to talk to Sam."

"Well, I know it was dumb of him to run away from camp, especially after you'd paid for it, and to run so far. Where did you ever get the money, Sammie?" His sister wanted to stay, obviously.

"Kimmie, downstairs," ordered her father. "You can tell Gwen all about the flight."

Kimmie looked from one adult to the other and then moved toward Gwen, who said into my ear, "I didn't realize I was coming over here to baby-sit."

"Sh-sh-sh," I hissed and went with them to the door.

"Carolyn," said Hugh. "If you don't mind staying . . ." Sammie looked so woebegone that I didn't make a fuss. "I'll be down in a while," I said to the two girls. "There's a nice café on the far side of the lobby from the elevators. I'll meet you there."

"Come on, Kimmer," said Gwen. "We'll tell secrets of our own and pig out on my mother's room bill."

Lord, I thought, *Jason will faint when he sees all the room-service charges and this tooth-decay fling in the café.* Once the girls were gone, I turned to find Robbie in one of the armchairs, Hugh and Sam sitting rigidly on the ends of the beds, and an armchair awaiting me. I sat down.

"Now, Sam, tell me why you came here," said Hugh, looking his son straight in the eye. "Did you plan to hurt Robbie?"

Pain and misery flashed across the boy's face. Robbie started to protest, but Hugh silenced her with a look and turned back to his son.

"No, I swear," said Sammie. "I wanted to tell her how sorry I was about being so awful and that I was going to straighten out, like you said, and I wanted to ask her to talk you out of sending me to military school." Staring back at his father, both voice and eyes pleading, he added, "Dad, I don't want to be sent away from the family. I already lost Mom." Hugh winced. "I don't think I can stand to lose you too, or even Kimmie. I —"

"Why do you think you killed this Isabel person?" Hugh broke in.

Sam blinked in confusion. "I hit her, and

she died. Robbie can tell you that she's dead. But I didn't mean to kill her. Or anyone." He shot an anxious glance at Robbie, who nodded reassuringly.

"I understand that the woman is dead, but how do you know that you killed her?" Hugh persisted. "Did you feel for a pulse?"

"Ah . . . yeah. I touched her wrist. On the inside. Like, where the pulse is supposed to be."

"Have you ever taken anyone's pulse, Sam?" his father asked.

"Well, no, but they do it all the time on TV, so I did it. I remember because that's when I pricked my finger on the needle."

"What needle?" asked Robbie. "You didn't mention a needle."

"Oh." He looked blank. "There was one on the desk. Like for shots at the doctor's office, but I didn't notice it until I got stuck. I was really scared, and —"

"And did you feel a pulse?" his father asked.

Sammie shook his head.

"But she might have been alive, nonetheless. What did you do next?"

Sammie squeezed his hands between his knees and stared at the floor. "I put the needle in my pocket."

"Why?"

"Because my blood was on it. Afterward I wiped off the lamp because I knew I could get my fingerprints off that, but blood you can't get all off. I've seen it on TV. They just spray this stuff around, and it lights up the blood."

"You watch too much TV," said Hugh.

"Yes, sir," mumbled Sammie without looking up.

"What did you do then?"

"Ran down the stairs. I was afraid to take the elevator because it was scary-looking and because I was afraid the guard would hear it and wake up and catch me. I ran all the way down to the basement, where I found this, like, window that I could force up with a metal bar, and I climbed out and pushed it back down and kept running."

"What else?"

"That's all. I ran and ran until I fell down in an alley. Then I crawled under a box and hid."

"What did you do with the syringe?"

Sam thought about it. "I don't know."

"Where was this box you slept in?"

"I don't know, Dad. I didn't know where I was. I've just been wandering around, scared the police would find me and arrest me or I'd starve to death or get knifed by someone when I was asleep somewhere."

"Ah, Sam." Hugh's eyes looked as pained as his son's had when the questioning began.

"It's not going to be a problem, Hugh," said Robbie. "Carolyn has it all figured out.

The three of you can get on a train to France. No one will be looking for him in France."

"But I can't do that," said Sam. "I can't let them arrest you for what I did. That won't put things right."

"Arrest *Robbie?*" Hugh turned to his wife. "Did you leave something out when you were telling me —"

"It's nothing," said Robbie. "I'm not going to be arrested because I haven't done anything. Just get Sammie across the border, and everything will be fine."

"Hm-m-m." He looked from Robbie to me. "You told the police that Sam was missing, so they are, in fact, looking for him?"

"Yes," I agreed, "but at that time I didn't know that he'd been in the museum the night of the murder."

"No one knows that as far as I can see," said Hugh. "If you go back to the police and tell them we've found him, they'll stop looking for him. If they've actually been doing that. Robbie said this inspector works homicides; he's not likely to be interested in missing persons. Just make an appointment. Or even call him on the telephone. Tell him you found Sam. Do you have a problem doing that, Carolyn?" Hugh eyed me sharply.

"Well, I guess —"

"I'm amazed that you all believe Sam killed

this woman," Hugh muttered bitterly. "He said he didn't hit her hard. He said there was a syringe on her desk. Robbie said her body was found several flights down in an art exhibit. Did you put her there, Sam?"

"Me? No. I told you. I ran."

Robbie and I stared at each other. We'd forgotten this important fact. "Someone must have moved her downstairs after Sam left," said Hugh in that reasonable scientist's voice. "This person is much more likely to have killed her than a boy wielding a bird."

"Of course," I agreed. "I've been too befuddled to see it. Looking at it that way, maybe I can figure out who did it. If we find the real murderer, that will clear Robbie and —"

"Fine," said Robbie. "You go tell the inspector he can stop looking for Sam, and Hugh, you take him home. Carolyn and I will work out the rest."

"I may send Sam and Kimmie home to Mother — I'll have to get her back from Mexico — but I certainly don't plan to leave until I know that you're safe, my dear wife. This dilemma obviously needs consideration by a scientific mind. Or two scientific minds. When does Jason get here?" he asked me.

"Tomorrow or the next day," I answered, somewhat piqued that he didn't think I could find the answer to Isabel's murder. When had Hugh ever smoked out a killer?

I'd found three out of four, more or less. And why did people keep dying when I was around? Jason would not be pleased.

35

More Input from the Interfering Senyora Blue

Inspector Pujol

Having received a number of reports from officers who had been interviewing in the neighborhoods of the suspects, I was about to leave for the day. The only interesting tidbit that turned up was the appearance of Senyora Hecht at her apartment with a man and a young girl. The girl called the man Daddy, and Senyora Hecht seemed very fond of both, according to my officer. He had waited down the hall to see what else would happen and had observed them leaving within twenty minutes, the man looking grim and the little girl chattering to Senyora Hecht. I wasn't sure what that meant, but I'd find out.

Bacigalupi had gone from my office to a bar and drunk himself into a coma, mumbling about his honor. Two of his employees admitted to following the comte from time to time but denied they had been on the job on the night in question. The comtessa's neighbors wouldn't talk to my men and threatened to reveal their visits not only to the lady herself but also to various important persons of their acquaintance. The neighborhood attitude seemed to be that the police were overreaching themselves in asking questions about a personage of such high rank and esteem. A frustrating case, which became more so.

With my briefcase in hand, I was stopped at my door by the breathless arrival of Senyora Blue. "I'm so glad I caught you, Inspector," she exclaimed. "I have several pieces of information for you."

"They can't wait until tomorrow?" I demanded. "Or better, Monday?"

"I suppose they could," she replied, looking taken aback at my attitude. "One thing, however, would save your men some time."

I sighed and motioned her into the office. Even my aide was gone. If note-taking were required, I'd have to do my own. "What is this matter that will not wait, Senyora?" I asked, holding a chair for her and taking one myself, which involved, on both our parts, alarming creaking and groaning of the wood. No doubt the judge would cry budget concerns when it came to replacing my office furniture until someone was injured when a chair collapsed. Not me, I hoped.

"Well, it's about Sammie," she replied. "First, of course, I want to thank you for all you've done in trying to find him."

"Very gracious of you, Senyora, but I can do nothing but pass on the photo to the proper authorities." Actually, the picture was still in my desk. I'd forgotten to do anything about the missing boy.

"Exactly. I do appreciate your concern, as does his stepmother. But I have good news. I myself found him. He's safe with his family, so the police need not look for him any longer."

"Excellent," I replied, glad that I hadn't passed the picture on. "Where did you find him?"

"On Passeig de Gràcia. I had been looking at Gaudí buildings, not to mention those of other modernists, and there he was. I took him straight back to my hotel and called his stepmother. Today his father and sister arrived, so the family is happily reunited."

"Good news indeed." That explained the man and girl at Senyora Hecht's apartment, also the man's grim visage when he left. Bad enough to have a son run away, but to run so far. Where did the boy get the money? Stole it, perhaps. Happily, that would not be my case. They could take the young fellow home and deal with him there.

"Well, if that's —"

"And Gwen arrived today, as well. I do

274

hope we can arrange a meeting between our daughters. I worry about her in a strange city, and knowing that she has a friend from such a nice family — well, it would —"

"By all means, Senyora. I will have my daughter call yours. Do you have a phone number for her yet?" Would the woman never leave?

"She's with me at the hotel, but she'll soon be moving into a dormitory."

"Fine. Let me give you my home phone number. You or your daughter can contact Magdalena." I wrote down the number, which I passed to my visitor.

"There was one thing, Inspector, that I feel bound to report to you, since it concerns a crime. Narcis Ramon Berenguer. The artist?"

"The fellow who took you to Bacallà?"

"Yes. I fear that he is not a very nice person."

"That is unfortunate, but not necessarily a crime, Senyora."

"You may remember the Englishman, Sir Cecil. His watch was missing, and —"

"He accused one of my officers. Yes, I remember. Also that the officer did not have the watch. Ah. It was this Narcis who made the accusation. Are you saying he lied?"

"Worse. I'm sure I saw the watch on his wrist this morning. Of course, he said it was his own watch, and Professor Toda and

Senyora Brusi were very unpleasant to me for accusing him. Even more peculiar, it seemed to me that they are both — ah — infatuated with Narcis, and he, in turn, seems to be infatuated with the count. Maybe there is some sort of — love quartet there that might have something to do with Isabel's murder. It's just a thought," she added defensively.

"But I do know that Robbie — Dr. Hecht — is not infatuated with any of them. Maybe one or more of them hit Isabel and killed her? They all have keys to the building. Well, not Narcis, if he's to be believed, but who's to say he didn't steal a key? He did, after all, steal the Englishman's watch and then blame your officer. But it might have taken several people to get her downstairs to the exhibit."

"As it happens, Senyoreta Almirall may have been killed downstairs in the bed or upstairs after being hit with the bird, but she did not die of the blow, which was, it seems, very minor."

"It was?"

My visitor looked amazed and delighted, and I wondered for a minute if she herself had struck Senyoreta Almirall with the bird. But no, the victim had evidently died before the American lady arrived from the States.

"Senyoreta Isabel died of an overdose of heroin, according to our toxicology reports." Why was I passing confidential police information on to this woman?

"Then Isabel killed herself?" exclaimed Senyora Blue. "Inadvertently or on purpose?"

"That's doubtful," I replied. "There was no syringe at either site and no evidence that she had used drugs before the fatal dose. At any rate, I must ask you to keep this information confidential." Then I had a thought. "Do you know if any of these people take heroin or have connections with dealers?"

"No, but I can certainly try to find out," she replied eagerly.

"That is not necessary, Senyora Blue. You have done more than enough to help with our inquiries."

"Oh, it's no trouble at all," she protested.

"I must insist that you not look into the matter. Citizens put themselves in danger when they interfere in police business."

"I certainly did not mean to interfere, Inspector," she said somewhat indignantly.

Ah well, better an insulted American woman than a dead one, whose death I'd have to investigate.

36

A Night Out

— But Who Gets to Go?

Carolyn

I left the inspector's office in a state of euphoria. Sammie had not killed Isabel! He had, in fact, inflicted only a minor injury, more in the nature of a nudge to the head than a blow. On the other hand, I had been sworn to secrecy and couldn't ease the minds of my friends. At least I was relieved to know that my daughter and I would not be sharing our hotel room with a murderer.

When I arrived, Gwen, Sammie, and Kimmie were watching Spanish TV and howling with laughter. The show was a tapas cook-off, with various portly, mustachioed chefs in tall hats presenting platters of tapas to a wildly enthusiastic studio audience, while a master of ceremonies chattered loudly and hugged several curvaceous young women with long hair and low-necked gowns.

I'm not sure why the children were so amused, but the show did convince me that Spanish television is even worse that our own at home. Gwen bounded out of the chair where she had been sprawled with both legs over a curved wooden arm and announced that Comte Miquel Xifré i Fontdevila, whose name she thought was so "cool," had invited us to a flamenco dinner and show that evening. "For some reason, Dr. Fauree thinks Kimmie is too little to go," Gwen added, "and Sammie can't go either, although no one would say why."

For a minute I thought Sammie should be allowed to go, poor dear, since he hadn't killed Isabel and didn't need to hide. However, it might take a while before the word got out to police officers on the street that the boy wasn't still missing.

"Then Dr. Fauree decided *I* should babysit," my daughter continued indignantly, "but I said I didn't see why I should have to stay home. After all, I am in college. I'm certainly old enough to accept the invitation."

"Gwen, that wasn't very accommodating, much less polite. Robbie's the only reason you got to come here." I didn't much like the idea of my daughter going to a flamenco club with a group of people, one of whom was probably a murderer.

"Well, it's okay, because Dr. Fauree changed his mind again and decided he'd stay here since he hasn't seen Sam in a while."

"He probably wants to give me a piece of his mind," said Sam gloomily.

"You could use a piece of his mind, dummy," said Gwen, laughing. "Running away to Barcelona? That *was* a little over the top."

"Yeah, dummy," Kimmie chimed in.

"So Dr. Fauree is coming over here to baby-sit his own kids," said Gwen before I could cut into the argument, "and you and I and Dr. Hecht — she said I could call her Robbie when we're not at work — are going to the party. But what do we wear to a flamenco party, Mom?"

"I have no idea," I replied. Obviously, although I was tired, there'd be no time for me to catch a little nap, especially with a room full of children. I would have offered to baby-sit, but the party was a chance to find out who had administered the lethal dose of heroin to Isabel. Could Robbie and Hugh investigate? No, because I couldn't tell them how Isabel had died. I had to go myself, tired or not. "Let's look in the closet," I said to Gwen.

Then I called room service and ordered two meals for the children — more charges on our hotel bill. Maybe Hugh would offer to pay for Kimmie and Sam. Or not. He was probably as thrifty as Jason. I joined Gwen at the closet to examine our pedestrian wardrobes — my tourist clothes, Gwen's school clothes. We agreed that people probably dressed up for a flamenco club. "We could go out and buy something neat," she suggested.

"I wouldn't know where to go," I replied hastily, again thinking of Jason's reaction to an even bigger credit card bill at the end of the month. He looks at every charge, checks it against the receipts, even asks me about some of mine.

"Robbie will know," said Gwen, and dashed to the telephone to call her. I wondered what the call would cost. Many hotels charge for calls, even within the city. I remember Jason's reaction to phone charges I ran up at a hotel in New Orleans. Fifty or more calls at seventy-five cents each add up.

"Okay," said Gwen. "How do we get there?" She made notes on the pad thoughtfully provided by the hotel.

Did the hotel charge for the pad if you used it? Restaurants in Europe charge if you eat "bread" from the breadbasket they provide — without mentioning that it isn't a free offering. I remember Jason's reaction the first time he studied a European restaurant bill and asked what the *pan* charge was. I knew that *pan* meant "bread" and was equally amazed to find that we'd been charged for the three pieces we'd used to sop up a wonderful sauce. No wonder Europeans think doing that is perfectly polite. No doubt, the restaurants encourage it. Not that I don't find it a lovely custom in a country where wonderful sauces are the rule rather than the exception.

Then I realized that if Gwen and I made a short shopping trip, we'd have to leave Sam and Kimmie on their own. I explained why we couldn't go. Sam protested that he could baby-sit his sister. His sister said that she wasn't a baby. Gwen said that we wouldn't be gone that long, not when we had the name of only one shop, although we might spot others on our way. Which would leave the children alone all the longer, I pointed out. Then all three of them ganged up on me, protesting their maturity and good sense. I finally had to settle for a short, private talk with Sam.

"You'll have to stay inside the room and be very quiet."

"I thought you just went to the police and told them they didn't have to look for me," he replied.

"I did, but they have to get the word out. You *don't* want to be picked up. Besides that, your parents would have a fit if they thought I was letting you wander around on your own."

"I did okay on my own before," he retorted sullenly.

"Sam, you were filthy, hungry, and really glad to see me when I grabbed your arm on Passeig de Gràcia, so stop arguing with me and entertain Kimmie as quietly as possible — no TV since you're not supposed to be here, and don't open the door to anyone."

I was interrupted by a knocking at the door. Room service. I pushed both Fauree children into the bathroom and accepted the cart. Of course, Kimmie wanted to know why I'd done that, but I grabbed Gwen's arm and fled. Gwen wanted to know too, but was soon diverted by my description of dresses I'd seen well-dressed Catalan women wearing since I arrived. I should have kept my mouth shut. We both ended up with filmy, floating outfits whose skirts had uneven hems that showed other layers beneath. Very pretty, feminine, and expensive. *Ah, Jason,* I thought as I turned in front of a mirror and allowed myself to be talked into a pale green number with pale flowers and darker blue and green underskirts. I was horrified when the saleswoman insisted that we were not to wear slips under these thin dresses.

"Of course we can't, Mom," Gwen agreed. "With all these different lengths a slip would show." Her skirt ended halfway up her thigh on one side. They were stunning dresses, but where in El Paso could I wear such a thing? And would my husband approve if I tried it?

283

37

The Refusal of an
Inappropriate Proposal

Inspector Pujol

Sebastiana and I were sitting in the garden under the grape arbor enjoying the evening as it cooled and whispered around us, when Magdalena came flying out of the house in a state of high excitement, which usually signals her wish to do something I don't approve of.

"Papá, guess who's on the phone," she cried.

"Fernando," I replied. Fernando was her latest boyfriend, a fellow student who was studying, of all things, French literature. I did not see a knowledge of French literature as likely to produce an income that would support my daughter in an acceptable manner, should she be so foolish as to decide that she was in love.

"No, Papá, it's Senyora Blue, that nice lady

you brought home to eat."

My wife did not look pleased, although she had seemed to like the woman well enough. I certainly was not pleased. My workday had already been lengthened by a visit from Senyora Blue.

"She's invited all of us — you, Mamá, and me — to a flamenco party at Poble Espanyol. It's being given by that comte. The one in your murder case. Remember?"

"I remember my case," I said. What was the woman thinking of?

"Dinner and a show and dancing. He's taken a huge table down front. Can you imagine? And she can invite friends, so she's invited us. But we have to hurry. We only have two hours."

"The party is to take place tonight?" asked my wife, frowning. "Last invited, least respected," she added.

"He's an impulsive man. He just thought of it. Senyora Blue herself only heard of it a few hours ago and had to go out to buy a dress. What should we wear, Mamá?"

"We will not be going," I said before my wife could reply.

Magdalena pouted. She said that I never wanted to do anything exciting, and if we didn't go, we'd insult Senyora Blue, who wanted us to meet her daughter, and she, Magdalena, might never get to meet a real comte. I was not moved by any of these arguments and said so. "Well, you talk to her, then," said Magdalena, and flounced off, calling over her shoulder, "She's still on the phone waiting to talk to you."

My wife was eyeing me with disfavor. "What?" I asked. "You want to go too? You just said that last-minute invitations —"

"I'm wondering why Carolyn is inviting us to parties," said my wife coolly.

She was jealous. I sighed and said, "She's an American. Who knows why Americans do anything? They seem to believe in instant friendship."

"Or love at first sight," said Sebastiana.

"The woman does not love me," I retorted. What an unsettling thought. I went inside to speak to Senyora Blue, in case she was still waiting. What if she *had* become infatuated with me? Some women do find a man of the people attractive. Perhaps her husband, the professor, was an effeminate, cold-natured type. "Inspector Pujol," I said into the phone, feeling rather disconcerted by the situation.

"Inspector! Turn off the TV."

"What?"

"Oh, I'm sorry. I was just telling my — ah — daughter to turn off the television."

It sounded to me as if there were several people in the room. "My daughter, Magdalena, tells me that —"

"Yes, yes. I hope that you and your wife can come tonight. It occurred to me that it would be a lovely chance for our daughters to meet. Gwen is so anxious to see Magdalena."

"I'm afraid —"

"And I had another reason for inviting you." She lowered her voice. "The museum staff will be there, not to mention the count's wife and daughter and goodness knows how many of his friends. You might be able to learn something of importance regarding the case. Being a professional, you'll know what to look for, what questions to ask, whereas I —"

"Senyora Blue, I believe I have already told you to leave my case alone. I would hate to hear that you have been murdered at a flamenco party."

"That hardly seems likely," she replied, laughing. "There will be so many people there, besides the dancers and singers, and the waiters and busboys and other customers, of course. It would be very hard to —" again she dropped her voice — "murder someone with such a crowd looking on, and if you come, no one would dare, would they? So it should be perfectly safe."

"I'm sure you mean well, Senyora Blue, but your proposal is quite inappropriate." Unfortunately, this was true, although I must admit that I was tempted because the comtessa was to be there, a lady who refused to speak to me or to any of my officers. The idea of confronting her at her husband's party was very tempting. "Quite inappropriate. Investigators such as myself do not interact socially with suspects in our cases."

"But it's such a wonderful opportunity," she persisted. Then in a whisper, "The murderer is sure to be there."

"What if the murderer was her drug dealer? Do you think he'll be there?" I asked, hoping to discourage the woman.

"But I thought you said Isabel showed no signs of addiction."

"Be that as it may, I must refuse your thoughtful invitation."

"What about Magdalena? Can she come?"

"Absolutely not. I do not want my daughter associating with — murderers. I'm surprised you plan to take your daughter."

"She rather bullied me into it," Senyora Blue admitted, then whispered, "Well, if you won't come, could you tell me what I should look for in a heroin addict? Needle marks on the arm, I suppose."

"An excellent place to start," I agreed dryly. "Although some addicts inject themselves between their toes."

"I'd never be able to discover *that* without being obvious."

"In which case, perhaps, you should give up the idea of doing anything at the party but enjoying yourself and keeping a wary eye on your daughter."

"Very well," she agreed. "But we still haven't arranged for our daughters to meet. Or do you disapprove of that idea?" She sighed. "I suppose you're too polite to say so, but I do wish you'd tell me. I don't want to get Gwen's hopes up for nothing. I told her what a charming and intelligent girl Magdalena is, and —"

"I have no objections to their meeting, in proper circumstances," I replied.

"I'm so glad, Inspector. Maybe they could have lunch together tomorrow."

"Fine," I said, and called my daughter to the telephone.

38

Flamenco!

Carolyn

Hugh arrived to spend the evening with his children and told me that Robbie would meet us at the flamenco club at 9:00. I do hate those late dinners, but there was nothing for it, so Gwen and I, dressed in our new finery, took a cab. We could have walked and seen the fountains on our way if she hadn't been wearing ridiculously high-heeled sandals. No one could walk more than a block in those shoes. I had hoped that the example I set by wearing flats would influence my daughter, but then Gwen is short, like her father's side of the family, so she will wear dangerous shoes. I'm always afraid that she'll break an ankle.

Then when we got to the gates of Poble Espanyol, the driver wouldn't or couldn't drive in, so we had to walk to the club after puzzling over directions given in broken English. The area was almost deserted at night, only a few restaurants and clubs open and the occasional couple wandering by. I did manage to point out to Gwen some of the examples of architecture native to various provinces of Spain and promised to bring her back in the daytime to visit the busy shops.

At the club, we had to introduce ourselves as guests of Comte Xifré i Fontdevila. Otherwise, we'd have had to pay a ludicrously high price for tickets. Once checked off a list, we were led to a badly lighted room crowded with tables on different levels and choking with cigarette smoke. The count's table was, as promised, at eye level with the stage. There were fourteen chairs, three empty. Arriving just ahead of us, Robbie had to remind the comte that Hugh wouldn't be coming. One of the three empty chairs was removed by a waiter, leaving thirteen. My first thought was that thirteen is an unlucky number. Then I told myself not to be silly.

After that, I noticed where Gwen and I would be sitting, to either side of Narcis, of whom I did not think well after our dreadful evening at Bacallà. On my left would be a priest and beyond him at the end, the comte's wife, who looked very chic but not very friendly. To Gwen's right was Robbie, a relief to me, and beyond her at the other end of the table, the comte, who rose to greet us and introduce us to those we hadn't met: Monsignor somebody; Comtessa Violante,

291

who nodded regally; Pau — I didn't catch his last name — who was a famous journalist and poet, according to our host — Pau rose and kissed our hands; Dolors, whom I knew — she rose and kissed my cheek, which earned me a glare from her mother; beyond Dolors, Martí, the son of Pau, a young man employed in his grandfather's shipping company — he rose and kissed our fingers, Gwen's a little longer than necessary, which earned him a frown from the comtessa; Madrona and Jordi from the museum, neither of whom looked very pleased to see us; and on the comte's right, Ceci, Pau's wife, another very chic socialite type. At least she smiled and said she was pleased to meet us. Then we took our seats to either side of Narcis.

"What charming dresses," the comtessa said to me. "Do you and your daughter always dress as sisters? I suppose that makes the mother feel younger and the daughter more mature." I was so astonished that I couldn't reply, so she continued. "But aren't you chilly in such thin dresses when fall is upon us?"

"We don't have fall," said my daughter. "Not at home or where I go to school. Just summer and a mild winter. We couldn't resist these dresses because we'll be able to wear them most of the year. Isn't that so, Mother?"

"Yes, indeed," I said, getting into the spirit of the response. "And they're washable and pack nicely. Wonderful for travel. I travel a lot, and Gwen, being a student, likes to be able to dip her clothes into the sink and hang them to dry."

"Woolite," said Gwen enthusiastically. "It's the very best soap for delicate fabrics that must be hand-washed. Do you have it here in Barcelona, Comtessa?"

"I really wouldn't know," said the comtessa.

"Mother, you must send her some," Gwen suggested. Then she turned to Robbie and gave her a hug.

I turned to the monsignor and asked what he thought of the Pope's Marian doctrines and whether it was true, as rumor had it in the United States, that John Paul hoped to declare the Holy Mother the intermediary between Catholics and God. That gambit saved me from having to talk to Narcis or the comtessa for some time because the monsignor was unfamiliar with pronouncements made by the head of the Marian Society in the States. I wouldn't have been either, but Jason read me an article about it. While chatting with the priest, a wide-shouldered man of middle age with a shining pate edged by gray hair, I tried to keep up with other conversations going on around me.

Narcis told Gwen that she was very pretty,

and she replied that he was very pretty too. I glanced toward them when I heard his breath hiss between his teeth. His eyes were narrowed. She had turned back to Robbie to tell her about our quick shopping trip. The comtessa, having been attentive to my conversation with the monsignor, asked if I was Catholic and tried to look sympathetic when I said no. She pointed out my heathen status to her daughter, who said that I was a very kind lady, nonetheless.

Martí broke off a rather desultory conversation with Dolors and asked Gwen if she was vacationing here in Barcelona. Once she explained her internship with Robbie, the two young people began a lively conversation about the sights of Barcelona, which he would be happy to show Gwen.

"Oh, I'm sure you're much too busy with your duties at your grandfather's firm to play tour guide, Martí," said the comtessa. "If Senyora Blue doesn't have time to show her daughter around, perhaps Dolors can do it to save you the trouble."

Dolors looked embarrassed, Gwen put her napkin to her lips to hide a smile, and a loud strumming of guitars caught our attention. We'd been served only cava, but it seemed that now the flamenco show was about to begin. Before dinner. Or had I been mistaken in thinking we were to have dinner? I, for one, was starving and had been hoping that food would overcome the queasiness produced by breathing in so much cigarette smoke.

Spotlights illuminated the stage, and the smoke spiraled up thickly through the light. In a circle at the back and sides of the stage were seated — in those dreadful rush-bottomed chairs that were even now cutting into my thighs — a number of slender women with black hair pulled tightly back, wearing figure-hugging dresses with flaring skirts and clunky-heeled shoes; two male guitarists; a thickset man with a ponytail and pitted face; and a middle-aged woman, also thickset, in a glittery black dress and brightly fringed shawl.

Guitars were strumming, fingers snapping, palms clapping with the sharp sound of gunfire, when the woman in the center stood up and began to sing in a powerful, hoarse, mournful voice. A whip-thin young man in black walked to the center of the stage and faced the singer. Her voice seemed to challenge him, and he began to dance, boot heels cracking hard against the wooden floor. Two dancers, then four rose and joined him, whirling, their skirts circling up their thighs, bodies lithe, arms and hands graceful, castanets clicking while the seated members of the company clapped and shouted encouragement, and the dance became wilder and faster.

I forgot the smoke, my hunger, and our unpleasant hostess, turned my chair for a better view, and wished Jason was there to see the dancing and enjoy the music. No smiles touched this company. Both their postures and faces were severe. Those sitting sat ramrod straight, spines not touching the chair backs. The guitarists played with fingers that flew in a blur of motion. The male singer's voice was so gravelly and powerful that one imagined he had suffered terrible tragedy, not to mention injury to the vocal cords. It was a stunning performance, especially the dance that involved women wearing long trains, which they whipped in circles as part of the dance pattern.

Prosaically enough, I found myself wondering if the costumes were washable. Could the trains, dirtied on the floor, and the tight, long-sleeved dresses, no doubt wet with sweat by the end of the performance, be dumped into a washing machine before the next night rolled around? Perhaps they needed to be told about Woolite. I had to stifle a giggle. Hunger and cava must have been making me giddy.

"You find flamenco amusing?" asked a voice, breathing the question into my ear. It was Narcis, who slid a narrow patent-leather shoe alongside my foot to give me a little nudge.

I jumped, and I don't think I meant to

bring my heel down on his toe, but the incident certainly wiped the flirtatious smile from his face. "I'm so sorry," I murmured, and turned back to the last number of the show. Everyone in the cast sang, strummed, or danced in a whirl of color and clicking heels. It occurred to me that the dancers probably suffered from early-onset arthritis from all the pounding their feet and legs received.

39

Catalan Goat Number Two

Carolyn

When we turned our chairs back to the table, the waiters had refilled our cava flutes, and the comtessa remarked to the table at large that the greedy Catalans were responsible for the death of Spanish vineyards when phylloxera arrived on the continent. "Madrid ordered that fifteen miles be cleared of vines so that the bugs couldn't get into Spain, but the Catalans wouldn't do it. All the vineyards had to be replanted."

Her husband gave her an angry look and lifted his flute in a toast. "To the fine wines of Catalonia and to my dear guests — family, friends, colleagues, and our three lovely American ladies, thank you for accepting my invitation. I hope you have enjoyed the performance. After dinner, there will be dancing for our party on the stage and the opportunity to meet the cast members." This prospect met with applause. "Those of you who aspire to learn flamenco, this is your opportunity."

Most of the party laughed. Because I was light-headed as a result of having my cava flute replenished too often on an empty stomach, the prospect of dancing flamenco held no appeal whatever.

"As for dinner, we have with us an American food writer whose career began as the result of a wonderful goat dish she sampled here in Barcelona."

He was talking about me. Good grief. He wasn't expecting me to cook the dinner, was he? I could feel my face turn red, and I darted a resentful glance at Robbie. He must have heard the story of my first newspaper article, "Goat Is Better Than You'd Think," from her.

"In honor of Senyora Blue's new career, I have arranged to have a fine Catalan goat roasted for our dinner," he continued.

Ceci, wife of Pau and mother of Martí, although she didn't look old enough to be the mother of a businessman, laughed with delight. "Goat!" she exclaimed. "How very fanciful of you, Miquel!"

"It is out of season," said the comtessa from her end of the table. "Baby goats are not weaned this time of year, and adult goats smell bad and are tough and greasy."

"Money can buy even a baby goat out of season, my dear Violante," he replied cheerfully.

"And how very bourgeois of you to mention your money, Miquel," she retorted. "You have asked for goat, Senyora?" she demanded of me.

"I knew nothing about it," I replied, although the idea of repeating that wonderful meal certainly appealed to me, but then I was hungry enough to fancy just about anything moderately edible. Did the comte know about the delicious glaze that had covered my first goat leg? Could his money reproduce that too?

"I planned this meal," said the comtessa, "and I did not order goat."

"But I changed the menu, and I did order goat," retorted her husband. "The rest I left to you, so no doubt we will be served a host of dishes not to the taste of good Catalans."

"Since when were Catalans known for their taste in cuisine?" snapped Violante. "Who else would name their most famous market La Boquería? It means 'a place for selling goat meat.'"

"It means 'meat market'," said the comte.

"Please don't," whispered Dolors in a tiny voice that we heard only because people at other tables had stopped talking in order to listen to the argument.

The comte looked conscious-stricken and assured his daughter that he wouldn't say another word to her mother. Dolors sniffled and blinked her eyes. "Talk to your young man, my pet," Miquel said to Dolors. She turned red. Martí, evidently "her young man" in the eyes of her parents, looked startled.

Gwen leaned forward and asked Dolors if she had attended the university that had dormitories for girls and if she knew what the rules would be for undergraduates. Dolors lifted her chin, smiled bravely through tears, and said she had gone to a Catholic girls' college, but friends of hers said that the housemothers in the dormitories were very kind and reliable and saw to the safety of their charges, even to investigating their boyfriends. Laughing merrily, Gwen replied, "You have just made my mother very happy."

Dolors nodded solemnly. "I am glad to have brought you happiness, Senyora Blue. Any help I can offer you or your daughter would give me joy."

Gazpacho was served, and the comte glared at it. "Andalusian," he muttered and cast a hard glance at his wife.

"Chosen to please the foreigners in our midst," retorted his wife.

I tasted it and said, "It's lovely, Comtessa. I make it myself at home, but this is excellent. I wish I had the recipe to pass on to my readers."

"I shall ask the chef," she replied, trying but failing to look displeased. "Monsignor, I am thinking of making a pilgrimage. What advice can you give me?" she asked, turning to her priestly guest.

He looked up from a ferocious attack on his soup and replied, "The reason for a pilgrimage often determines the site. For instance, an illness might send one to Lourdes in France or Loretto in Italy."

"I am not ill. I go to show my devotion to God, not to ask for favors."

"Have you ever been to Santiago de Compostela?" I asked wistfully. "I have always longed to go there but never had the chance. It's ironic, don't you think, that people came, often on foot, in the Middle Ages from distant lands on that pilgrimage, and now, in an age of modern transportation, the trip is difficult to schedule."

"What is your particular interest in Compostela, my child?" asked the monsignor.

"The history," I answered. "The discovery of the bones of St. James, the building of the cathedral, the hostels set up for pilgrims by the Cluniac monks.

"Do you know that there is a virtual-reality computer in Paris that allows a person to visit the monastery at Cluny as it was in the Middle Ages? My husband has seen it. What a wonderful experience it would have been. But Compostela is *there*. One can walk the very stones on which those many pilgrims walked and knelt to pray — without resorting to computers, marvelous as they are."

"For a non-Catholic, you seem very interested in our church," said the monsignor.

I shrugged, embarrassed that I had become so excited. No doubt all the Catalans at the table had been to Compostela and found my enthusiasm amusing. "The history of the church is the history of Europe in large part," I mumbled.

"It is the history of the faith," the comtessa corrected.

"Still, Compostela would be a good choice," said the monsignor. "St. James is the patron saint of our county, and Compostela is his place."

"So, Senyora, you are a journalist?" asked Pau as the soup plates were cleared and the goat served with a delicious scalloped potato casserole, its layers alternated with allioli. "We share a profession."

"You are very kind," I murmured, "but I am not a poet and write only about food and the history and enjoyment of food, whereas I believe there is a tradition, at least in this century and city, of journalists who are also men and women of letters."

"And whom would you cite as an example of this tradition, Senyora?" asked the comtessa.

"Violante, are you harassing Senyora Blue?" the comte called from his end of the table.

I saw Dolors wince at the prospect of another war of words between her parents. "Not at all," I said hastily to the comte, then to the comtessa, "I think a good example would be Quim Monzo. I have read some of his newspaper pieces, in translation, of course, and thought they were very witty, and I understand that he has won prizes for his short stories."

"Well spoken, dear lady!" cried Pau. "Did you by any chance read the bit on names, and a person's right to call himself what he wishes?"

"Yes," I exclaimed. "Pablo Casals should not have his name changed to Pau Casals just because Pau is Catalan for Pablo. And what about the man who would only speak Catalan to the 'common folk'?"

"And Monzo's explanation that the politician who wanted prostitutes kept from plying their trade on the streets was actually advocating the reestablishment of brothels," added the comte.

Amid the laughter and citations of other amusing Monzo articles, the comtessa said, "How did you come across Quim Monzo, Senyora? Surely that is not standard reading material in the United States."

"Mom reads all kinds of stuff before she visits a new place," said Gwen. "History, of course, and travel books, but a month ago she told me I should read some Catalan novel about doves."

"Rodoreda?" asked Dolors. *"La plaça del diamant?"*

We smiled at each other. "Even in translation it's a beautiful book," I said. "So sad. The time during and after the civil war must have been very hard in Barcelona."

"Not for Miquel and his family," said Violante. "They were making money through it all."

"Well, my father did too," Ceci chimed in. "What's wrong with that?"

"Nothing, dear lady," said the comte. "Better to be rich than poor."

"Senyora," said Narcis as the conversation around us shifted, "do you no talk to young men?"

If I don't, I should, I thought. *Here I came to find out what I could about Isabel's murder. Who better to ask about drugs than Narcis, who has either a fetish for low places or a desire to shock sedate women.* I forced myself to smile at him and said, "Of course I talk to young men. I talk to my son all the time, and he can't be much younger than you. Tell me about yourself, Narcis. I find your name fascinating. Are you descended from the Ramon Berenguers, Counts of Barcelona, perhaps from Petronella, the princess of Aragon who married a Berenguer?"

"Maybe," he replied playfully. "But I am man of mystery, no family, no home, no name until I discover by comte, my patron, and given place in life."

I wondered if Inspector Pujol could solve

the mystery of this too pretty, too slippery young man. I'd suggest it again, but the inspector had told me to stay away from his case. I finished my decidedly French dessert, hoping the count had forgotten his idea that we should dance and mingle with the flamenco cast.

"The goat was lovely, Comte," I called. "Thank you."

40

Dancing for Clues

Carolyn

After dessert, we were served tiny chilled glasses of a white liqueur and required to toss them down in a toast to Catalan nationalism. *Alquardent de casa*. It tasted suspiciously like grappa and burned all the way down. I heard the comtessa murmur to the monsignor that her husband liked to talk about Catalan nationalism, but he wouldn't want to see it come about because that wouldn't be good for business. After the drink, tiny cups of strong coffee were served. I passed on that, hoping to return to the hotel sometime soon and get a good night's sleep.

The comte rose and ceremoniously asked his wife to dance. Pau asked his wife, Ceci; Martí asked Gwen, and Narcis asked Dolors, who said she didn't care to dance. Her mother, who was keeping an eagle eye on the table, was angry, evidently, that Martí had not asked Dolors, but approving when Dolors refused Narcis. I was hoping to go unnoticed, as there were more women than men, but Jordi bowed to me. Reluctantly, I rose as Robbie invited the monsignor to dance with her.

He looked quite astounded and suggested that they sit together and talk, but my friend laughed merrily and hopped up onto the stage to catch the hand of the male flamenco dancer. What a pair they made. Athletic woman that she was, Robbie managed to do a fair imitation of every step he showed her. Then she taught him a few, using her scarf in flirtatious ways. He actually broke into a smile by the time the dance was over, as did several of the women dancers who were watching them. Monsignor leaned back in his chair, benignly watching the fun and sipping another glass of the detestable alquardent de casa, which was eating a hole in my small intestine.

Nonetheless, I had questions to ask — about heroin, since Isabel had died of it. Because I was dancing with Jordi, I asked him, explaining that I had heard rumors of drug use among supposedly respectable people, especially young people, and was worried about bad influences on my daughter.

"Does your daughter take drugs?" he asked. "Everyone knows, of course, that they are part of American culture."

"They are not," I snapped, "and Gwen does not take drugs. In fact, drug use is down in the United States, although I believe that I read that heroin use is up. Is heroin a problem here?"

"I'm sure I wouldn't know," said Jordi. "*I* don't use it."

"What about younger members of the staff? Gwen will be working at the museum. Did Isabel —"

He looked shocked. "Of course not. Isabel? What an idea."

"Well, no one knows exactly how she died," I said defensively.

The music stopped, thank goodness — Jordi had stepped on my toes several times and in each instance gave me a pitying glance as if it were my fault. He stopped dancing abruptly and said, "If anyone would know about drugs, it would be Narcis. I wouldn't let him dance with my daughter, if I were you."

However, it was too late to intervene. Violante, protecting her daughter's interests, had just insisted that Narcis dance with Gwen, and Martí with Dolors. While she was directing Martí to the seated Dolors, who didn't look particularly pleased with her mother's machinations, the comte had taken Robbie's hand and pulled her into some dramatic South American dance. Before I could escape, Pau smiled at me and put his hand on my waist. "I don't know how to do this," I protested.

Much good it did me. I soon found myself stalking up and down the floor, twirling, and stalking back. I'd have died of embarrassment if I hadn't had so much to drink. Really he was quite a good dancer and kept me from making a fool of myself. Meanwhile Robbie and the comte were showing off unabashedly and having so much fun that I couldn't help laughing with them. Jordi and the comtessa engaged in a more stately version of the same maneuvers, both looking very politely bored with each other, the comtessa paying more attention to her daughter and husband than to the director of her husband's museum. Occasionally I heard her make some remark about the frivolous buildings of Gaudí and the nonsensical painting of Miró as compared to, for instance, various cathedrals she admired and religious painters of the past. Jordi, without denigrating the two art inspirations of Esperit, always murmured that her tastes were exquisite.

I was almost shoulder to shoulder with the comtessa when the music stopped again. "Your friend Senyora Hecht is very — ah — how to say? — flamboyant. I am surprised her husband does not make her stay home unless he escorts her."

Feeling rather giddy at having managed to get through a samba or whatever it was without injuring myself or my partner, I replied, laughing, "None of her other four husbands managed to keep her at home. I don't imagine Hugh even plans to try."

"She has been married five times?" gasped the comtessa, too horrified to take the news with sophistication.

We had been escorted back to the table by then, so I didn't have to answer. I could see that Narcis planned to dance with my daughter again and dropped down beside Madrona, whispering, "Please, please, dance with Narcis, would you? He's much too sophisticated for Gwen."

Madrona, delighted to oblige me, sashayed right up to them and nipped Narcis away. Maybe she had been right to say he had a thing for her. Martí immediately appropriated my daughter, leaving poor Dolors standing. Violante hissed under her breath with displeasure, Jordi glanced at her nervously, vacillated for just a minute, and then rushed up onto the platform to bow in front of Dolors. Robbie had stayed on the stage and snagged the flamenco dancer and two of his female partners. The comte glanced at Ceci, but asked me to dance, and Pau took the comtessa out onto the floor, making her look as good as he had made me. What an amazing man.

"So, Senyora Blue, how goes the investigation of my poor Isabel's death? Has the inspector finally realized that she must have fallen on the stairs and dragged herself into the exhibit to lie down?" the comte asked.

"That's not how she died," I said indignantly, forgetting for a moment that I had promised to keep secret the heroin. "How do you know she didn't kill herself?" I added, trying to make up for my slip.

"How would she kill herself?" he asked, astonished.

"Perhaps she overdosed on something. That is a common way for a woman to commit suicide, I believe."

"And why would she do that?" He was frowning.

"Unrequited love," I suggested. She had, after all, been his mistress, and he didn't show any signs of leaving his wife.

The comte looked troubled.

"Maybe she was a drug addict," I suggested. "I'm told heroin is easy to get hold of here."

"Believe me, Isabel was not a drug addict. I do not approve of drugs and would not have an addict on my staff. I'm surprised that you would say such a thing."

I shrugged. "Then we don't know what happened to her, do we? What a shame you don't have security cameras. I imagine most museums do. They would have told us just what did happen."

"I suppose so," he murmured, looking bemused.

"Carolyn." Robbie was by my side, cell

phone in hand. She urged me away and murmured, "Hugh just called. He wants someone to come back to the hotel so he can go home to bed without leaving Sammie alone. I think he's afraid Sammie will run off again. And speaking of Sammie, did you throw away that syringe he mentioned?"

"If he didn't lose it, it's probably under the bed in a laundry bag with the clothes."

"You kept those? I thought I told you —"

"I'll have to look," I hissed back, rolling my eyes toward the comtessa, who was within earshot. What a time for Robbie to bring up Sammie's involvement.

She nodded. "Let me know. And do you think Gwen would be willing to relieve Hugh?"

"She's not going to want to."

"Well, someone has to, and you and I need to stay and talk."

"Have you heard anything?"

"I'll tell you later, but we also need to stay and see what else we can find out."

Reluctantly I went off to speak to my daughter, who was not happy to be sent home to baby-sit. Neither were Martí and Narcis happy to end their competition for her attention, Narcis while dancing with Madrona. "Please, love," I murmured. "Hugh needs to get home, and he's afraid Sam will take off if —"

"Oh, all right."

"I'll call a cab and walk you to the entrance," I said, although I didn't want to walk back by myself. I was saved when Martí offered. I took him up on it because I could see that Narcis had the same thing in mind. Gwen was much less put out now that she was to be escorted to a cab by a handsome young Catalan shipping magnate. The comtessa, on the other hand, was furious, and even more so when her husband followed me to the table and complained at having his dance cut short.

"Don't you have a husband of your own?" she snarled in my ear.

"Yes, and I love him dearly. He's in Salamanca at the university giving a paper."

Then I hustled Robbie off in search of the ladies' room, leaving the comte and comtessa to entertain each other. She was saying, "You could at least have served a good cognac, Miquel, instead of that Catalan acid. I noticed that it made your dear American friend cough and gag."

"But she got a true taste of Catalonia," the comte retorted, "unlike the soup and dessert you chose."

Robbie shook her head. "I've heard about them, but I've never seen them together. Maybe she did kill Isabel."

41

Grand Finale to a Flamenco Evening

Carolyn

"What is it you found out?" I asked as Robbie and I washed our hands and peered at ourselves in the mirror.

"I heard Madrona tell Narcis she had found his pen in her office the morning after Isabel was killed. The pen was a special gift from Miquel." Robbie dropped her lipstick back into her purse and turned to me. "That means he was in the museum that night. Maybe he picked up that bird and hit Isabel really hard after Sammie ran away, or maybe he did something to her before Sammie got to her."

"Why would he?" I asked.

"How do I know?" Robbie retorted. Her cell phone rang, and she spoke briefly with her husband. "He's back at the apartment and wants to know when I'll be home," she told me after she'd closed the phone. "I'm going to have to go."

"I'll go with you," I said immediately. "You can drop me at the hotel."

"Carolyn, you need to follow up on this. Someone carried Isabel down to the exhibit, and it wasn't Sammie, so it must have been Narcis."

"Or he could have left the pen in Madrona's office at some earlier time, and she only noticed it when she came in that morning."

"It was *his* exhibit, Caro, and he does have a weird sense of humor. Why else would he take us to that seedy café and start a fight? Not that it wasn't fun."

"Fun?" Robbie was a lot more adventuresome than I am. I'd thought it was awful, except for the food. That had been good.

"So you've got to stay and talk to him."

"I don't like Narcis."

"There. You see. A murderer is bound to be someone you don't like."

"That wasn't necessarily true in France," I pointed out.

"Oh, France." Robbie waved a dismissive hand. "How often does something like that happen? If he's the one, we need to weasel an admission from him. Since I have to go home, it has to be you. Ask him to dance. He might let something slip."

I shuddered at the thought of dancing with

Narcis, but Robbie was right. He really did seem to be the person most likely to have access to heroin, the cause of death about which I couldn't tell Robbie. Now we had evidence that he'd had opportunity to kill her — maybe. Motive was the problem. "Why would he have done it? Can you think of a reason?"

"I never noticed that he had anything against her. Unless it was that the comte paid her a lot of attention. Narcis has a thing about Miquel. The big patron. You know. Miquel is his big chance in life."

I thought about what Narcis had said to me — that he'd had no name or home before Miquel took him on as a protégé. Of course, the way he'd said it — there was no way to be sure whether he was serious or just being, as he'd called himself, "a mystery man." I sighed and agreed to talk to him. I'd at least know what direction to angle my questions — although how did you ask about heroin when you were asking a person who might actually use it or have used it to kill someone? "I'll talk to him," I said reluctantly. "After all, I can't let you be arrested for a crime he might have committed."

"You're a doll," Robbie exclaimed enthusiastically. "And now I've got to run. I have a grumpy husband waiting to be sweetened up, and I'm the lady who can do it."

I returned to the club, where Dolors was

dancing with Martí, looking a bit more animated, while her mother and father glared at each other. Ceci and Pau were putting on a fine show doing some intricate South American dance, and Madrona was again dancing with Narcis. Sighing, I headed in their direction and arrived in time to hear her say, "I do know what Isabel knew, Narcis, but if you're sweet to me —"

"Ah, here is Senyora Blue," said Narcis. "She looks like lady wants to dance with soon famous artist." Madrona's lips compressed, and I wasn't any less irritated. I had wanted to hear what else she would say. What did she and Isabel know? Something that gave Narcis a reason to kill Isabel? "We talk later, dear Madrona," Narcis murmured, and swept me into his arms. Madrona stalked back to the table and sat down beside the monsignor, whose clerical collar was beginning to wilt under successive doses of alquardent de casa.

I immediately launched into the tale of the encounter Robbie and I had had with the two passport and drug-control officers who wanted to look at our passports, our billfolds, and our money. "I still don't know whether they were real federal officers. They said lots of drugs come into the port and that they could spot drugs on our money. Does that sound likely?"

"Much money pass through drug dealer

hands and pick up product. No?" said Narcis. "You maybe have money with cocaine."

"I did read, now that I think of it, that most money in Miami has cocaine on it. But goodness, do I look like someone who would be a drug user?" I laughed and flipped back the floating sleeve of my dress. "See, no needle marks."

"And pretty arms," he said, smiling.

"That's sweet," I replied, trying to sound pleased. "But of course, it's the young people who are into drugs. How about you, Narcis? You're young and — ah — hip."

"What is *hip?*" he asked.

"Ah — a swinger. Popular. A man of his time."

"Sí, sí. I most certainly — hip."

"But are you a user?" I managed to produce a giggle. "Let me see *your* arms?" And I playfully pushed up the sleeves of his black silk shirt.

"Senyora," he protested, pushing me away before I could get a look. "I am insulted. Would you like if I push up your skirt?"

I blushed, and he turned away and left me on the dance floor. Well, that hadn't been very successful. Or even subtle.

"What? You have frightened off Narcis?" the comtessa called.

"Stop picking on Senyora Blue," her husband ordered.

"What is *picking on?*" she demanded.

They began to argue, Dolors turned pale, and I denied frightening off anyone.

"And who is frighten off? Not me." Having returned, Narcis took my arm and walked me to the table, where he sat down beside me with an arm around my shoulders. "How could I be frighten off by such pretty, laughing lady?"

"Ah, sí, laughing ladies. Laughing American ladies," said the comtessa with acid in her voice. "My husband likes these laughing American ladies, don't you, Miquel? And other ladies. Miquel likes many ladies not his wife." She turned to the monsignor. "What do you think of such a bold adulterer as my husband, Father?"

The monsignor looked embarrassed and at a loss for words.

"He brings scandal on his family when his mistress is murdered. Probably by someone at this table. Maybe another lady who desires him and has not yet had him."

Much to my dismay, she looked directly at me. Then she turned her eyes to Madrona and even gave Ceci a venomous glance. "Where is the flamboyant Senyora Hecht? Has she lost interest in you, Miquel? Perhaps she is afraid to be murdered like your Isabel."

"And maybe, Violante, you murdered my Isabel, as you call her," snapped the comte.

I could hear the soft gasp of Dolors. "Mamá," she whispered unhappily. "Papá."

"Be that as it may, I really doubt that Isabel was murdered," said Miquel coolly.

"Then perhaps she committed suicide because you did not come to enjoy her wonderful paella and her young body that night. Little did your Isabel know the perils of paella. She was cooking, and you were chasing after a fado singer."

"I am certainly known for my patronage of the arts," he replied, voice now cold.

"And your sins," said Violante. "You are even more famous for your sins."

Dolors burst into tears and declared, "I am going into a convent. Tomorrow I shall go to become a nun. Monsignor, you must advise me."

"Well, I —" The prelate looked befuddled.

"You will do no such thing, Dolors," snapped her mother. "You have a duty to your family."

"What family? I have no family." Holding a lace-edged handkerchief to her eyes, the girl ran out of the room with her father right behind her.

I quickly clasped my handbag and tried to slip away, but Narcis grabbed my arm and asked, "Leave so early? Show may no be over. You no want to see if noble couple come to blows? But then the comte is too much fine gentleman to strike harpy wife.

Harpy? Is right word? You go for a taxi? I escort you."

That was the last thing I wanted, but he folded my hand in his arm and walked me all the way to the gate, where he found a cab waiting, although no one had called one, as far as I knew. Never was I so glad to see a taxi, especially when Narcis helped me in without insisting on accompanying me. I thanked him for his courtesy, gave the driver the name of my hotel once the door was closed, and fell back against the seat in relief. Finally this dreadful evening was over.

42

The Assassinee

Carolyn

With eyes closed, I relaxed against the upholstery of the car seat. Just a few minutes and I'd be in my hotel room, shared, admittedly, with Gwen and Sammie, but I could go to bed and sleep peacefully, a perfect escape from the death of Isabel Almirall and all its attendant ramifications. There was Narcis, who may have been in the museum the night she died. Someone gave her the overdose of heroin before Sammie arrived, and took her downstairs after he ran. It well might have been Narcis. Madrona knew the same things about him that Isabel had known. Were they bad things? Did he trust Madrona not to tell, or was she in danger, as Isabel had been?

Or had Isabel actually killed herself? The inspector said no because there was no needle on the desk or beside the bed, but that was because Sammie had taken it away, afraid luminol and DNA would link him to her death. But then how had she gotten downstairs? Unless Sammie was lying about not moving her body. But why would he take her downstairs? It made more sense for him to panic and run, as he had said. And if she had been alive, she might have staggered downstairs to die when he was gone.

Then there was the comtessa, who was jealous of anyone who came in contact with her husband, even me, and I hardly knew the man. She definitely had the motive and the temperament to have killed her husband's mistress. She —

I opened my eyes and noted that we were not passing the fountains leading to my hotel. "You're going the wrong way," I said, tapping the driver on the shoulder.

"No anglès," he muttered, and continued down a street I'd never seen.

"Wrong way," I insisted, and repeated the name of my hotel.

"No anglès."

"And why isn't the meter on?" I had just noticed that as I leaned forward to talk to him. The man was driving all around town without the meter on, planning to charge me some enormous amount for the trip. But now the streets were darker and meaner with only a few people skulking in the shadows. Where was he taking me?

"Stop," I commanded. He ignored me. Was I being kidnapped? Did he hope to hold me for ransom? Or sell me into white slavery? Well, no. That was a silly idea. I was too old to be a candidate for white slavery, unless they were looking for a maid or food writer. "Stop!" He didn't even turn his head. I glanced at the door. Should I throw it open and jump? It would be dangerous. And the neighborhood was looking worse and worse. If I survived the fall, I'd be afoot and lost in a strange, scary place.

"Please take me back right now," I said, but I'm afraid I sounded more pitiful than commanding. He said nothing. In desperation, as he slowed to turn a corner, I lunged for the door. It wouldn't open. I tried to pull up the little thingy, but it wouldn't pull. The door handle wouldn't move. Then the cab slewed around another corner and pulled into a lightless, trash-filled alley. A deserted alley.

"Give purse," he ordered, and reached a hand up to take it.

Thank God, I thought. *He just wants my money, and I never carry much.* I handed him the purse.

"Give watch and ring," he said.

My wedding ring? And the watch Jason had bought me for Christmas?

"Now. Watch and ring."

Shivering, I handed them over, after which I heard the locks snap up.

"I can't get out here," I protested. "You can keep the money and jewelry, but please take me back to my hotel."

When he climbed out himself and reached for the door, I saw the knife in his hand. The man wasn't going to eject me from the car. He was going to kill me. I dove across the seat, got the far door open, and tumbled out as he reached across for me.

"Estúpida americana," he muttered. I scooted to the front of the car and ran with his heavy footsteps clumping behind me in an odd rhythm. "Ask too many questions. Die," I heard him shout. I speeded up, heading for the end of the alley where a street crossed, my feet hardly touching the rough, trash-covered surface. If I fell, I was lost.

"No mind own business. S-s-s-t. I kill." His voice sounded close, but he was winded, more, for a wonder, than I. I wasn't even breathing hard yet, and at the end of the alley, I'd find people on the street. He couldn't kill me then.

Mind own business, he'd said. *About what? Isabel's murder? Narcis? Or Violante? Who had hired him to attack me?* The stink of garbage, mold, and clogged sewers gagged me, but I reached the street ahead of him. It was empty, narrow, and dark, except for dim lights behind shades higher up in the scabrous walls of buildings. I screamed, hoping to attract the attention of whoever was up there. And I ran faster, glancing over my shoulder. He was there, still armed with the knife, but limping. Not gaining ground on me. I had to find help before he caught up or I ran out of breath.

I stopped screaming because I couldn't afford the oxygen it took and because no one was paying any attention. No one was on the street. In the ensuing silence, I heard only my own accelerating breath, his hoarse gasps and clumping steps — and a lone car? Muted voices? I cut through another alley to another narrow street, terrified and shivering, even as the sweat of exertion broke out on my skin. Still, I could hear him behind me. Farther behind, I thought, but there, coming on.

Once on the second street, I saw lights several blocks away. From what? Businesses? Bars? A police station? Was the last too much to hope for?

I headed toward a place where a few, not many, men staggered on the cracked sidewalks and young women called out to them. He couldn't kill me in front of these people. Hurtling up to the women, I ensconced myself in their midst. Girls in tight, short skirts that barely covered their underwear, if they were wearing any, low-cut tops displaying breasts, not all of them young or even shapely, big hair, and very high heels. Prostitutes? I didn't care. They were people. When I glanced over my shoulder, I caught sight of him at the corner, glaring. Then he was gone.

43

Barri Xino

Carolyn

The women stared at me and crowded closer, sneering at me and snarling in unfriendly voices. One grabbed my skirt and laughed. "Does anyone speak English?" I asked.

"Anglès. Anglès," they said to one another and jostled me roughly. Farther down the street I could see light streaming from a doorway. Whatever it was, it couldn't be worse than this. I ran until I reached the hoped-for sanctuary, with the girls hooting at me and calling out threats and insults in Catalan. A bar. Worse-looking than Bacallà had been. Patrons mostly male and less respectable-looking than the den of sailors where Narcis had taken us, Robbie and me. I leaned against the door frame, breathing hard and studying the room. The walls were stone and stained with moisture and dirt. Splintering wooden shutters covered the few windows. The air reeked of smoke, alcohol, and unwashed bodies, but the bar was straight ahead, while behind me on the street, the women were heading in my direction.

Maybe the bartender spoke English or could at least understand my request to use their phone. What was Spanish for telephone? *Teléfono*, I thought. With any luck the Catalan would be similar.

I gathered my courage and headed for the bar, keeping as far away from the rickety tables and their frightening occupants as I could, but I was noticed. "¿Anglès?" I asked the man dispensing drinks. "¿Habla anglès?" He was huge — tall and broad-shouldered with a great ball of a head on top of a short, wide neck and a jaw like a granite tombstone, mossed over with bristly black hair. "¿Teléfono?" I asked.

"Whiskey?" said a man beside me, his smile exposing rotted teeth.

"No, thank you," I replied, and repeated my request for a telephone. The bartender stared, then served the man who had asked if I wanted whiskey. Or maybe he had wanted me to buy *him* whiskey. No, the fellow flashed blackened teeth and bare gums and pushed the glass toward me. "Whiskey," he repeated.

I felt like crying. "Doesn't anyone speak English?" I asked without hope. I could now hear the voices of the prostitutes who had resented my arrival on their street.

"Me," said a voice, and a little man with bowed legs and canvas pants pushed through the crowd. "Me . . . anglès. San Francisco."

"Oh, thank God!" I exclaimed. "You're from San Francisco?"

He nodded vigorously. "Houston."

"Houston?"

"New York. Long Beaches."

"Are you a sailor?"

"Sí. Spik anglès. You like have fun?"

"What?"

"How much pesetas? Dólares?"

Good grief. Was the man asking to purchase my . . . favors? "I . . . am . . . not . . . a . . . prostitute," I said slowly.

"No?" He looked disappointed. "Got money." He pulled some from his pocket. One of the women from the street made him an offer.

"Not . . . a . . . prostitute," I repeated. "I . . . am . . . an . . . American." Various men nodded and repeated my nationality. "A writer." Confusion greeted this announcement. "*¿Escribir?*" Didn't that mean to write? But in what language? "About food."

"Food?" asked the sailor. "*¿Aliment?*"

"Sí, aliment," I agreed, making the leap to alimentary. "Escribir aliment. For newspapers."

"Ah. Newspapers." The sailor beamed. "*Diari,*" he announced to the other drinkers.

I breathed a sigh of relief. There was a

newspaper in Juarez, across the border from El Paso, called *Diario*. Now that I had established myself as a non-prostitute, it was time to reintroduce my need for a telephone. However, before I could do that, the bartender shouted through a curtained door to the back of the establishment, and a very fat woman, dripping with sweat, responded, wiping her hands on a heavily stained apron. The bartender — or was he the owner? — sent a machine-gun rat-a-tat of Catalan toward the woman, whose face lit up.

"*¿Americana?*" she asked.

I nodded.

"*¿Escriptora?*"

Assuming that meant writer, I nodded again.

"*¿Aliment per diari?*"

I agreed. She was obviously the cook. Maybe *she* would let me use the telephone. Before I could ask, she rushed through the curtain and returned shortly with a plate. Oh dear, I was obviously expected to try the things on it. I selected. I chewed. I exclaimed with delight, having no idea what I was eating. The little fish bits in a red-hot batter, fried crisp, were pretty good. They insisted that I have a mug of beer. It was awful, smelled like sweat, but I drank it, hoping that on top of all that cava and goat and alquardent de casa, I wouldn't get sick, right here over her offering.

She pointed to the fish and asked, *"¿Bona?"*

"Sí. Bona."

She nodded, pulled a pencil from the knot of hair on top of her head, demanded that the bartender provide paper, and wrote what I took to be the recipe.

"Mila gracia," I said, accepting the paper. Was that Italian? At least she seemed to understand. "Per diari," I added. She beamed. I was learning Catalan. "¿Teléfono?" I asked hopefully.

"Sí. Telèfon," she replied, then touched the paper I was putting into my pocket. *"Per diari."*

"Sí, per diari," I assured her, and she led me to the telephone. The only Barcelona number I remembered, because I had called it before leaving for the flamenco club, was the home number of Inspector Pujol, so I called him. And why not? He was a policeman. And I was in trouble and penniless. Besides that, I had information for him about the case.

Inspector Pujol was not happy to hear from me, and I didn't know where I was. *"¿Dónde está . . . aquí?"* I asked, again hoping my Spanish was understandable and they would understand it. The sailor and the cook fed me the address one word at a time. Inspector Pujol was horrified to hear my location and arrived in twenty minutes. In the meantime I was fed more samples of the house fare and given another glass of beer, which I sipped as slowly as possible.

The women I took to be prostitutes edged closer to me now that they knew I was not foreign competition trying to lure away their customers. Through the sailor, they asked how much "whores" made in America. Of course I had no idea. They persisted, and the sailor translated, "How much per . . . mano?"

What does that mean? I wondered, and stared at him helplessly.

Spurred on by a girl in a red satin blouse, he asked, "Per . . ." He made sucking noises. Thinking that I caught his drift, I felt my face turn red. Much laughter followed.

Then, thank goodness, the inspector appeared, and a murmur ran through the room. "Policía." Women disappeared. Patrons and owners looked at me askance. I rushed to meet him, calling, *"Adiós. Muchas gracias,"* to my most recent Catalan acquaintances. Unfortunately, or perhaps not, I lost that recipe.

44

A Reluctant Rescue

Inspector Pujol

The department provides me with a pager
that can be set to beep or vibrate. When my
wife and I retire at night, I strap it to my
wrist so that, should I be called, I can return
the call without disturbing Sebastiana. However, I do not encourage night calls. When a
man has worked his way to the rank of inspector, his subordinates should be able to
take care of crimes until he reaches his office
at a reasonable hour in the morning. Consequently, I was not only rudely awakened but
also shocked when the telephone rang. At
first, I thought I must have neglected to
switch the pager from sound to vibration. I
did that, and the noise continued.

"Ildefons, who could be calling?" my wife
asked with sleepy irritation. "Are you waiting
for me to answer the telephone? At this hour
it must be some drunk calling a wrong
number."

I crawled out of bed and went to the hall where our telephone hangs, a good placement. The need to stand to use the instrument discourages long conversations. Colleagues tell me that their teenaged daughters lounge in comfortable chairs chattering on their telephones for hours. Our Magdalena does not do that, although she met me in the hall that night, curious about the late call.

"Pujol," I muttered into the receiver.

"Oh, thank goodness. I was afraid I had remembered the number wrong. Inspector, this is Carolyn Blue."

"Senyora Blue?" My wife was now standing beside me and looked very unhappy when she heard who was calling. "What is the hour?" I asked reproachfully.

"I don't know," the woman replied. "The cab driver stole both my purse and my watch after stopping the taxi in a dark alley."

"You are calling from a dark alley?" I asked, confused.

"From a tavern. Could you come and get me?"

"I am not a transportation service, Senyora Blue," I said sternly. My wife nodded her approval. Magdalena, giggling, went back to her room.

"But I have no way to get home and don't even know where I am. You're the only person whose number I know. And the taxi driver wanted to stab me, something about not minding my own business, which I take to mean that information I gathered to-night —"

"Madam, I told you to leave the case —"

"— has made the murderer see me as a threat. And I'm afraid. I'm in a drinking establishment where I was . . . propositioned. And on the street, prostitutes tugged at my clothes, pushed me, and called insults. Then they followed me in here and asked embarrassing questions."

I fear that I cursed, something I try not to do in front of women. To Senyora Blue my words meant nothing; she did not speak Catalan, but Sebastiana frowned at me. "Where are you, then?" I could hear the noise in the background, then the woman asking where she was.

Other voices prompted her answer. Senyora Blue had good reason to be frightened. She was lucky to have lost only her wallet and her watch. "I will come for you within fifteen minutes," I said.

She sounded very grateful, as well she might — getting herself into trouble in the middle of a man's sleep. I told her to make herself inconspicuous until I arrived, and I hung up. Even my wife, when she heard where in Barri Xino the woman was, agreed that I had to go after her, although I could see that she was not pleased to have me riding around Barcelona in the middle of the night with a blond American. However, I was too cunning for Sebastiana. I asked her to come with me.

Being a sensible woman who likes a good night's sleep, she refused and went back to bed. I dressed and set out, reluctantly, to rescue Senyora Blue.

"It must have been the murderer, don't you think? Someone arranged to have that man pick me up. The cab was waiting although I didn't call it," Senyora Blue told me once I got her out of the lowlife dive that she had entered to find a telephone. Astonishingly enough, she called and waved goodbye to the clientele, who seemed to like her. They knew that I was not their sort and lowered their eyes when they saw me, while the prostitutes simply disappeared into the crowd. Well, Americans, just as I surmised, seem to believe in instant friendship, even with the least respectable people.

"Cabs do wait where people will be looking for them," I remarked, "and Poble Espanyol has clubs and restaurants that are open at night. Unfortunately, there are taxi drivers who are also villains. As you said, he stole your purse and jewelry and threatened you with a knife to do it."

"No, I said he threatened me with a knife after I asked him to take me back to the hotel. Why would a simple thief want me to mind my own business — that's what he said — and try to kill me?"

"No doubt he wanted to frighten you to keep you from describing him or his vehicle to the police, so perhaps you should do that. I can put out the word and see if other tourists have had this experience."

"I never saw his face. He kept it turned away, and the street was too dark to see him when he tried to drag me out of the car and chased me. As for the car, it was a taxicab. At least, it looked like one initially. Now I'm not sure that it had a meter. I asked him to turn it on, but he didn't."

"You asked a man who was robbing you to turn the meter on? Did you plan to tell him to take the fare out of your purse?"

Unfortunately, she began to cry, which was very embarrassing. I had to apologize and give her a handkerchief since her purse, which had no doubt contained paper handkerchiefs, along with the miracle toothache reliever, was now gone. Then she apologized for crying, saying that she had had a very trying evening and was upset. I tried to sound sympathetic, but I myself was having a trying evening. In order to distract her, I asked whom she suspected of turning a villain loose on her.

After sniffing a few more times, she said her first choice was Narcis, the performance artist. "Robbie heard Madrona Brusi tell him that she had found his pen in her office the morning after Isabel was killed, which we took to mean that he had been in the museum at the time of the murder."

"Did he know you overheard that?" I asked.

"Well, no," she admitted, "but if he was the murderer, what followed might make him see me as a threat."

"I told you not to pursue your own investigation. What is this that followed?" I asked grimly.

"Before I found out about the pen, which the comte gave Narcis, I asked him about his background, and he told me nothing. Not a thing. He said he had no name or home before the comte discovered him. Of course, he acted as if it was a joke, but I found that very suspicious. A man who has nothing to hide would have more to say about himself than that, don't you think?" By then we had reached the Ramba, and she was peering out at the throngs walking among the trees and stalls that filled the park between the two motorways of the street. "Isn't it amazing," she mused, "that back there in — where was I?"

"Barri Xino," I replied. Her revelation reminded me that I had circulated the artist's picture and name, asking for information other departments might have, especially narcotics officers. I'd need to visit my office to-morrow to see if anything had come in. Sebastiana would be appalled if I worked both Saturday and Sunday. I rarely did that these days.

"I think I've read about Barri Xino," said the senyora. "Anyway, it's amazing that that quarter can be so dark and sinister, while out here on the Rambla, people are walking and conversing and buying things; students are standing in bookstores, reading. The city is so vibrant here, and so frightening —"

"Perhaps Narcis simply considered his background none of your business, Senyora," I interrupted, uninterested in her tourist observations on my city.

"After I heard about the pen," she went on doggedly, "I told him about the run-in Robbie and I had with the passport and narcotics officers, and asked about drug dealing and use in Barcelona. I even flipped up my sleeve to show him that I do not inject drugs and then laughed and tried to push his sleeves up. He became very angry and asked if I'd like him to flip up my skirt. Then he walked off. Not only was that rude and un-gentlemanly — about my skirt — but if he has nothing to do with drugs, why would he react that way? A respectable citizen —"

"— might think you a very strange woman, Senyora Blue," I finished for her. "I insist that you give up your investigatory activities.

And if you have told anyone about the cause of Isabel Almirall's death, I —"

"I haven't," she assured me. "Not even Robbie. And before you make me get out of your car" — we had reached her hotel — "let me add that he didn't just threaten me. He chased me at least four blocks brandishing his knife. If he hadn't been lame, he would certainly have caught me. As it was, I reached the prostitutes and barged right into their circle. Then, and only then, did he turn away. Does that sound like he was just threatening so I wouldn't describe him or his car?"

"Hmmm," I said. In truth, it didn't.

"And I have one more suspect for you. The comtessa was at the party, and I must tell you, Inspector, that she is a wildly jealous woman. She and her husband quarreled throughout the evening, and she accused him not only of his affair with Isabel and with some fado singer, but she also intimated that Robbie and I were after him. It was horribly embarrassing, especially for their daughter. A woman that volatile might well have killed a rival and then hired a cab driver to kill me since she seems to think I covet her husband."

"We are parked in a no parking zone, Senyora," I pointed out.

"You're a policeman," she retorted. "I doubt that anyone is going to arrest you.

And I have no key card to my room now. For that matter, what if that driver is waiting for me with a knife when I get up there? What if he's holding my daughter hostage?"

I sighed and turned the motor off. "I will escort you to your room and search it."

Then, as women will do, she changed her mind and insisted that I go home to my wife; she would ask a bellboy to accompany her upstairs. Now curious, I insisted on doing so myself. I arranged for the hotel to change the key card so that the taxi driver could not enter her room with it or sell it to someone else for purposes of burglary. Then we rode the elevator in silence and knocked at the door. It was opened by her daughter, to whom she introduced me. The girl, I was happy to see, wore a long, respectable nightgown instead of one of those embarrassing short bloomer outfits modern females sometimes wear to bed. My own Magdalena was given one as a gift. Naturally, I confiscated it.

I discovered almost immediately why Senyora Blue hadn't wanted me to come upstairs with her. An adolescent boy rose sleepily from a pile of covers on the floor and gaped at us. It seems that the recently discovered stepson of Senyora Hecht was sharing the room with Senyora Blue and her daughter. Why, I wondered, was he not staying with his stepmother? Not to mention his father and sister? Senyora Blue introduced the boy, who shook my hand politely, then more or less fell back into his blankets and went immediately to sleep. My own son, in his boyhood, was given to such abrupt departures into sleep.

Having met the occupants of the room — *where would they all sleep when the woman's husband arrived?* I wondered — I duly searched the bedroom, bathroom, and closet for the absent criminal, while the daughter giggled and assured us both that only she and "Sammie" were there. Having done my duty as a policeman and gentleman, I then said good night.

"What about the suspects I suggested?" the lady demanded.

"I shall certainly give everything you have told me careful consideration," I assured her. "Tomorrow. Better yet, Monday."

"And aren't you going to look for the limping taxi driver who tried to —" She glanced at her daughter and stopped in mid sentence. "Who stole from me."

"I shall certainly pass the information on to the proper officers," I replied, and escaped.

45

The Comtessa Speaks to God

Inspector Pujol

At 9:30 I was at my desk, much the worse for my curtailed night's sleep, going over information the picture of Narcis Ramon Berenguer had produced from my colleagues. A slippery fellow, suspected of many things, but never arrested. Before I could reach any conclusions, a woman strode into my office with my aide running behind protesting.

The lady was handsome and haughty, draped in a full-length fur coat and displaying a good deal of black hair done up in elaborate coils. It was no surprise to me when she announced herself as the Comtessa Violante Roca i Navis. "I have come to you, Inspector, after a night spent in prayer. You may take my coat."

Although I resented being treated like a footman, I rose to do so and hung the heavy garment on a peg attached to my wall. It would seem that Senyora Blue's speculation had been correct. The jealous comtessa had come to confess or at least point the finger at someone she had hired to kill Isabel Almirall. Very good. I would be saved the trouble of reading over the murky suspected misdeeds of Narcis, who had no name in our records but that. The Ramon Berenguer part had evidently been added to impress his patron, the comte.

"Do not put my coat on a hook," said the comtessa angrily. "That is not a proper way to deal with a fine garment, although I suppose a policeman would not know that."

"If you are suggesting, Comtessa, that a policeman's wife would not be wearing furs, you are correct. What would you like to do with the coat? Hold it over your arm? Our facilities here are very simple, as befits the offices of public servants who devote their time to the safety of the citizens of Barcelona rather than the cosseting of fur coats."

"If you were more successful in your assigned duties, my visit would not have been necessary because Isabel Almirall would not be dead." She sighed, took the coat from me, and draped it carefully over another chair. The chair creaked, causing her to look surprised, then worried about the safety of her coat. Then she seated herself in the second chair, which also creaked, and began to talk.

"As I said, I have prayed over the matter and come to the conclusion that God wishes me to put an end to this investigation, at least as it reflects on my family. My poor daughter, being a devout and sensitive girl, is very upset and threatening to do something foolish."

Was the mother about to tell me that her daughter was the murderess and had decided to commit suicide rather than join a convent to expiate her sin? "You daughter is considering suicide?" I asked.

"*Suicide?* You little know my daughter, Inspector," said the comtessa indignantly. "I am shocked that you would suggest such a thing. Suicide is a mortal sin, and she is not *that* upset. But please do not interrupt me until I have finished what I have to say. Then if you must, you may ask a question or two, taking into consideration that I am a busy woman with other engagements today."

I folded my hands on my desk and stared at her, thinking that she was an appallingly arrogant woman, but what else would one expect of a comtessa?

"Good," she said with satisfaction. "You are following my suggestion. As I said, after consultation with my God, I have decided that I must put aside family pride and make a statement. My husband, Comte Miquel Xifré i Fontdevila, did not kill Isabel Almirall. The fact that he is a sinner does not make him a murderer. His sins are of a different kind. If you doubt my statement,

346

you may consult one Orfeó Bacigalupi, a man who does private investigations. He can tell you everything my husband did on the night in question. What you hear will not reflect well on my husband, but it will clear him of any involvement in the murder."

Evidently Bacigalupi had not confessed to her that he had broken her confidence. I would not break his. "Very good. We will check that out," I replied, expecting to be chastised for speaking. "But what of you, Comtessa? What were you doing on the night in question?"

"You suspect *me?*" Her face flushed.

"You are a jealous woman, Comtessa, from all I have heard, and the victim had a . . . relationship with —"

"No need to speak of that." She thought for only a moment, then continued, "I did not kill her." The comtessa spoke as if her statement settled the matter.

"Unfortunately, the word of a suspect who has motive and no explanation for her time that night, as far as we know, is not enough."

"Outrageous. Very well. You have my permission to speak to the nuns of St. Eulalia. I joined them in prayer that night in the chapel at their convent."

"Very commendable," I replied. "For how long?"

"For the whole night, of course."

"I shall seek to establish that as well."

"I find this most embarrassing. It's bad enough that you have been harassing my servants, my daughter, and my neighbors —"

"Such is the duty of a homicide inspector."

"And a very distasteful profession it must be. Perhaps I may suggest another way to satisfy your inquiries without further embarrassing my family. There is an employee of my husband named Roberta Hecht, an American and, I think, a loose woman."

I had had the same impression and did not disagree with the comtessa. In fact, I was interested in what she had to say about Roberta Hecht.

"This woman is obviously in love with my husband. Just last night she was dancing and flirting with him outrageously. I have no doubt that she killed the Almirall woman to dispose of a rival for his affection. I might add that I heard her say a very peculiar thing to one Senyora Blue, whom you may not know. She is interested in my husband as well."

So the senyora had been right on that score. The comtessa was jealous of anyone who even saw her husband. Still, I myself had been suspicious of Roberta Hecht. "What was said between the two women?" I asked.

"The Hecht woman wanted the Blue woman to send her daughter home, no doubt so that the girl would not see her flirting with my husband and tell the Hecht woman's husband about it. Then the Hecht woman asked if the Blue woman had disposed of the syringe and became very upset when her friend did not know where it was. I have no idea how this would bear on the murder of Isabel Almirall, but no doubt it does. It is for you to find out how, Inspector."

A syringe? The comtessa may not have known how a syringe bore on my case, but I did, and so did Senyora Blue. Most interesting. "Thank you for this information, Comtessa. Have you anything else to add?"

"I do not. You may help me on with my coat." She rose as if she were the queen of Spain and gestured to the coat. I held it for her.

46

A Confrontation with Madrona Brusi

Carolyn

Still tired and upset, I woke to the thought that if Narcis had tried to have me killed because of what I suspected, he might do the same to Madrona Brusi because of what she knew. Robbie and I had to get to her, question her, and hope she was still alive to be questioned. Gwen and Sam were sleeping, so I edged silently from my bed and slipped into the bathroom, which had its own phone. Closing the door softly behind me, I called Robbie, who answered, as if out of breath, and told me that my timing was bad.

Neither apologetic nor embarrassed, I whispered, "You have to get dressed and meet me somewhere — at the museum — no, I don't want to go there alone. Anyway, somewhere we can talk without the children hearing us. Then we have to get to Madrona

Brusi while there's still time."

"Caro, I don't know what your problem is, but I'm sure it can wait a few hours. After all, my husband —"

"The driver of a cab into which Narcis put me last night tried to kill me, Robbie. You sent Gwen home. You went home yourself to be with Hugh, and left me there to —"

"Come on, Caro! Someone tried to kill you?"

"That's what happened. Now get yourself dressed and over to the coffee shop downstairs. I mean it. Right now." And I hung up on her. All the time I was talking to Robbie, the picture of that driver opening my door was in my head, the knife in his hand, me scrambling across the seat, tumbling into the alley, and running for my life. If he hadn't had a limp, he'd have caught me.

I pulled clothes from the closet and underwear from my suitcase, and went back into the bathroom to dress. When I reemerged, both kids were still under the blankets but now more or less awake. "I'm going out, Gwen. You stay here with Sammie."

"Mom, I'm getting sick of being stuck in this room," she complained. At the same time Sammie was saying, "I don't need a baby-sitter. I can stay here by myself. When's my dad coming over?"

"Do what I say. Both of you." I grabbed my purse.

"I hope you haven't forgotten that Magdalena is picking me up for lunch," my daughter said in a voice that verged on a whine.

"I'll be back before that, and I expect to see both of you here." I left before they could argue. Two cups of coffee later, Robbie appeared in the coffee shop.

"Okay, what's this that happened last night?" she asked, looking grumpy but sitting down and waving to a waitress for a menu.

I told her as soon as the waitress had gone. "We need to get right over to Madrona's and pray to God that she's alive and at home. Then we need to find out about the pen and anything Isabel might have told her about Narcis that would have given Narcis a reason to kill Isabel."

"If my husband dumps me because I'm not around to fulfill my marital obligations —" Robbie began.

"I'm sure you can make it up to him this afternoon," I finished for her. "After we've talked to Madrona. Or the inspector, if she's disappeared."

"Come on, Caro. You think, even if he did kill Isabel, that he's going to risk killing Madrona? And you?"

"He probably thinks I'm dead," I snapped. "If I see him, I'm going to faint."

"Well, Madrona isn't at home. She's at the museum on Sundays."

Narcis was nowhere in sight when we entered the museum and went upstairs. Madrona was in her office, alive, thank goodness, but not very cooperative. "I don't know what you're talking about," she said when Robbie asked about the pen Madrona had discovered.

"I heard you tell Narcis," Robbie retorted.

"You must have misunderstood. Why were you eavesdropping on us?"

"Madrona," I said quietly, "last night I asked Narcis some questions he apparently didn't like. Then he walked me to the front gate and put me in a cab. The driver took me into Barri Xino, stole my purse and jewelry, and then tried to kill me in an alley. Narcis could arrange the same thing for you if he thinks you're a danger to him."

She turned pale. "Narcis wouldn't hurt anyone. He's a beautiful boy."

"Oh, for Pete's sake, give your hormones a rest, Madrona," Robbie snapped. "Narcis is scary and dangerous. He took us to a café down by the waterfront and picked a fight with some scruffy sailors."

"He took the two of you out?" She glared at us.

"And we were lucky we didn't end up in jail or a hospital," said Robbie. "Ask Caro. The inspector told her that the cops arrested everyone in that place." She would have elaborated on the subject, but her cell phone rang. "Roberta Hecht," she answered sharply. "I don't really have time for . . . What? Am I under arrest? . . . So, okay, I'll come down." She closed the telephone. "Your buddy Pujol," she said to me. "He wants to talk to me, and if I don't get myself down to his office, he'll send the gendarmes for me. What did you tell him last night when he picked you up?"

"That I came close to getting killed and then had to find a phone in a horrible neighborhood full of prostitutes and their customers."

"Well, I've got to go, I guess. He didn't sound very friendly. You find out what Madrona knows. It may save my hide if Pujol has decided I'm the murderer."

"They never did get along," said Madrona smugly once Robbie had left. "Isabel and Robbie. She's much more likely to have killed Isabel than Narcis."

"And if she didn't," I retorted, "you're next. Maybe he'll have another shot at me too, but I'd like to see him in handcuffs before that happens."

"I don't have to tell you anything."

"You mean you helped him kill Isabel because you wanted him for yourself?"

Madrona turned a dusky red and stammered a denial. "He wasn't interested in Isabel."

"Madrona," I said with as much patience as I could muster, "by your own evidence, you proved that he was here the night of the murder. If he didn't kill her, why hasn't he come forward to tell what he knows?"

"Well . . . he's not likely to trust the police."

"Why not? Does he have a criminal record?"

"No. Not exactly."

"Then what is it that Isabel knew about him? This is your skin too, you know."

"My skin?" She looked confused.

"Your life is in danger as much as hers was and mine is. Now tell me what she told you."

"Oh, it was just that she'd heard rumors about him. About what he'd been before he became an artist. Things that the comte wouldn't like if he knew."

"And she tried to blackmail Narcis?" I asked, realizing just how dangerous that would have been.

"Not blackmail him. Just warn him off. She didn't like all the attention Miquel was paying Narcis. They went out together some evenings when she thought Miquel should have been with her. She even thought that Narcis might have a — a sexual interest in Miquel. Of course that's nonsense. Narcis isn't a pervert, no matter what she heard."

Everything Madrona said made my skin crawl. "Isabel thought he was gay?"

"Happy, you mean?"

"No, homosexual."

"Of course he isn't, but she'd heard that he sold himself to older men when he was a boy, and that he did other things, criminal things. But if he had, he'd have been in jail. I told her she was wrong."

He's got a motive, I thought. *And opportunity. And if he has criminal connections and is so touchy about drugs, he'd had the means to kill Isabel, whom he must have seen as a threat to his position as the comte's protégé.*

"Madrona, I want you to think about what you've told me —"

"Please, don't tell Narcis that I —"

"— and what I told you, and stay as far away from Narcis as you can until this is resolved."

"What are you going to do?" she asked, alarmed.

"I'm going home to check on my daughter and Robbie's son," I replied, "and I'm going to think about all this as carefully as I hope you'll think about it. We're both in danger, whether you want to believe it or not." I stood up and glanced at my watch. I had no watch. It had been stolen by the man with the knife. "Could you tell me what time it is?"

"Eleven-thirty," she replied, and agreed when I asked to use her phone. If I didn't get there in time, I wanted to be sure that

Gwen stayed with Sam until I arrived. "Gwen, it's Mom. I'm on my way back. Please be sure you stay with Sam until I get there . . . Robbie can't. Inspector Pujol has insisted that she come into the police station. . . . He didn't tell her why. . . . Well, just ask Magdalena to wait in the lobby. . . . When you're not out front waiting for her, she'll park and have the desk call you. Then you can tell her to — Gwen, just do what I ask. I'm not having the best day, and I don't feel like arguing." I thanked Madrona, warned her again to be careful, and left her office.

But I still had to get out of Esperit without seeing Narcis. And I was afraid to take a taxi. I'd insisted that Robbie and I come here on a bus, and I was going back to the hotel on one, although I had to skulk, fretting about how late I'd be, in a doorway at least fifty yards from the bus stop. After a good half hour, the bus I wanted to catch arrived.

47

An Unexpected Confession

Inspector Pujol

Since I already knew that Bacigalupi could alibi the comte for the night of Isabel Almirall's murder, not that I had told the comtessa that, I sent an officer out to interview the nuns of St. Eulalia about the comtessa's alibi. While waiting for that information, I interviewed Senyora Roberta Hecht, who was not happy that I had ordered her to my office. The whole of her response to my questions revolved around her insistence that she had not been at the museum that night, while Narcis Ramon Berenguer had. "Why haven't you called in that nasty little prick for questioning?" she demanded. "I know Carolyn told you about his taking us to that place down near the port. We had to run for our lives after the fight started.

"And she's convinced that he tried to have her killed last night. You know that too because you had to pick her up at some combination bar and brothel. And let me tell you, Inspector, my friend Carolyn Blue is not a person who appreciates being hassled by a bunch of whores."

"Actually, she seemed to be on quite good terms with the crowd from which I rescued her."

"I don't know what you mean by that, but if it's anything immoral, you've got the wrong woman. She's as respectable as a nun. If they liked her at that place, it was because she's polite to everyone and programmed to think the best of people. Which I suppose explains why she likes you. Furthermore, Narcis was at Esperit that night. He left a pen in Madrona Brusi's office. Didn't Carolyn tell you that? He was there, and I wasn't. Now if you're planning to arrest me, do it, and I'll call Mr. Barkley at the American consulate. If not, I have a family to take care of and some people to ask about Isabel's death. I wouldn't have to do that if you'd do your job."

"Madam, I have a very respectable witness who thinks you killed Isabel Almirall because you were jealous of her relationship with the comte, your employer. Add to that the fact that you cannot account for your where-abouts the night of —"

"Well, your witness didn't see me kill Isabel, because I didn't kill Isabel. Who's your informant? Miquel's half-nuts, insanely jealous wife? She thinks everyone has the hots for her husband, her estranged husband, I might add. She even thinks Carolyn is after him, if you can imagine. It never occurs to her that we might be in love with our own husbands and couldn't care less about where Miquel is sleeping. No, I take it back; it wouldn't be his wife who told you to hassle me. She's too stuck on herself to even talk to a policeman."

If the comtessa hadn't appeared in my office that morning, I'd have agreed with Senyora Hecht.

"So go talk to Narcis. And put a guard or something on Carolyn. She thinks she has to save me from being arrested, so she's running around asking questions that get her into trouble. I should never have agreed to help her. I could get myself killed and, obviously, I'm not going to be arrested for Isabel's murder, no matter what you think, because I didn't kill Isabel. Okay? So do I leave, or go straight to jail?"

What a pushy woman, I thought, and dismissed her, remembering only after she was gone the comtessa's eavesdropping tidbit: Senyoras Hecht and Blue had argued about a missing syringe. I'd have to pursue that avenue later. Disgusted with myself, I went back to my perusal of the information I had on Narcis. It wasn't definitive, but it didn't look good. Suspicion of being a male prostitute, suspicion of beating up and stealing from a customer, suspicion of killing a customer, suspicion of pimping female prostitutes, suspicion of aggravated assault, suspicion of drug dealing. The notes went back nine years, and he was only twenty-three. But no arrests. A lot of smoke, but no fire.

I was mulling over the discovery of his pen in Madrona Brusi's office the morning after the murder — of course *she* hadn't mentioned that to me; she had implicated Senyora Hecht. And hadn't I heard from someone that Brusi was infatuated with Narcis? What a den of intrigue and violence the Esperit was proving to be. Would Brusi implicate Narcis? No way to know without interviewing her.

"Sir, there is a young man who insists on seeing you," said my aide, knocking twice and poking his head in the door.

I glanced at my watch. It was time for my midday meal. Sebastiana had promised me a special favorite to make up for the sleep I had missed last night. "Get his name and ask him to come back around three," I said.

A boy, gangly and dark haired, pushed past my officer and said, "You have to talk to me. I've come to confess."

"And you are?"

"Henri Samuel Fauree," said the boy. "Gwen told me that her mom told her you were going to arrest Robbie, but you can't do that. She didn't kill that woman in the museum."

"Did your stepmother send you here, young man?" I asked. Obviously, this was the pushy Senyora Hecht's stepson. "And how do *you* know she didn't kill the woman in the museum?"

"Because no matter what my dad says, I'm pretty sure *I* killed her. Not that I meant to, but I did hit her with the bird. The Miró bird. Well, I thought it was more of a poke, but — well, anyway, Robbie didn't send me. The doorman at the hotel told me how to get here, and I walked because I don't have any money."

"Sit down, young man," I said. This wretched case was going to make me late for lunch, perhaps miss it entirely. I motioned for my aide to bring his notebook into the office. "Now perhaps you can explain to me exactly what happened between you and Senyoreta Isabel Almirall. I assume that is the death you're confessing to."

"I guess," said the boy. "I thought she was Robbie. She looked like Robbie, but she wouldn't talk to me, and I had to talk to her. I had to say I was sorry for being so awful to her and to get her to ask my dad not to send me away. I ran away from home all the way here to talk to her, and she wouldn't even answer me or turn around. I even thought she was laughing. So I grabbed the bird and gave her a poke, and she fell onto the desk and died. I didn't even know it wasn't Robbie until Mrs. Blue told me and I saw Robbie alive."

"So your stepmother and Senyora Blue know that you allegedly killed this woman?" I was disappointed in Senyora Blue. Keeping information from the police. And I had taken the woman home to dinner. Given up a night's sleep to rescue her from Barri Xino. Never trust an American.

"Well, don't get mad at them. They didn't know what to do, and then my dad arrived and decided I couldn't have killed the woman. He said we didn't have to sneak out of Spain on a train to France because I wasn't guilty of anything and they should tell you that I'd been found because Mrs. Blue had reported me missing. Since my dad's a very smart man, we all believed him, but I guess I must have killed her, and now you're going to arrest his wife for something I did, and he's going to be very sad, and —"

"A moment," I cut into his headlong confession. I could see that my aide was falling behind in his notes and becoming very confused. "Your confession is that you killed Isabel Almirall, thinking she was your stepmother, by hitting her with a bird. Do we have that right?"

"Yes, sir," said Henri Samuel Fauree, and he began to cry.

I sighed. He was obviously very young. What had Senyora Blue said? Thirteen? Still, I hated to see a male cry. Especially one who obviously had no handkerchief. He had just wiped his nose with his hand. "Well, young Senyor Fauree, I appreciate your candor, but the fact is that Isabel Almirall did not die of a blow to the head. What else did you do to her?"

"I didn't do anything," he responded, confusion rounding his brimming eyes. "I ran out and down the stairs as fast as I could. I'd have taken the elevator if it hadn't looked so scary and I hadn't been afraid the guard would hear it."

"And who else did you see in the museum that night?"

"No one. I hid in the men's room till it closed and snuck upstairs later and found Robbie's office with a woman who looked like her at her desk, so how was I to know that —"

"You have neglected to tell me that you took the body downstairs to the exhibit on the first floor and placed it in a hospital bed."

"I didn't do that. Jeez, I couldn't carry Robbie downstairs. She's a half foot taller than me and weighs — I don't know — twice as much."

It would be amusing to see Senyora Hecht's reaction to her stepson's estimation of her weight. Women tend to be touchy about such things. "But it wasn't your step-mother. It was a much smaller woman, whom you might well have been able to move downstairs."

"But I didn't know that. I don't know who took her downstairs. And that's really weird. Why would someone do that? And if the bird didn't kill her, what did?"

"Heroin," I replied, interested to see his reaction.

"Wow. Heroin? You mean like the drug? I guess that explains the needle on her desk."

"There was no needle on the desk."

"I guess not when you got there, but I pricked my finger on it when I tried to find a pulse. Then I figured you could get my DNA off it. Even if I wiped it off, you'd use luminol and find the blood. Like on TV. So I stuck it in my pocket and ran away."

"I see. And how do I know you didn't inject Senyoreta Almirall with the heroin that killed her?"

"Where would I get any heroin?" he responded, astonished. "I spent my last money on the ticket to the museum. And I wouldn't know where to buy it if I'd had any money. And I don't know how to use a syringe. Maybe she gave it to herself. Maybe it was pure stuff, and she didn't know it and overdosed. I've seen stuff like that happen on TV shows."

"You obviously watch too much TV, young man."

"Yeah, that's what my father thinks," he agreed sadly. "I guess I'm in big trouble, even if I didn't kill her."

"What did you do with the syringe?" I asked.

"I don't know. I must have run about forty miles that night with it in my pocket. Maybe it's still in my clothes. The ones I wore until Mrs. Blue found me and took me back to the hotel. Of course, maybe she threw them away. They were pretty disgusting. She never said anything about finding a needle."

"I think we shall go to Mrs. Blue's hotel room and look for the needle."

"Okay," he said agreeably. "If we find it, maybe the murderer's fingerprints are on it. Are we going to take a crime scene expert with us? Like in *C.S.I.* on TV?"

48

Panic in an Empty Room

Carolyn

I was at least three-quarters of an hour late getting back to the hotel. Gwen was going to be furious. I scanned the lobby for Magdalena as I hurried through, but she wasn't there, which meant she had given up and left or Gwen had invited her up to the room. If so, what had Gwen done with Sammie, whom we were still hiding in case the police still thought he was a missing person? I should have remembered to ask Inspector Pujol last night whether Sammie's name had been removed from their list.

Now, with the new key card in hand, I let myself into the room, calling, "I'm back. Sorry to be so late." Silence. I scanned the room and saw no one. No Gwen. No Magdalena. Had Gwen left against my explicit instructions? Worst, no Sammie. And the bathroom door was open. I was alone in the room. If he had run off again, Robbie and Hugh would be furious. Although I really couldn't be blamed. They should be looking after him themselves.

Food. Sammie had the appetite of a regiment. With Gwen gone — I'd have a thing or two to say to her when she got back — he'd have had no way to order lunch. I looked around for signs of room service. There were none. Could he, in the desperate throes of adolescent hunger, have gone down to the coffee shop? If so, how did he think he was going to pay for his meal? Charge it to my room? Could he just sign his name and my room number? They probably wouldn't know the difference. Anyone off the street could come in and eat at my expense. Jason would kill me when he saw the bill.

I rushed to the elevator, downstairs, and into the coffee shop, peering at every diner at every table. Sammie was not there! I went outside and looked up and down the street. No Sammie. I described him to the bell captain, who didn't remember him. Oh my, he'd run away. I'd have to call Robbie. If she was home from the police station. If she wasn't, I'd have to tell Hugh. Wearily I went back upstairs and sat down on the bed, thinking how much I'd rather have a nice nap than make this call. My pillow looked so tempting. Just a half hour would do wonders for me.

Stop it, Carolyn, I told myself. *You have a duty to your friends.* I made the first call to

Robbie's cell phone. I'd rather confess this new problem to her than to Hugh. "Where are you?" I asked when she picked up.

"Home," she replied. "Where are you? More to the point, did you manage to get anything out of Madrona?"

"Yes, but that's the least of our concerns."

"Easy for you to say. Your inspector came right out and accused me of murdering Isabel. I think Violante put it in his head. He thinks I was jealous of Isabel's affair with Miquel. How stupid is that? So if Madrona told you anything more that implicates anyone at all, I'd like to know about —"

"Sammie's gone," I interrupted.

"What?" There was an ominous silence. "Gone where?"

"I have no idea. When I got home both he and Gwen were missing. If we're lucky" — This scenario had just occurred to me — "Gwen took him with her to lunch with Magdalena when I was so late getting back."

"Oh, that's just great. He's not supposed to be out in public. What if Pujol picks him up? What if Sammie confesses? Hugh will be livid. And why were you so late?"

"Because I'm afraid to ride in a taxi because I nearly got killed in one last night when you went off and left me. So I had to wait for a bus, and it was unbelievably late."

"Okay. Okay. Mea culpa. I'm on my way over. We'll find him."

"And where is Hugh, by the way? Why isn't he taking responsibility for Sam?"

"They're leaving tomorrow, so he took Kimmie out sight-seeing. I wish I could have taken her. I saw some darling dresses for girls and —"

"Sam," I reminded her. "We need to find him."

"Right. I'm on my way."

Again I looked wistfully at the pillow. It might take Robbie fifteen minutes to get here, which would allow me a little catnap. But she was going to ask me about the clothes and the syringe. Sighing, I got down on my hands and knees to drag the laundry bag out. Obviously the maids didn't vacuum under the beds. Then I sat cross-legged on the floor staring at the bag. I needed to look for the syringe. The syringe that had probably killed Isabel. The thought of it made me shudder.

Get a grip, I told myself, and loosened the string that held the bag shut. Gracious, what a smell. Boy unwashed for multiple days and sleeping goodness knows where. Probably in alleys like that one I'd run out of last night. Even if Sammie stuck the needle in a pocket, it must have fallen out during his homeless period, which meant I didn't have to go through the pockets, risking a prick from the death weapon. Needles carry dangerous viruses. People die from accidental encounters with needles. Oh, how I wanted to retie the bag and shove it back under the bed! Let Robbie search it if she was so intent on finding the syringe. She just wanted to throw it away, so we didn't really need to look for it. We could simply drop the bag, unexamined, in some Dumpster. Did Barcelona have Dumpsters? My panicky musings were interrupted by a knock. Robbie. At last. I rushed to unlock the door and throw it open.

Sam and Inspector Pujol, not Robbie, stood there. I simply stared at them, dumbfounded.

"We would like to come in," said the inspector politely.

"Have you still got my dirty clothes?" Sam asked as I stepped back.

Why were the two of them together? I wondered, aghast. Why was Sam asking about the clothes in front of the inspector?

"Don't look so scared, Mrs. Blue," said Sam in a kindly tone. "When Gwen said Robbie had been sent for by Inspector Pujol, I knew I had to go over and confess. But it turns out that I didn't kill anyone. It was heroin that killed her. I don't know why you couldn't have told me that or at least told my folks. They've been really worried."

"I promised I wouldn't tell," I said weakly.

"Another question," said the inspector, "is why you or your friend, Senyora Hecht, didn't tell me about this young man's involvement in my case."

"And rat out my own stepson?" exclaimed Robbie. We hadn't closed the door, and she stepped in. "Sammie, what the hell have you done?"

"He's told me the truth," said the inspector. "A commendable course of action when dealing with the police."

"We're looking for the syringe," said Sammie. "It's probably long gone, but I thought it might still be in my clothes. It would help the inspector because there might be fingerprints on it. From the murderer."

"And certainly from you," said Robbie dryly.

"Oh." Sam looked dismayed. "Yeah, I guess."

"The clothes, Senyora Blue," said the inspector. "Or are you guilty of destroying evidence as well as impeding the progress of my investigation?"

"Oh, knock it off," said Robbie.

"On the floor," I interjected hastily, gesturing toward my bed.

The inspector picked up the bag, donned rubber gloves, searched the clothes, and came up with the syringe.

"Before you go arresting Sam," said Robbie, "remember that Narcis Berenguer was in the museum that night. He dropped his pen in Madrona's office. Madrona Brusi."

"You told me," said the inspector.

"Narcis must have killed Isabel. Sammie ran off *before* her body was carried downstairs."

"So he says," the inspector answered, bagging the syringe.

"And Madrona told me something else this morning," I added. "Narcis had a motive. Isabel knew that Narcis had been . . . I glanced at Sammie. "Sam, maybe you could go into the bathroom."

"Hey, I'm the one who's under suspicion. Robbie and me. If you know something that will clear us, we should get to hear it."

"I believe Senyora Blue does not want to say anything about Senyor Berenguer's unfortunate past in front of you, young man," said the inspector. "Some things are better not mentioned in front of young people."

"Anyway," I hastened on, "Isabel evidently threatened to tell the comte about Narcis's past if he didn't stay away from Miquel. She was . . . jealous."

"Why would she be jealous?" Sam asked. "This Narcis is another man, isn't he?"

"Did you know about Narcis?" I asked Inspector Pujol.

"I have, as I promised, investigated him. He has a bad reputation, but no arrests. The problem we face is that even with the needle, Sam's testimony, the pen in Madrona Brusi's office, and her testimony about the conflict between Isabel and Narcis, I doubt that we have enough evidence to convince the investigating judge to issue a warrant."

"What judge?" asked Robbie. "I thought you were doing the investigation."

"Under the direction of Judge Enric Goytisolo. Our system of justice is not the same as yours." Robbie was sputtering, but the inspector overrode her indignation to say, "However, I think we will all call on the judge and try to convince him."

"All, who?" demanded Robbie. "Sammie isn't going anywhere without his father's permission. And a lawyer. The consulate can get him one. Goodness knows what you weaseled out of a naïve boy without anyone to look out for his interests."

"Robbie, I went on my own. I told him the truth. I think we should go see the judge." Sam's mouth set in a stubborn line. "Even if you tell Dad to send me off to military school for the rest of my life, this is the best thing to do."

"Military school wasn't my idea!" she exclaimed.

Inspector Pujol was using his cell phone to call the judge. "Yes, Your Honor, I think you need to hear what I have discovered on the Almirall case. I have some witnesses to bring in. Would a half hour be convenient? . . . Very well, we'll wait in your anteroom until you finish your dinner."

My goodness, but the inspector looked peeved. I wondered if he'd missed his own dinner because of Sammie's visit.

49

The Judge Reprimands Sammie

Carolyn

Poor Inspector Pujol, I thought as we took our chairs in the judge's office. The contrast of this fine office to the inspector's rickety quarters was certainly cause for sympathy. On the other hand, Judge Enric Goytisolo with his drooping mustache and eyebrows, his center-parted hair, and his nervous twittering made the inspector look like a movie star.

"You have altered suspect, Pujol?" asked the judge, eyeing Robbie and me suspiciously. I had to wonder if we had been the previous suspects, although why I should have been a target of investigation was beyond me. I hadn't even arrived when Isabel was killed. Perhaps the judge simply distrusted Americans. Inspector Pujol had certainly seemed to view me unfavorably when we first met. "Why," asked the judge, "are many foreign people in my chambers?"

"Each of them holds a piece of the puzzle," the inspector replied. "The boy is Henri Samuel Fauree, thirteen years old. He is the stepson of Professor Roberta Hecht, the lady seated in the middle. On the left is Senyora Carolyn Blue, a friend of the professor's who has taken an unusual interest in the case. May I introduce Judge Enric Goytisolo i Llull, my superior in this investigation. It is he who will decide if an arrest can be made."

"Who are we arrest?" the judge asked, after greeting each of us with little enthusiasm.

"One Narcis Ramon Berenguer, the artist who designed the performance exhibit 'Tapas Triage' at Esperit."

"Protégé of Comte Miquel Xifré i Fontdevila?" asked the judge, thick eyebrows raised in disbelief. "Person under comte's patron would no be —"

"Perhaps you would like to hear what these witnesses have to say, sir," Pujol interjected.

"Oh, yes," said the judge petulantly, "but I need very fine evidence to arrest of comte's new art finding. I hear fellow is a much talent. Even newspaper say is innovative in his exhibition, which bring much tourists to museu. Friend of comte's say increase each day. Comte much happy."

"I imagine the *murder* brought in the tourists," I said, taking an immediate dislike to the judge. "And actually, Narcis's work,

'Tapas Triage,' is somewhat derivative," I added, remembering the artist's own admission that he was influenced by an exhibit he had seen years ago at Fundació Miró. Perhaps the judge would be more willing to consider Narcis as a suspect if he thought the talent was questionable.

"You are art expert, madam?" asked the judge.

"No, I write an American newspaper column about food, Catalan food just lately."

"Ah. I am somewhat gourmet," said the judge. "What dishes you choose to write about, madam?"

"Your Honor, it is very kind of you to take an interest in Senyora Blue's research into our native cuisine, but, as you said, you have a busy schedule."

"Much busy. You, young boy, what you tell?" demanded the judge, sounding snappish now that he remembered his busy schedule.

I can't say that I was impressed with Judge Goytisolo, his English, or his name. It was as bad as that private detective's. Bacigalupi. On the basis of naming, Catalans have an odd language, not all that Latinate, in my opinion. Maybe the names came from the indigenous people in the Roman period and from Roman foot soldiers who might have been enlistees from non-Latinate Roman provinces. I couldn't help asking, "What is the linguistic origin of your name, Your Honor?"

"Is important to case?" he retorted, staring at me over round spectacles.

"No," I answered. "Just a point of interest."

"Senyora Blue is familiar with our language and history as well as our food," said the inspector, giving me a silencing look. "Senyor Fauree?"

"That's so cool. Being called Senyor," said Sammie. "Well, I'll have to start at the beginning so you'll understand how this happened. My mother died a couple of years ago, and . . ."

Sammie, much more relaxed than at any time since I found him on the street, perhaps as a result of having unburdened his conscience, began a very detailed account of his dismay at his father's remarriage, his inexcusable treatment of Robbie, and his father's threat to send him to military school. At which point the judge said impatiently, "Sí, sí. What this doing with murder of Senyoreta Almirall?"

"He ran away from camp to apologize to me and get me to intercede with his father," said Robbie.

"I can tell him," said Sam, who was obviously enjoying the spotlight. At least, he was no longer shedding tears.

"You are camping in Spain?" asked the judge, astonished.

"No, I flew here using my college fund."

379

"Does father wish to arrest boy for theft?" Goytisolo asked Pujol.

"Of course not," said Robbie.

"Jeez," said Sammie. "I didn't kill anyone. And the account was in my name too. My dad's mad at me, but he's not going to have me put in jail."

"Wouldn't that be a matter for the American judicial system?" I asked helpfully.

"Maybe yes," the judge agreed. He gave his mustache a little upward shove and side sweep to keep it from drooping into his mouth instead of simply down onto his jowls. "Please advance to Senyoreta Almirall's death, young person."

Sammie, looking disappointed, got on with it. "Okay, if we're in such a hurry, I snuck into the museum to see Robbie, thought the woman at the desk was her, gave her a poke with the bird when she wouldn't talk to me —"

"You have bird with you?" asked the judge, more bemused than ever. "Ha! Buy in bird market on Rambla. Very popular tourist place, but I think Catalans buy there birds more than tourists. You can no carry bird home. American government —"

"It was a metal bird, sir," said Pujol.

"Since the syringe on her desk had pricked me, I sucked the blood off my finger —" Sammie continued.

"Oh, my God," said Robbie. "You didn't

tell us that. What if the needle was contaminated? We'll have to have your blood tested immediately."

"Madam, stepson's health no concern of Catalan judge. Investigate boy's health other time," said the judge.

"I feel fine, Robbie. Honestly," said Sam. "Anyway, I stuck the needle in my pocket and ran away."

"The poor child lived on the streets for days," said Robbie, "thinking he was a hunted murderer, until Carolyn found him begging on Passeig de Gràcia." She stretched her arm out to give Sammie a hug.

He tried to smile, but I could see that he was embarrassed. When my son, Chris, was that age, he'd have died rather than let me give him a hug in public. Ah, boys.

"No begging legal in Barcelona, especial on rich streets," said the judge. "You not do that, young person."

"I didn't have any money," said Sam. "I spent the last of it on a museum ticket."

"And bird. Museum tickets and birds not necessary to buy if person poor. Parents should tell you save money."

"Yes, sir," said Sam. "Anyway, I didn't know who I nudged with the bird, and I didn't mean to kill anyone, and I didn't. She died of a heroin overdose, according to the inspector. I found the needle for him. It was under the bed at the hotel."

"Impeding progress of homicide investigation," said the judge sternly. "You should come policía immediate, with important evidence needle."

"You're going to arrest me?" All Sammie's confidence disappeared. "And put me in a foreign dungeon?"

"We do not have dungeons," said Pujol hastily, and passed the boy a handkerchief, "and there is no need for an arrest. The boy's testimony is important to our case. Wouldn't you agree, Your Honor."

"Sí, maybe," said the judge. "Who next?"

50

Judicial Remarks on the Reliability of Women

Carolyn

"I have information," said Robbie in response to the judge's call for another witness.

"You are boy's stepmother? You speak next," he replied.

"I heard Madrona Brusi — she's a researcher at Esperit — say to Narcis, the artist, that she had found his pen in her office the morning after Isabel was murdered, which means that Narcis was in the museum that night and said nothing about it. You think Sammie should have come forward? Well, he did, and he didn't kill anyone. Narcis hasn't said a word. Right, Inspector? And the reason he hasn't is that he killed her."

"He maybe drop pen in lady's office other time. Only thing comment tells is she *find* pen after murder," said the judge. "Is no much for arrest."

"Well, she told *me* just this morning," I intervened, "that Narcis had a motive. Isabel knew that he . . ." I glanced at Sammie, rose, and walked around the judge's desk to whisper in his ear.

"What's the big secret?" Sammie asked Robbie. She shook her head.

". . . that Narcis was a male prostitute before he became an artist," I continued softly. The judge looked at me, puzzled, and he didn't seem shocked enough. "His customers were both women *and* men," I whispered.

"Sex customers?" asked the judge, horrified. "Pujol, is this true?"

The inspector joined us at the desk for a conference. The judge had now swiveled his chair so that his back was to the others and motioned us to extra seats so that we could confer in comfort and confidence without revealing this part of the story to Sammie, who was saying "What can be *that* bad?" to his stepmother. "The guy murdered someone, for Pete's sake."

"He was prostitute and — what is the English for —"

"Sodomite," said Pujol.

"Excuse please, madam," the judge murmured to me. "Most improper this discussed with you here. You return to seat."

"Unpleasant as it is," I replied, "I did bring it up. I hope you'll excuse me, but

384

when a life has been lost —"

"Sí, sí. You are brave lady," said the judge.

Actually, I just wanted to hear Pujol's description of Narcis's police record.

"So, Pujol?" asked the judge.

"He was, according to various sources, just what the senyora said, not to mention guilty of attacking his customers and injuring, perhaps murdering them, as well as selling drugs, which would explain his method of killing Senyoreta Almirall."

"He has arrests? Why comte not knows this? Big shock when he hear."

"Unfortunately, there are just notes in our files of crimes for which we were unable to arrest him, but those stretch back to the time he was fourteen, perhaps further."

"And Madrona Brusi thinks Isabel threatened to tell these things to the count unless Narcis stopped flirting with him," I added.

"Flirting? You slander comte —"

"No, no," I replied, seeing that the judge would not allow any aspersions cast on Miquel, even though the man was a scoundrel. Did the judge know of his record with women? "Isabel was very jealous of anyone the count paid attention to. She mistook the relationship of patron to protégé for something it wasn't."

"She should know own lover was no —"

"No doubt she should," I said hastily. "But

she knew the ugly proclivities of the murderer, and insane jealousy does tend to cloud the judgment."

"Ah, sí," said the judge thoughtfully. "Women known for unfounded jealousy."

I felt like pointing out that the count had been with a fado singer, according to his wife, the night poor Isabel died, but I thought better of it.

"Still, how we know comte's protégé actually what victim think? No arrests say such. Only rumor. I better like trust comte's think about protégé's character than jealous woman, or gossiping policemen who never find cause for arrest in what is much disgusting crimes."

I could see that the inspector was fuming when he said stiffly, "I went to a lot of trouble to gather this information, sir, and I consider my sources credible."

"We not so much evidence for arrest warrant. Hearsay only. One woman say other woman say artist have reason to kill victim. What is that? Nothing. Hundreds years women not even allowed testify in courts."

I'd love to have sicced my mother-in-law on this judge. His opinions were enough to make a rabid feminist of me, the least confrontational of women. "Perhaps you would be interested to know that Narcis tried to have me killed last night, Judge Goytisolo," I said angrily.

He gave me a condescending glance. "You seem healthful."

I told him that story, but it was no use. He said I had no evidence that Narcis had hired that cab driver to chase me with a knife through the streets and alleys of Barri Xino.

"Then it must have been Comtessa Violante who hired him," I retorted.

"Madam," said the judge. "Saying so is outrageous."

"Why?" I asked. "She is a jealous woman as well. She thought Robbie and I were after her husband. If Narcis didn't try to have me killed, she probably did because she saw me as a threat. You yourself remarked on the jealous nature of women."

"Noblewomen not buy lower-class taxi drivers to kill husband's mistresses."

"I am not anyone's mistress. I am a happily, respectably married woman."

"Then why husband not here with you?"

"He's in Salamanca giving a paper on science at the university."

"Still," said the judge, "you americanas have withhold information from police. How you know stepson not murderer? He think so. You should report confession to Pujol, not hide boy. Is as I say —"

"We solved your case," said Robbie indignantly.

"Not solved," said Judge Goytisolo. "No arrest without more evidence."

"Why?" snapped Robbie. "Just because there's a count involved? That's bullshit."

"Remove woman from my chamber," ordered the judge.

But Inspector Pujol's cell phone had rung. "Very well, send him in," he said into the telephone. "Your Honor, it seems that the comte himself has arrived with information. Perhaps we should hear what he has to say."

51

The Ultimate Art Movie

Inspector Pujol

I can't say that I was surprised at the judge's refusal to provide an arrest warrant or at his reaction to the arrival of the comte, who strode into chambers looking serious and important.

Goytisolo poked his mustache up on each side. Sometimes in my dreams he misses his mustache and pokes a finger into each nostril. That did not happen on this occasion, but one can always hope. "My dear comte," he exclaimed. "We are honored by your visit. Pujol, please take these people away." He waved his hand at the boy and the two American women.

"Not at all necessary, Judge," said the comte. "I am sure that they will be as interested as anyone at the shocking news I bring. And perhaps we should all speak in English as a courtesy to our American friends."

Disappointment shadowed Goytisolo's face.

He had wanted the comte to himself, perhaps pictured himself serving coffee and buns to his noble guest. Instead he had to put up with three Americans and even speak their language — badly.

"Last night Senyora Blue said something to me that proved to be both important and embarrassing," the comte continued.

What now? I wondered. Was he going to blame Senyora Blue for the murder? Perhaps he was unaware that she had been on a transatlantic flight at the time. I glanced at her and saw that she looked quite puzzled.

"If this americana has offend you any way, dear comte —" began the judge, casting a look of admonition at Senyora Blue.

"Not at all," said the comte. "I was not too pleased with her remarks initially, until it occurred to me that she had reminded me of something important. Hard to believe, under the circumstances, that I would forget such a thing, but I am a busy man and naturally upset over the recent death of my dear friend and employee, Isabel Almirall."

"Who was a victim of sexual harassment in the workplace, it would seem," Senyora Hecht muttered under her breath.

The comte didn't hear her and continued with his remarks. "This most intelligent American lady, Senyora Blue —"

Much to my disgust, the lady in question blushed at his compliment. *All it takes to turn*

*a woman's head is a compliment from a no-
bleman,* I thought. *Had I said to her that she
was intelligent, she wouldn't have turned a hair,
but then I am only a simple man of the people.
And the Americans think themselves so tolerant
of all classes!*

"— asked me why my Esperit has no security cameras and pointed out that if it did,
we would have known immediately who killed
Isabel. I was astounded."

"Much discourteous," agreed the judge.

"Not my point at all, Goytisolo," said the
comte. "The fact is that we *do* have security
cameras. It had simply and not too surpris-
ingly slipped my mind."

"I asked your security people about cameras the morning after the murder, Comte," I
said. "They assured me that there were
none."

"Of course. They don't know," he replied
breezily. "The cameras are my little secret.
How do I know if I can trust the guards? If
they knew of the surveillance and planned to
steal from me, they would simply turn them
off. That is the beauty of my setup. If there
is a theft, naturally I would have the tapes
reviewed immediately. If not, a fellow named
Bacigalupi runs through them at the end of
every month looking for strange happenings
that I might want to know about. As soon as
Senyora Blue mentioned cameras to me, I realized, to my embarrassment, that I probably

had the murder on tape, if it was a murder. If Isabel fell on her head and staggered into 'Tapas Triage' to die, as I personally thought, we'd have that on tape."

"She was injected with heroin," I said shortly.

"So it would seem," the comte replied, beaming at me. "At any rate, as soon as my guests departed, I called Bacigalupi —"

"But he is employed by your wife to spy on you," I pointed out. The judge looked amazed.

"True," said the comte, laughing in a good-humored fashion. "But since I knew about it, I took the opportunity when I opened the museum to employ him to monitor the tapes from time to time." He stopped thoughtfully. "I wonder if he knows that I know he is employed by both of us. Well, no matter. I called him last night and insisted that he monitor the tapes from the night of the murder. It's an amazing system that replaces full tapes with new ones and files the old. Excellent. No one needs to do a thing to it until we want to see the movies."

"And what did Senyor Bacigalupi find?" I asked, somewhat impatiently. The judge gave me a reproachful look. Evidently I hadn't been deferential enough to the comte to please Goytisolo.

"A picture is worth a thousand words, as they say," said the comte. "Bacigalupi pieced together the whole incident from various tapes — every room including my office is covered by a camera — spliced them or some such thing, and presented me with a new tape. The ultimate art movie." He held the cassette up. "Perhaps, Judge Goytisolo, you could send for a monitor so we can all see what happened to poor Isabel."

The judge couldn't comply with the comte's request fast enough. "Then you have tampered with the originals?" I asked. "They will not be acceptable in court if —"

"Not at all. They are in my limousine in the care of my chauffeur. There are so many that I didn't care to bring them all up or subject you to the evidence bit by bit. Ah, here we are."

The judge's secretary wheeled in a television set and VCR, accepted the tape from the comte, and slid it into the appropriate door. Then the comte insisted that we all move our chairs so that we would have a good point of view from which to watch the entertainment. Never have I investigated a more peculiar case, peopled by such irritating people.

The film began with a shot of Isabel Almirall sitting at the desk in the office of Senyora Hecht, busily reading and making notes on some papers. Evidently she *had* been stealing the American's work.

"What a nitwit," said the Hecht woman.

"That paper was a joke. I was going to show it to you, Miquel, so that we could have a good laugh."

"There is no reason then to think Miró was painting parasites into his work?" asked the comte. "Well, I did think her idea rather strange."

As they spoke, Narcis came into the office, and the two argued — Narcis and his victim. There was no sound, but I could imagine what the problem was. When she turned away from him, he injected her with something that froze her in place. Then he pushed up her sleeve, tied her arm with a rubber tube, and slipped a second hypodermic syringe into her vein. The effect in terms of seizures was immediate but brief. Then the needle wielder turned away from his handiwork, peered down the hall, rushed back in to wipe her mouth with a handkerchief, remove the tube, and drop the needle on her desk. After staging the scene to his satisfaction, he slipped out of the office and into another.

"Wow," said the boy. "Who was that?" No one answered.

The film jumped to another office, lit only by street light through the window, where Narcis stood at the inner window peering through blinds into the next room. "That is Madrona's office," said the comte.

The film jumped again to show the Hecht

boy coming into the first office and speaking to the woman at the desk, who was hunched over the papers, shaking slightly. I could see why he might have thought she was laughing. The camera showed his face, which became more and more desperate until he snatched up the metal bird and, as he had said, poked her. She slumped flat onto the papers.

The boy looked alarmed and spoke to her again. Then he approached cautiously and reached around her head, drawing his hand back suddenly and sucking his finger. Once more he reached around and touched her wrist; then, looking terrified, he spoke desperately to her, but not once did he get a good look at her face, which explained why he thought that he had killed his stepmother.

He stood trembling, biting his lip. Then he wiped off the bird statue, which he still held in the other hand, and replaced it. Again he paused, staring at her or the needle; I couldn't be sure which. Senyora Hecht now had her arm around him and was murmuring consolingly to him as they watched. On the film, he picked up the syringe, wrapped it in his handkerchief, stuck it in his pocket, and pelted out of the room. A camera picked him up running down the stairs, down a second flight, and finally disappearing through a door that evidently led to the basement. I saw lighted steps going down from the ground floor into darkness before the door closed behind him.

Then the camera came back to Senyora Hecht's office, which was being entered by Narcis, who seemed quite amused. He contemplated his victim, felt for a pulse, looked for the needle, then hoisted her body onto his shoulder and carried her downstairs. The last shot was of Narcis Berenguer, or whatever his name was, tucking her into a bed in his art exhibit, arranging her hair and hands, and calmly walking out of "Tapas Triage." At no time had I seen a museum guard on the film. The artist punched in a security code, let himself out the front door, and the film ended.

"That was Narcis Ramon Berenguer," I said to the judge.

"Such a shame," said the comte. "He was so talented and, in his way, witty."

"I am much sorry, Comte," said the judge, "that we must issue warrant for his arrest."

"I would expect nothing else," the comte assured him.

"Think of how many crimes went unsolved in years past," murmured Senyora Blue, "because women were not allowed to testify or even considered reliable."

The judge gave her a resentful look. I had to stifle an impulse to congratulate her on her excellent rebuke to Goytisolo. However, there was no time. I had an arrest to make.

52

You Should Be Proud of Me

Carolyn

Inspector Pujol sent us home in a police car. We were all elated that the case had been solved without any of us being jailed or killed. Robbie said, "I think we should go out for a drink. Or two. Or three." Sammie said, "I'd rather get something to eat. I didn't get any lunch, you know." I said, "Why don't you two stop somewhere. All I want is a nice nap back at the hotel." Naturally they both gave me that how-can-you-be-so-boring-when-it's-time-to-celebrate look. Well, they hadn't been up half the night under terrifying circumstances, then out of bed early in the morning. I was tired! I'd celebrate later.

So we went up to the hotel room, Robbie to call Hugh, Sammie anxious to tell his father how he had extricated himself from his problem, and I — well, I just hoped they'd leave and let me have a nap.

It didn't work out that way. After I'd inserted the key card, Gwen was opening the door before I could turn the knob. "Look who's here!" she cried.

It was Jason, and he did not look delighted to see me. "Where were you last night, Carolyn? I called repeatedly to tell you I'd be in today."

"I told you she was at a party, Dad," said Gwen, "but I didn't get to tell her you called because I went to sleep before she got home, and then she came home with the cop, which confused me, and then I was so sleepy this morning —"

"You mustn't be angry at Carolyn," said Robbie. "She was lucky to get home alive last night. She's a heroine!"

Jason looked from one of us to the other until his eyes came back to me. "Oh, my God, Carolyn, what have you been doing?"

I gave him the briefest possible rundown on our week in Barcelona. Gwen interrupted every so often to say, "You didn't tell me that, Mom."

Jason asked if Sam intended to keep sharing our hotel room. Robbie said, "You're really not getting the whole story, Jason. Carolyn saved herself last night from a knife-wielding assassin *and* a gaggle of jealous whores and amorous drunks."

My poor husband groaned while I glared at Robbie. She didn't have to tell him *that*.

"Carolyn, how many times have I asked you not to get mixed up in dangerous situations?" he asked in a voice replete with anger and reproach.

"Friendship imposes duties on us, Jason," I said stiffly. "I couldn't let Robbie or Sam be arrested unjustly. And I really think you should be proud of me. You're always nagging me to get more exercise. Well, I'll have you know that last night I outran a man with a knife and a group of angry — ladies of the evening."

From: Pujol, Ildefons
To: Blue, Carolyn
Sent: dimecres, 8 octubre 2003 14:33
Subject: Stolen property

Dear Madam:

During the pursuit of our investigation of Senyoreta Isabel Almirall i Corberó's death, we were fortunate to find the taxi driver who stole your belongings. As soon as his trial is over and he has testified against Narcis Ramon Berenguer, we will return to you your watch, wedding ring, and handbag. If you had money in the handbag, it was gone, but your credit cards and identification seem to be intact. I will return the key card to your hotel.

The department thanks you for your contributions to our investigation.

Respectfully yours,
Ildefons Pujol i Serra
Homicide Inspector
Barcelona Police Department

From: Hecht, Roberta
To: Blue, Carolyn
Sent: divendres, 10 octubre 2003 14:30
Subject: a new job

Caro, the damnedest thing happened. Miquel closed down the Esperit, so I'm off to France to look at Miró ballet sets. I got some funding from the university. Hugh and the kids are coming for Christmas. Think I'll do a book — MIRÓ IN THE THEATER. Books look good when they pass out the raises. Sorry I can't fund Gwen too, but she's taken care of. Miquel and Violante are getting back together. They'll remodel Esperit and live there — Miró on the ground floor, crucifixions and paintings of the Virgin upstairs. You want to bet which one kills the other before the year is out? Dolors really shook them up when she said she was going into a convent. No heirs to the family name and all that garbage. So they live unhappily ever after, and she promises to get married and produce the babies. She's dating that Martí we saw at the big flamenco party. What a night that was. Jordi went back to the university and Madrona to Fundació Miró. Narcis is — where else? — in jail. What a creep he turned out to be.

Hugs,
Robbie

From: Blue, Gwen
To: Blue, Carolyn
Sent: dissabte, 11 octubre 2003 9:03
Subject: change of plans

Hi Mom,
The internship at Esperit fell through. Robbie will tell you about that. But not to worry, Jordi arranged for me to get into the U. here at midterm and I have a job teaching English. Some foreign student deal. And the Pujols offered to let me stay at their house. Magdalena is so cool. We're seeing the whole city on weekends. I'll share her room. I could have their son's room. He's working in Madrid, which for some reason the inspector hates, but Magdalena and I decided we'd rather share. See you at Christmas.

Love and kisses,
Gwen

From: Blue, Gwen
To: Blue, Carolyn
Sent: dissabte, 1 novembre 2003 21:35
Subject: All Saints' Day

Hi Mom,

Today is Todos los Santos (All Saints' Day). Last night Magdalena and I and her mom made *panellets*. They're marzipan cakes that Catalans eat on November first. Today we took the train to Emporda and visited the graves of Inspector Pujol's ancestors. They're buried in niches in walls. Weird, huh? But we had a great time and ate all the panellets, not to mention all kinds of other stuff. I'm sending you the recipe for your column. You get about 24 of them.

  7 oz. or 1 3/4 cups of ground almonds
  2 1/2 oz. freshly cooked mashed potatoes
  grated rind of 1 small lemon
  corn flour
  1 egg white, lightly beaten
  2 1/2 oz. pine nuts

Grease and flour a baking tray.
Mix really well the almonds, potato, and lemon rind.
Divide the stuff in half and divide each

half into 12 small balls.

Roll the balls in 1. corn flour, 2. egg white, and 3. pine nuts (Mrs. P says you can use dried coconut or chopped almonds instead of pine nuts if you want).

Place balls on a baking tray and bake 15 minutes in a preheated 450° F oven or until coating is browned.

Don't eat them until they're cool or you'll get a blistered mouth. Guess who did that. Store them in an airtight container. Mrs. P. used a clean pickle jar. I just love Barcelona. What would you think of my spending Christmas here? I'm invited and it sounds so cool.

Love,
Gwen

From: Blue, Carolyn
To: Blue, Gwen
Sent: Sunday, November 2 2003 8:30
Subject: Christmas in Barcelona

Dear Gwen
Absolutely not. Your father and I would be devastated and cut off your allowance if you do not come home for Christmas.

You'll be happy to know that my handbag, ring, and watch came in the mail yesterday. Please give Inspector Pujol my thanks and extend my greetings to Mrs. Pujol. It was very kind of them to take you in and a source of comfort to me. Not that I don't worry about you in a city where I had several frightening experiences.

We look forward to your speedy return and expect you to make the panellets over the holidays, not to mention telling me about all the other things Catalans eat on All Saints' Day. It should make a wonderful column. Thanks for the recipe.

Love,
Mother

Recipe Index

About the Author

Nancy Fairbanks is a pseudonym for Nancy Herndon, who is the author of the Elena Jarvis mystery series for Berkley. She has also written historical romances under the name Elizabeth Chadwick. She lives in El Paso, Texas, with her husband, Professor Emeritus of Chemistry at the University of Texas at El Paso, who is still an active researcher. She travels widely and frequently with her husband throughout America and Europe, enjoying new places, interesting people, good food, opera, and scientific conferences.

Visit her website at www.nancyfairbanks.com

The employees of Thorndike Press hope you have enjoyed this Large Print book. All our Thorndike and Wheeler Large Print titles are designed for easy reading, and all our books are made to last. Other Thorndike Press Large Print books are available at your library, through selected bookstores, or directly from us.

For information about titles, please call:

(800) 223-1244

or visit our Web site at:

www.gale.com/thorndike
www.gale.com/wheeler

To share your comments, please write:

Publisher
Thorndike Press
295 Kennedy Memorial Drive
Waterville, ME   04901